The Devil's Library

The Devil's Library

short stories

Joachim Glage

JACKLEG PRESS

JackLeg Press
jacklegpress.org

joachimglage.net

Cover art: *Electric Discharges 1909*, a collection of colorful and different
drawings of electrical currents.

Praise for *The Devil's Library*

Glage has given us an utterly captivating collage of essays that is, in the truest and best sense, *sui generis*. With its unerring instinct for unearthing intellectual gold in the inexhaustible, labyrinthine, and stubbornly persistent realm of printed matter, *The Devil's Library* stands in the lineage of Thomas Browne, Coleridge, Borges, and Sebald. Ranging from the abstruse to the fantastic, the complex paradoxes and insights here reclaimed from philosophical, theological, anthropological, or biographical miscellany and brought to life so vividly in these pages are not just being rescued from oblivion. Rather, in Glage's tonally varied and subtly propulsive telling, they are in a deeper sense redeemed. Few books better stage the absorbing delights of voracious, disinterested, and eclectic reading of everything from treatises to telegrams, from Scriptural exegesis to newspaper clippings. Glage's responsiveness to the unexpected enriches us all.

—Thomas Pfau, Alice Mary Baldwin Professor of English & Professor of Systematic Theology, Duke University

Joachim Glage's fiendishly entertaining collection combines the pleasures of deciphering an ancient scroll, curling up with a good detective story, and stealing an accursed manuscript from a crypt. Erudite, inventive, and marvelously sly, *The Devil's Library* will delight readers of philosophical speculative fiction until it dissolves in a plume of evil-smelling smoke."

—Sofia Samatar, author, *The White Mosque* and *A Stranger in Olondria*

Browse the stacks of *The Devil's Library* at your peril! You'll find obscure but fascinating treatises demonstrating that God cannot be perfect, labyrinthine heretical arguments against traditional morals, and reports of the mysterious deaths and murders of authors. A demonic alternative version of *Genesis* turns sacred history upside down. Who knew that the devil was not only a humorist but the author of frightening underground books? Discover them here.

—Gary Shapiro, author, *Nietzsche's Earth: Great Events, Great Politics*

Hoax meets homage in this glorious collection, an imaginary where bespoke apocrypha and wishful thinking invite us into a labyrinth of possibility, association, and a kind of readerly revisionist collaboration. Funny, subversive, and authoritatively anti-authoritarian, Glage finds no tradition unassailable or otherwise invulnerable to his joyful repurposing. What Stanley Crawford did for travel writing in *Travel Notes*, Glage does for storytelling and bibliophilia. Joachim Glage is not only a writers' writer but writing's writer. Borges is dancing in his grave.

—Andrew Tonkovich, editor, *Santa Monica Review*

Table of Contents

Part 1. Books, Devils

A Note on a Note on the Paraclitans   1

The Book of Ahaziah   4

Les Maux de la joie   24

"That Which We Truly Don't Know, We Don't Know That We Don't Know," by Glenn Trollip   56

Some Pages Concerning the Demise of Dr. Conrad Faintly   69

The Devil is a Shape in the Brain   80

Being and Fiction (a Fragment)   114

The Eighteen Possible Plots   116

Missive on an Old Refutation of Time   135

HAPPINESS('ha-pē-nəs), n._[pl. happinesses ('ha-pē-nəs-əz)]:   139

Epilogue   145

Alternate Subtitles for the Present Volume   160

Part 2. Apparitions, Ghosts

The Secret of the Tulip   163

The Black Square   171

The *Gehenna* of Saint Augustine   178

The Ambivalent Moller Gitch   184

When the Ghostmen Came to Mothview   191

Acknowledgments   219

Part 1. Books, Devils

A Note on a Note on the Paraclitans

In the original edition of Gaddis and Miller's *Encyclopaedia of Ancient Greek Thought* (London: 1959), on page 277 of the 14th volume, you will find a short entry, written by one Flynn Barrey (whose institutional affiliation, if he had any, was not recorded), devoted to that little-known pre-socratic philosopher called Paraclitus. The mysticism of this essay—to which Barrey gave the ostentatious title, "Paraclitus and the Glory of Finitude"—must have embarrassed the editors, for the entry does not appear in any of the *Encyclopaedia's* subsequent editions. To my knowledge, only Maurice Blanchot has ever referenced it (somewhere in *L'Entretien infini*, of course, that inexhaustible book; you will forgive me if I omit the exact citation). I reproduce here Barrey's entry in full, so that you may judge for yourself whether the near-oblivion into which his essay has fallen is deserved:

I offer the following note on the ancient Paraclitans, that sect (descended from the early Eleatic School) known for preaching the notorious doctrine that the one *sine qua non* of perfection is *finitude*: "One cannot say of anything that it is perfect until it is finished," or so Paraclitus himself has it in one of his more famous fragments. A great deed might achieve perfection, as might a poem or a military ruse or a political speech or a tulip, or even a human life, but "the proof will not be had until the thing in question has reached its end, and can no longer ruin or detract from itself." This doctrine would lead its later adherents, in the early Christian era, to the heresy that the only object in the universe which in principle *cannot* be perfect is precisely the infinite God. "The incorruptible ALL must wilt before the perfection of a single melting snowflake," writes the paraclitan monk Philoxenus in the fourth century A.D. (before being flayed for it in Constantinople): "God can only dream of so faultless a completion." And even before that, in Plato's time, the doctrine had led already to a number of philosophical perversions, among them certain morbid creeds that professed to find majesty in death. According to one tidy legend, a friend to the young Plato perishes by leaping headfirst from atop the newly-built Theseion in Athens, after having been mystified by the syllogisms of a nameless paraclitan disciple. Outraged by this tragedy, the heroic would-be philosopher sets out on his fateful mission to refute Paraclitus once and for all, by proving the *true* perfection of the eternal and the timeless. (Which is to say, he seeks out the dialectician, Socrates.)

As Christianity eventually spreads through Europe, the principles of paraclitan philosophy come to be perceived as traps laid by the devil; indeed there even arises the superstition, among certain Renaissance occultists, that a reader of Paraclitus's fragments might be induced by those texts to perish spontaneously. "Not only falſe, but a friuolous fable," writes John Dee as part of a petition to Elizabeth I, "nay a moſt grieuous Sclaunder, and damnable, to ſay, with PARACLITUS, that Death is Perfect." For centuries the writings of the Paraclitans, wherever they are found, are consigned to the flames.

Of the few extant pages that have survived from this despised tradition (and I know some of them are kept in the rare books room at the University of Leyden), their magic, should they possess any, is undoubtedly greater now because of the dark history that trails behind them. (I am referring here, of course, to Eccles' Ratio, the inverse relationship between the dissemination of a work and its occult power.) Such a prospect, I submit, justifies our patient analysis of these texts, no matter what supernatural risks we may thereby incur. Perhaps, if one should study the paraclitan mysteries today, even after all the time they've endured, and after the long contempt visited upon them through the ages, they could yet bring about one's death.

In the relevant volume of the 1959 *Encyclopaedia* that I now hold in my hands, inside the left margin of these passages, there can be found inscribed, in pencil, and in a supremely steady hand, the following two sentences, like twin revelations:

> *Or perhaps some other words you've read, some secretly effective words—perhaps these very words—are killing you even now, without you knowing it, and it is already too late to do anything about it, you've already read too much.*

> *A text, after all, is not a road; it's not like you can turn back the way you came.*

I choose to believe that Barrey himself was the one who defaced these pages: a sign, perhaps, that he had a good deal more to say. Perhaps he hoped to warn us of something (he may yet succeed in doing so). Or perhaps he perished many years ago, his face over a parchment or an old book.

The Book of Ahaziah

The mysteries that surround the life and cruel demise of Perry Dankworth (1899 – 1957)—that briefly prominent scholar of the Bible whose theories (on morality, on biblical exegesis) were, among respectable deputies of Christianity, even more briefly in vogue, and whose consignment, following his death, first to mere unfashionableness but at length to infamy (that ever more populous city), did not disappoint even one theologian of good standing—may be encapsulated in the questions that follow. If you are not already familiar with Dankworth's lurid tale, the substance of these questions may seem vague or even shocking to you, but rest assured: all will be illuminated, at least to a partial degree, in the course of our commentary below. We shall leave ornament aside, for what is to be said must be said plainly or no one will believe it; anyway art and poetry become more sublime when, in the main, they are avoided. (For the Ancients—in the odes of Pindar, for example—both the lyre and careful discourse were necessary when entreating the gods; in our more profane endeavor, we will require only the latter.)

Here then are the questions: *Did Perry Dankworth write three books about the Bible before his strange and ghastly fate came to pass, or only two? If he did complete a third, what was its subject matter? Did that mysterious third book (assuming it exists or once existed) hold some connection to his demise? Finally, what are we to make of the gruesome fact, preserved for posterity in the crime photographs, that not only was Dankworth found in his secluded Scottish home dismembered and beheaded, but also that his torso had been inscribed—postmortem, according to the records of the procurator fiscal—with signs and sigils no one has yet been able to decipher?*

Before offering our own speculations in regard to these questions, we should establish that Perry Dankworth, an unaffiliated scholar and migrant Englishman who spent most of his adulthood in the north of Caithness in Scotland, and whose murder there in the winter of 1957—in a remote crofting hamlet called Diabhalton, of all places!—has never been solved, was not, at least to our best knowledge, a member of any denomination of the Christian Church. When pressed about his faith, on those occasions he deigned to appear at a conference, for example, Dankworth, upon drawing to a squint his deep-set eyes and turning up his imperial, would offer always the same cryptic sentence in reply: *I count myself among the people of the Book.* That this very sentence might furnish a clue for solving the Dankworth mystery is an idea we shall propose and expound upon later in these pages. In the meantime, let us simply note that although he had "probably read the Bible cover to cover more times than any other person alive" (to quote his fellow theologian and only known friend, Dr. Basil Black of Cambridge, whose own death last year at the age of one-hundred went unannounced in the usual bulletins), Dankworth seems nonetheless to have had a distaste for so-called "world religions." At the very least there are those who have opined as much: some say he boasted he never once attended an actual religious service; others recount how he spat if anyone said the word "amen." It is also rumored—mainly among excitable gossips in humanities departments—that the man refused so much as to *set foot* in a church. ("Perhaps there's a worry he'll burst into flames," a particularly pious provost at Oxford is supposed to have quipped.) Tall tales, or so I once told myself, though I no longer do. In any case, whether rumors like these are credible, and since most of the details of Dankworth's day-to-day life have eluded us, I will here propose that, if we are to gather his personal metaphysics, then it is not with any established religion that we should begin, nor even with Dankworth's scant biography (and much less with rumors), but rather with the secrets contained in his writing. Any insight we might gain into his spiritual heart will first have to be gleaned there, from his books. We will have occasion to look at his abundant notes, too, to be sure (which were curated and have been made available to me by the Centre for Research Collections at the University of Edinburgh), but first and foremost we will look to his books. In this regard fortune favors us, for he published only two.

(You may be asking yourself why we must bother with Dankworth's personal spiritual beliefs in the first place. Am I proposing that they are somehow relevant to his murder? The answer to this can be revealed only slowly, in careful steps, and in the fragments from history and religious lore which bear on the matter, sometimes from a great distance, and which I've searched out and assembled below. I beg your patience; the truth is bigger than you imagine.)

…

I have said that Dankworth *published* two books; the rumor, popularized some years ago by gossip[*] in *Theophany Today* (that tabloid for dons and lectors), i.e., that Dankworth actually wrote—though could not find anyone who would publish—no fewer than *ten* other books, and that those several manuscripts, shortly after his death, were mysteriously appropriated and then hid away within the *piani superiori* at the Vatican Archive, has not been substantiated and, in my opinion, has no basis in fact. The more standard view, reflected in Dankworth's own notes (and affirmed by Basil Black and others), namely, that he had been at work on a *single* book—his third—for the last eighteen years of his life, is by far the more plausible theory (and, as we'll soon see, the more ominous of the two). On only one point shall we agree with that otherwise execrable piece in *Theophany*: it is true that no manuscripts were found among Dankworth's papers in 1957, and it is therefore all but certain that, if any copies of his final work existed, then indeed they must have been pirated away by someone—most likely by his killer.

It will be objected that we are wading already into the waters of speculation, and too deeply. Let us then withdraw to dry land, and consider for the moment only those works that are verifiably

---

[*]   "The Prodigal Magus" by Montcrief deserves no further citation.

from the man himself. In 1937, Perry Dankworth, a complete unknown in the world of theology, publishes his first book, *Suicide and the Bible, A Defense* (London: Kegan Paul, Trench, Trübner & Co.). Many are the detractors who hurry to despise this work, often on the basis of its title alone. (*A defense of suicide? Sacrilege!*) The book's apologists—fewer in number though no less excited—rush to point out that the "defense" is not of suicide but indeed of the Bible (or, more specifically, of how suicide is treated in biblical texts). In actuality neither faction has it quite right, which is also to say that neither is wholly wrong; but we shall let the man speak for himself, as he does in the following excerpt from the book's preface:

> In its first half, this book maintains, contrary to doctrines that grew out of the middle ages (from Aquinas to the Council of Trent and then on to our own more solicitous custodians of souls), that the Bible, but for a tepid verse or two in First Corinthians, does not report anything particularly objectionable about suicide, and certainly nowhere condemns it outright. Self-murder, taken even in its broadest sense, is in fact exceedingly rare in both Testaments (by my count there are only nine such acts), but when it does occur it typically is treated as a matter of course. What could be more natural, after all, than that the words, "Then he went away and hanged himself" should follow from "I have betrayed innocent blood," or than that God should approve Samson's vengeful (and suicidal) prayer? This of course was in keeping with antique attitudes regarding suicide more generally; Seneca's was only a late but quintessential formulation:

Agamus Deo gratias, quod nemo invitus in vita teneri potest.[*]

I also could have cited Plato or Epicurus or Plutarch or Tacitus or Marcus Aurelius or any number of Stoics or Cynics or even Homer and the authors of the ancient epic poems; and even as late as the thirteenth century there proliferated Christian sects, among them the highly-literate Cathari, whose doctrines found nothing intrinsically sinful in suicide. So what then of the view, seemingly taken for granted by most orthodox Church authorities for a thousand years now, that suicide is to be condemned as a sin most grievous? that it is in fact a transgression for which repentance—and even forgiveness—is unavailable? As the mighty Burton expressed it in the early seventeenth century:

He that stabs another can kill his body; but he that stabs himself kills his own soul.

Damnation may well be the outcome for those who, in the lovely phrase preferred by Burton, "make away with themselves;" but whence this sureness, whence this disdain? If we succeed here in nothing else, we shall at least declare with confidence that any such prejudice against the right of self-destruction, no matter how venerated, can be rooted only in something *other than scripture.*

Dankworth proceeds to make the even more astonishing claim that, although there are at least a few instances of self-murder in the Bible, most of them are not *"real* suicides, true and

---

[*]   Let us thank God, that no one is forced to live against one's will.

pure." In most cases, Dankworth writes, they are but "phenomena of fate":

> Kings Saul and Zimri, for example, are about to be captured and are doomed already. Samson is in the clutches of the Philistines and badly tortured, soon to breathe his last. Abimelech is mortally wounded, and disgracefully, at the hands of a woman. Accordingly, these men do not *want* or *choose* to die; they are *going* to die. They merely select the means. Even Judas—having grasped the terrible magnitude of what he'd done, and having understood that his life lay already in the devil's hands (as confirmed by Luke 22:3)—has *no other option* but to annihilate himself.[*]

In its second half the book turns philosophical. On the first page of this second part we read the following lines, which Dankworth no doubt intended to be provocative, if not blasphemous:

> There can be no greater proof of belief in the life of the soul, and thus in God, than that willingness, seen in martyrs, to lay down the body for reasons of the spirit. It cannot be denied that the Bible teaches dualism, and that within that binary structure of the universe the soul is supreme over the flesh. The

---

[*] The only "true" suicide in the Bible, in Dankworth's view, is to be found in a single verse from First Samuel (specifically, the fifth verse from chapter thirty-one), and it is performed by the armor-bearer to King Saul. "Having witnessed the doomed and too-merciful King take his own life," Dankworth writes, "the armor-bearer, moved purely by grief and love, throws himself onto his own sword." Dankworth describes the servant's deed as "gently touching, but in no way exceptional; the verses proceed without a second thought to it. He is not even named."

doctrine of transubstantiation is a wicked lie: *even the Savior's body was wretched.*

In the next hundred pages or so (which, to be sure, grow increasingly abstruse, and are accompanied by frequent references to Husserl), Dankworth attempts to refine his position down to its most basic and phenomenological form:

> Human thinking is intrinsically affirmative and productive. A conscious mind cannot but create. As a result, pure *nothingness* may not be conceived by us, or even dimly imagined. Hamlet understood this, and was pained by it. Whatever conception of empty infinite black one might come up with, it is after all just more *being*, rumbling on and on and away forever. Every thought of suicide contains implicitly this warning, i.e., that existence might very well be endless. *Every suicide is a confrontation with immortality.*

It is not our place here to evaluate these notions. That in the months following its publication Dankworth's book incurs substantially more criticism than acclaim, at least from academic quarters, is perhaps telling enough. Bertrand Russell argues that the moral proofs in the second half of the work are at best pedantic; Schweitzer judges it more generally to be "lean fare." Karl Barth describes *Suicide and the Bible* as but an instance of "vogue theology." Still, the work is a financial success, selling many thousands of copies and all but guaranteeing a publication contract for Dankworth's next book.

Readers would not have to wait long for the latter. In the summer of 1939, in the same week that the world's fate is sealed by the Molotov–Ribbentrop and Anglo-Polish pacts, Dankworth publishes *The Bible's Axiom* (again with Kegan Paul). It is however not until the German translation of the book— published only after the war and transcribed by Dankworth himself, doubtless out of zeal more than necessity—that the clarifying subtitle is added: *die Undankbarkeit der Kinder* [The Ingratitude of Children].

In Dankworth's view, this axiom comprises the fundamental moral principle of the whole Bible. "Search the sacred books for as long as you like," he proclaims,

> you'll scarcely find a handful of verses that speak well of children. Far more common, by a factor of a hundred at least, are sentiments like those found in Proverbs 17:25: *A foolish son brings grief to his father and bitterness to the one who bore him.* The prime biblical truth is that human children are not born innocent and faithful, but are by their very nature wicked.

This principle, Dankworth contends, is "the very essence in the idea of original sin, *the sin of the infant*," and it is found as well

> in the angels that fell after turning their backs on the Father, in the first humans who could not keep from violating the one rule of Eden, in Cain's savagery, in Job's long complaint, in the wasteful son, in the doubt of Christ, and indeed in every follower of false gods, and in all of the godless, too, and even in the bored lad sniveling in the pew, as in every well-rested head that wakes without prayer or thanks, every sot, every banker and every warmonger, every plump and limp bureaucrat, every chancellor and gleaming dignitary, every ill-used body, and all everywhere the bitter faithless: *the children are ungrateful, and the Father grieves for it.*

We shall leave this second work—more blasphemous and even more despised than the first—without saying anything more about it, other than to note that, in the years following its publication, the name Dankworth began its descent into opprobrium.

...

In both *Suicide and The Bible* and *The Bible's Axiom*, one finds in the front matter the same dedication: *For Howard.* To my knowledge no one has yet made any serious effort to identify this person. Rumors have accumulated, of course: some speculate it must be a secret lover; others think "Howard" is somehow a pet name for Basil Black. For a long time I myself imagined it might be the name of a lost son, though I never found any evidence that Dankworth was ever married or fathered a child.

But: *I now know who Howard is.* Not only that: it is my belief that this information bears directly upon Dankworth's bizarre and brutal murder.

(Once more I will ask for your patience, however. The secret I am to unveil must be handled carefully, and can be told only in the context of the whole tale. We've only begun preparing the proper place for it.)

I made my discovery while studying Dankworth's notes in Edinburgh. There are many thousands of pages of them, going back even before his first published book; they are written in multiple languages, and are full of ancient Greek and scriptural verses (though there are many variations of these last which doubtless were composed by Dankworth himself). There are strange symbologies, as well as what appears to be an attempt at a translation of the Egyptian Book of the Dead. Vast tables of Hebrew letters are also found, arranged non-syntactically (it seems that, for a time at least, Dankworth had been seduced by the lures of divination and Hebrew numerology). The greater portion of these notes, however, is devoted to Dankworth's various translations of apocryphal books, notably the pseudepigrapha of Enoch and Jubilees. But it is for that least-known apocryphal text, the so-called Book of Ahaziah, that Dankworth, throughout the notes and with increasing vehemence towards the end, reserves his most serious and sustained attention.

You will forgive me if I presume your unfamiliarity with this last text. Of all the Apocrypha it is the one most reviled—and most successfully suppressed—by the Church. Most catalogues of apocryphal books omit it entirely; to my knowledge it has been translated into modern languages only twice, first into French by François Bartolomeu (Paris, 1843), and more recently into English by Elizabeth Nisben (Chicago, 1928).[*]

An historical anecdote may be illuminating here, and will serve to introduce this impugned and oft-disputed text. Shortly after the publication of Bartolomeu's translation, John Vianey, the famed *curé* from the village of Ars, wrote at once to his friend Edward Pusey at Oxford; the letter contained, among other invective against Bartolomeu, the following distraught line:

> *All spheres of the Church and every congregation must be shielded from this abomination, which pretends to the rank of Genesis, and purports to say how Man really was made, and the Devil's role in it.*

Pusey, equally alarmed, recommends in a letter to the Bishop of London that the book be formally condemned:

> *'Tis a leading trait of this book that it contains a myth, whose long-lying slumber on the sea-bed of Satanic theology and devil-lore, among many other doctrines thankfully and long-ago discarded, has not been disturbed for two-thousand years. Now, perversely, it rises.*

---

[*] Rare is the book dealer today who still possesses an original copy of either of these volumes; as far as I am aware Bartolomeu's translation no longer exists in any form other than the facsimile edition printed in 1917 by *La nouvelle revue française.*

The origins of the Book of Ahaziah remain mysterious. Although incomplete versions of the text are found in some of the older Ethiopic Bibles (dating as far back as the eighth century; there is one preserved at Istifanos Monastery in Lake Hayq, for example), the first *complete* version that can be verified was not compiled until the late middle ages, and by Florentine occultists. This version was drawn from multiple sources in both Hebrew and Greek, and from different times and places of the ancient world; as a result the book's earliest origins can only be guessed at. Nisben estimates its date of composition as being sometime in the sixth century B.C. (though this claim rests almost exclusively upon her conjecture that a verse from the book is quoted in the twenty-fifth fragment from Xenophanes). There is at least partial evidence that, in the fourth century, the Council of Laodicea possessed a complete copy of the book, and refused to condemn it, though they elected at last not to dignify it as canon. Bartolomeu opines that Ahaziah's original sources pre-date the Book of Genesis itself (which he deems to be an inferior and derivative work), and so constitute a kind of "proto-Genesis." Professor Pfau of Heidelberg more recently has denounced the text as a Renaissance hoax. But what does the book actually say?

In contrast to Genesis, the Book of Ahaziah contains no cosmogony. The earth and the heavens and the waters are all given from the start. Nevertheless, its opening chapters clearly resemble those of the first book of the Bible, insofar as both begin with the doings of that same plural deity, *Elohim*, and with a story of how humans were made. Also making an early appearance in Ahaziah are the so-called "sons of Gods" or "sons of Elohim;" it is implied that these latter are angels, or at any rate celestial beings, though admittedly the Hebrew phrase *bene Elohim* is amenable to more than one construction.[*]

---

[*] Wholff, for example, perhaps making too much of a verse from Isaiah, insists that they are literal stars, and demonic or "Luciferian" in essence; F. Edmondsen says they are just the same ancestors of giants as in the Book of Enoch. Here we will follow both Nisben and Bartolomeu and call them

In the Book of Ahaziah these angels gather in Elohim's presence so that they might bring forth challenges, and in a manner that will seem either good-natured or bellicose depending on if your translation of the Hebrew leans toward Nisben or Bartolomeu. For the most part these challenges are phrased so as to confound the very notion of omnipotence; that is, they are what we today might recognize as merely scholastic paradoxes: "Form a mountain so vast even you cannot move it," says Azazel, one of the sons; "Create a speck of dust so small even your eye cannot perceive it," says Jomjael (Ahaziah 2:16-19; Nisben 77). Another challenge, from the angel Rameel, seems almost to have the spirit of a riddle: "Teach us, then, what is the shape of the sky?" (Ahaziah 2:21; Nisben 77). Naturally, God is able to answer these challenges instantly and effortlessly, though just how He does so is not explained (anyway such feats must remain unfathomable to us).

Finally, they come to "the scribe of the Lord," who is not named, but whom both Nisben and Bartolomeu associate with Samael, that early angel of death (a precursor, surely, to the Accuser of later Judeo-Christian lore). This son of Elohim—who is referred to as "the serpent" and as "the bringer of dawn,"* and also as "inventor of letters"§ and the personage "destined to preside over the birth of Esau but not of Jacob" (Ahaziah 2:35-40; Nisben 78)—proposes a challenge of a different sort.

---

angels. Indeed in most of what follows, except where otherwise noted, we shall consult primarily Nisben's excellent translation as reproduced in *Ahaziah: Text and Commentary*, U. of Chicago Press, 1948.

* It is clear from his notes that Dankworth saw a connection between this figure and the Egyptian Apep, the serpent that the god Ra, with his retinue, must repel each night so that the sun may rise again.

§ Dankworth links this epithet, perhaps too hastily, to a passage from Agrippa, in which "that devil *Theutus*" is mentioned, who is cited also in the *Phaedrus* as the god that "invented numbers and arithmetic and geometry and astronomy, also draughts and dice, and, most important of all, letters."

Knowing that all things composed of earth are, *ipso facto*, governed by that substance ("locked into the realm of causality," as Sartre has put it), the serpent-scribe challenges God to invent a creature "formed of clay, without spirit, yet who nonetheless would be free in mind and will" (Ahaziah 2:37; Nisben 78). Bartolomeu, perhaps truer to the concise Hebrew verse, has simply: *Montrez-nous votre puissance: donnez à cette poussière la liberté.* [Display your strength: give this unspirited dust freedom.]

This challenge evidently proves more difficult than the others, for Elohim's answer does not come for seven days. After that time, the serpent is brought to a garden in which now lives *adam* (or Man, or humankind), a term rendered idiosyncratically by Bartolomeu as *terrehommes* ["earthmen"], and more poetically by Nisben as "the people of the dust" (these beings, after all, as in Genesis, were brought forth from the dust of the soil, i.e., from *aphar adamah*). They are non-angelic and non-celestial; their life flows not from any ghostly essence but rather from red blood (*see*, perhaps, Leviticus 17:11). Nonetheless—and miraculously— they possess intelligence, and they are free.

Humiliated that his challenge was successfully answered, the serpent goes to the people of the dust and whispers to them the following lie:

> Though you are formed of clay, know that God
> has hidden spirits within you; your bodies only
> enrobe them. As spirits you will surely not die, but
> will live long after your blood has run dry and your
> flesh is torn asunder and your bones are turned back
> to dust. (Ahaziah 2:46; Nisben 79)

"The truth I bring, you already keep," the serpent adds in a subsequent verse, "for even you are frightened by the sight of blood, and can see that it is foul" (Ahaziah 2:49; Nisben 79). And then, almost teasingly: "Does your Father despise you? Surely your flesh is bondage, to be thrown off" (Ahaziah 2:51; Nisben 79). The people of the garden, believing the serpent, begin covering their bodies in shame. Elohim—now called Yahweh—grows angry upon seeing this: "Why do you cover yourselves? Who told you you were naked, or that death shall not lay hold of you?" The people of the dust, struck dumb by fear, cannot bring themselves to answer. "Depart from me then," says the God, "for by believing the serpent you dishonor the miracle I have done" (Ahaziah 2:54-55; Nisben 80).

Much of the rest of the Book of Ahaziah is roughly similar to Genesis as we know it. An exalted pair is introduced as the principal progenitors of the human race, and mention is made of a murderous brother and also of Noah and a great calamity, and then of Abraham and his prolific brood, and so on. The doomed descendants, and the nursery of kings that blooms from them, are followed from generation to generation, the curse of the first sin being passed down to them all—not only through the blood, but also through the ancient lie to which the bewildered members of humanity still cling, to wit: that they are not in fact *miracles* of clay but, somehow beneath their flesh, mere souls.

Most of this, as I've mentioned, should sound more or less familiar to readers of Genesis ("like twins, the books resemble one another in their differences, and most especially when they are opposite" says Bartolomeu). All, that is, but for one early chapter in Ahaziah: chapter three, which deals at length with the *punishment* inflicted upon the serpent, the former scribe of God. In Genesis, there are but two verses devoted to that judgment;* in Ahaziah, by contrast, just over a *hundred* verses deal with the Liar's fate. And it is to these verses, and that third chapter, that Dankworth, in his copious notes, devotes more of his attention than to any other subject.

---

* So the Lord God said to the serpent, "Because you have done this, cursed are you above all the livestock, and all the wild animals! You will crawl on your belly and you will eat dust all the days of your life. And I will put enmity between you and the woman, and between your offspring and hers; he will crush your head, and you will strike his heel. (Genesis 3:14-15)

…

Permit me in this brief digression to make the following conjecture: the mysterious "third book" that Dankworth was working on for eighteen years was indeed a translation—though not, as you might expect, of the Book of Ahaziah more generally. Instead, he confined his labors to *the third chapter alone.*

Eighteen years, spent on a hundred verses!

That is the first astounding possibility I ask you to entertain. The second one is this: as the name "Howard" appears with increasing frequency in the notes whenever the Book of Ahaziah is the subject, we should at least humor the prospect that something spiritual, and perhaps even a "substance magical" (as Dankworth often describes the matter and the forms of words in Ahaziah), beyond any ordinary intrigue, somehow attaches itself to that name.

To be sure, the jottings that mention "Howard" or "HWD" in Dankworth's notes (the two terms are used interchangeably) are often impenetrably vague; they consist mainly of awkward fragments such as: *Sly writer Howard, goading god*; and: *Take courage, Hwd soon arrives*; and: *Infinite Book! Howard pretended so that he might write it*; and: *Sly father hwd has his own book to make.*

There are clues in these stray phrases. I ask that you keep them in mind as we continue.

…

Chapter 3 from the Book of Ahaziah is of all the chapters the most enigmatic. Nisben and Bartolomeu render key verses in wildly different ways. I do not know if I can adequately summarize it; the following, however, may serve as a basic review of the most important points.

As punishment for his lies, the serpent-scribe is banished. "I cast you away from me," is God's simple decree (Ahaziah 3:6; Nisben 82). This may be enough to establish that the serpent has been sent to hell (or some place akin to it), though it is important to note that the word *sheol* is not used (wherever the serpent ends up, it is not the realm of the dead). If it is hell, it is a dark and arid hell, a hell not of flames but of dust: "You will eat dust in darkness, and you will breathe dust, the very thing you hold in disgrace" (Ahaziah 3:13; Nisben 83). Astonishingly, the serpent is given leave by God to continue to *test* humankind; more specifically, he is permitted to influence, through his whisperings from exile, "half of letters" (Ahaziah 3:22; Nisben 83). Dankworth interprets this last phrase to mean: *half of all the writing ever made in the world.* And so, for example—I now paraphrase from Dankworth's notes, and from his own rather unusual speculations about the New Testament—for every verse that is holy or angelically inspired (e.g., *he that is not against us is for us*, Luke 9:50), there is a corresponding verse composed or influenced by the serpent (e.g., *he that is not with me is against me*, Luke 11:23). Indeed, when the Lord God says, in the Book of Ahaziah, in a sentence that either repeats or prefigures Genesis, "the asp strikes the heel that crushes its head" (Ahaziah 3:76; Nisben 101), this is a figure, like that of Jacob and Esau in the same womb, for the coexistence of the loved and the hated, or of the angelic and the demonic (or perhaps even of truth and falsehood) in the scriptures themselves. "It is up to humankind to discern the difference," Dankworth writes,

> since its failure to do so has always been its first
> and most fateful sin. In the eyes of God, the original
> transgression was not eating from the forbidden
> tree, but heeding the snake.

Equally astonishing: in but a fleeting verse, God commands the serpent to continue "to keep parchment and to write on it" (Ahaziah 3:52; Nisben 85). It is difficult to tell if this command is meant as a consolation or as a further torment. Presumably, as God's scribe, the serpent once kept a record of the entire universe; but now, in only dust and darkness, what is there to record? As Dankworth puts the question: "What sort of writing can an angel thus severed from the Lord, and from the Creation, and from any and all beatitude, possibly bring himself to make?"

As in the second chapter, the serpent is not given a name in these verses, but instead is addressed by a series of epithets. He is now one who "signs" or "records" (*roshem*) while in the dark; he is *ha-kotev ba-choshekh* and *sofer ba-chasheikhah*, the one who writes in darkness and is a scribe of darkness. Dankworth, in the notes, soon settles on a *single phrase* for rendering all these epithets: *He that writes in the dark.*

After reading that phrase many hundreds of times in Dankworth's notes, even in the earliest entries, I began to see how several of the threads in this mystery tie together. And then, all at once, an image of the thing coalesced.

Dankworth wrote two blasphemous books (including one that all but promoted suicide), and cited the Bible as his justification. Echoing the serpent's lies in Ahaziah, he championed the doctrine of the soul as a separate and non-bodily existence, and sought—once again citing scripture—to demonize children and to drive a wedge between generations. He dedicated his books to "Howard," or who is also called "HWD" in the notes—an abbreviation which, I now have no doubt, is short for *He that Writes in the Dark.*

The conclusion is all but unavoidable: Dankworth wrote his books for the devil.

. . .

What possesses a man to celebrate the devil? Of course there are those who but pray for their own advantage, and so seek out magic. (A brute Calvinist principle stirs here: *You might bargain with the devil, never with God.*) Such lures, however, attract only the basest and coarsest among us, the types that hardly ever are seen shuddering in the throes of religion. Beyond vapid self-interest, however, there are other and more sophisticated forces that might drive a person to devil worship. Some devotees, for example, hold as a matter of principle that God's verdict against humanity was unjust. (*Were we not tricked?*) Others merely sympathize with the *punished* (and surely no being in all the universe has been punished more than he who went from Paradise to the Pit). Still others exalt the powers of imagination and fiction, which are embodied most supremely in the Father of Lies.

What in particular moved Perry Dankworth to love the devil we may never know. Perhaps he had a vision of a resplendent but wronged archangel; perhaps he saw phantoms, with arms outstretched or bound in grave-clothes, who somehow pressed him into their service. Perhaps he found something hidden in the scriptures, or in the Book of Ahaziah, from which he could not look away.

One might be satisfied to leave the mystery there; alas, as I was studying Dankworth's notes I felt no such satisfaction. I sensed I was on the cusp of understanding something more about his murder. I'd already managed to catch a glimpse of it through the haze, after all, and, like storm-beset travelers who see a glow in the distance, and infer from that a window, and a fire, and a hot bowl—or in my case, something infinitely more sinister, yet still irresistible—I felt my feet as it were press on.

I obtained a copy of a photograph of Dankworth's corpse— a file from the criminal investigation undertaken in 1957. The photo is the only document I know that shows clearly the mysterious script left upon Dankworth's mutilated body. It is hard to say if the signs inscribed there are symbols or hieroglyphs, or letters; they are unlike any other writing I've seen. They were drawn, according to the investigation files, with ink made from ocher, which also contained a subtle acid that caused the inscription to burn slightly into the flesh.

For two years I searched, profitlessly, for any person or book that could help me decipher these symbols. Of course, for all I knew at the time the markings might not even be *writing* at all; perhaps they were only the dashings of a murderous madman. Again, though, impelled by strange and unknown forces, I pressed on. I began to focus my efforts on a large symbol located near the bottom of Dankworth's abdomen; the fact that it was complex, and set off from the other signs, seemed of significance to me. Perhaps it is a signature, I thought, the mark of an author who could not resist taking credit for his work. Or perhaps it is instead a title, and one is meant to read the lines upwards. Once again, however, my searches were made in vain.

It was almost by chance that I happened into a conversation with the famed book collector, Holling Laertus (a young and precocious genius, I might add), after I'd been granted permission from his foundation to consult a copy of *De Bluotfluchjen* at his private library in New York.

Impressed with his knowledge of the occult (and seemingly of every major heresiarch of the Christian and Jewish traditions), I showed him the photograph of Dankworth's marked-up cadaver, drawing his attention especially to the large symbol written at the bottom of his torso. Laertus did not gasp, but only wrinkled his brow, and then frowned; after a moment he opened up one of his locked bookcases and pulled out a worn, antique-looking volume. Its title, embossed in lettering of faded crimson, was in a language I did not recognize. "*The Numbering of the Swindler,*" he told me, "by the Andalusi mystic known only as Ibn Hashim of Iber. Composed in the twelfth or thirteenth century, or so the story goes, and transcribed for this partial edition in 1622. No copy of the original survives—if one ever really existed." For several minutes he looked through the book, seemingly struggling to understand it himself.

"Ah yes. You see, right here." He placed the book carefully on a wide and burnished table and pointed to a page inscribed with characters so minute they were scarcely legible. "It's a numerical system. Ibn Hashim notoriously attributed it to the devil. See, this mark indicates one quantity, that mark another, and so forth. This here is a computational sign. In fact, this whole symbol you've shown me is itself just a computation."

"So it's a number," I said, almost to myself.

"A number, yes." He took out a piece of paper and, looking back and forth to the photograph, wrote some figuring upon it. "The number forty-four-thousand-seven-hundred-and-seventy-seven, to be exact."

...

I won't burden you with any detailed description of the agonizing searches I undertook, whereby I tried to determine the significance of this number, 44,777. Surely there had to be some special meaning to it! I noticed, for example, that it is a prime number; the three sevens, too, might suggest some sort of satanic association. For weeks I racked my brain, and pored over occult numerologies, until finally it dawned on me. *There is no special significance to this number, because it is a page number.*

I remembered the sentence that Dankworth is reported to have uttered whenever anyone asked him about his faith: *I count myself among the people of the Book.* I then understood: *he meant it literally.* I now believe that Perry Dankworth (possibly along with thousands of others over the course of centuries, or millennia) willingly allowed himself to be turned into a page in some vast and monstrous book, a book which no human, and perhaps no creature of any kind, will ever possess as a whole. This last fact is incidental, of course, since no word is ever written that is not read by God.

Les Maux de la joie

1.

*Handwritten note, from Hélène Carrère
d'Encausse, permanent secretary, Académie
française, to Jean d'Ormesson, dean, Académie
française. November 2009.*

The dossier enclosed was delivered anonymously to my office about a week after Claude's death. I only found the time to look it over thoroughly a few days ago. I'm bewildered; is this perhaps a gag? Could René be up to something? The pages do however appear to be properly tender as with time and use and, as far as I can tell, the typeset and the ink and the occasional letterhead in each case look to be authentic. As terrifying as it is to imagine, I think these papers might be genuine. If they are forgeries, then they were fastidiously done.

The documents also appear to have been carefully assembled—but by whom?—not in chronological but in a kind of narrative order. They've been labeled too; there's some sparse bibliographic information scrawled, in pencil, at the top of each document (not by me!). I am enclosing the translations of the Portuguese texts I had Thomas write up for me.

I'm at a loss as to what to do with this. Should we send these documents to Laurent Lévi-Strauss? Or to Sarkozy? Should they be archived, or just consigned to the fire?

Do read them all.

Hélène

2.

Telegram from "Ruy" to F. Durão, District Commissioner, Indian Protection Service. June 1921.

[The header contains several abbreviations; I assume they are codes for the telegraph office. I don't know what any of them mean. The body of the text reads as follows. —Thomas]

MADE CONTACT WITH TRIBE. THEIR WORLD IS BEYOND BELIEF. RECOMMEND KEEPING EVERYTHING CLASSIFIED. SENDING ARTIFACTS. REPORT TO FOLLOW.

RUY

3.

Unfinished manuscript, Senator Filinto Müller. June 1973.

Someone, some future editor or someone in charge of curating my papers, will—I cannot doubt it—feel compelled to give these remarks a title, or a heading at least, and so I may as well attempt to proffer one myself (though this may seem overly stately and artificial). Something simple, "My Confession" perhaps, or something more functional: "To Be Published On The Occasion Of My Death" or "A Last Word." I know at any rate that no one will believe the fantastic thing I have to say here, at least not if I say it while I'm alive; and so, whoever you are, you may take your pick.

—F.M. 6/19/73

[The above paragraph in pen, presumably in Müller's own hand. The rest of it typed. —Thomas]

After a life of public service, faithful service to the great nation of Brazil—long may you gleam, oh spire of America!*—I, Filinto Müller, many times a senator for Mato Grosso and now head of the senate, former federal police chief and once-advisor to the noble Getúlio Vargas (and, I dare say, his political conscience), soon to turn seventy-three years of age and sensing the finitude of my life, am now moved to make the following confession.

Some of you, I am sure, are already licking your teeth. He is to apologize, you are thinking, for a career in brutality, for being a torturer, a Nazi-sympathizer, a thug in a politician's garb; for his role in suppressing the rebellions of the thirties; for being among those who transformed President Vargas into a dictator; for urging censorship; for helping to implement the "draconian" policies of the Estado Novo, all while sneering at his foes' calls for leniency . . .

No. Whatever public concessions I may have made over the years, in my heart I apologize for none of it. I always did what had to be done for the good of Brazil. I'll not throw down my plume at this late hour.

I have among my memories of public life but one haunting source of regret. Before I unburden myself, however, I wish to supply the proper context. Confession, after all, is a narrative act, just as the issuing of a moral verdict—at least if the latter has been allowed to mature—is really only a species of history. I feel confident that only those who have not prejudged me will have the patience to follow along. I smile at this, the flagging muscle of my detractors! How they lack the stomach for truth, for all that

---

* *florão da America!*—"florão" meaning, here, I think, a crocket, a finial, a flower- or leaf-shaped ornament atop a structure, typically architectural; somehow I feel "spire" best captures the melodrama. —Thomas

is unhandsome in life, for the disfigured, uncountable bits of the world as it really is!

It was late in 1935, and I, as every schoolchild knows, was the chief of police for the federal district under President Vargas. The word out from Moscow, we'd learned, was that the germs of revolution were bursting open all across our continent, and that in Brazil especially the roots had already caught hold and would soon be pushing up those hearty flowers which, like the future itself, "come through the soil already blossomed." All that was left, or so the Comintern assured anyone who saluted them, was for the local communist groups—in our case, the scoundrels of the *Aliança Nacional Libertadora*—to prepare the ground for the coming wave and, perhaps with some violence here and there, to break open a few cracks in the already-wobbly edifices of state power (built up by the likes of Vargas), so that those structures might be toppled once and for all. The natural swells of history, and the workers' own fervor, would surely take care of the rest.

The Brits tipped us off. We knew the insurrections were coming, and we planned accordingly. This is all well-documented. Besides a little trouble we encountered in Rio Grande do Norte, the insurgents were all put down efficiently (and generally for good) within a few days. Some publicized summary punishments followed, reprisals of a sort, though we inflicted them without pleasure. Shows of strength are necessary in such circumstances; the revolts themselves provided the political cover we needed.

But make no mistake! This was a time of chaos for us. Vargas—whom many still regarded at this stage as a merely temporary figurehead—was fighting tooth and nail to keep hold over the various local, and still largely independent, governing powers. We felt we were struggling for our very existence.

You will naturally imagine my exasperation when, during this same turbulent time—it was by now almost November of that terrible year—our good President repeatedly attempted to divert our attention and our limited resources to the wetlands of Mato Grosso. And why were his worries focused there? Because of some foolish swamp legend! Nothing less than the fountain of youth!

Word had reached Vargas, from an informant at the Indian Protection Service, that some tribe living out in the swamps—with reportedly purplish skins and a robust culture that the IPS had been keeping under wraps for nearly a decade—had learned the secret of immortality. Absurd, I know. And yet Vargas became obsessed; in time he could think of nothing else. "What if our enemies should lay their hands on this knowledge? We'll be done for!"

Perhaps this flies in the face of your remembrance of our good former president. Noble Getúlio, you imagine, must have had more dignity than that! Indeed you might just as well think that putting a bullet into his own heart in '54 was a shrewd or masculine suicide (you'd be wrong: Vargas just wanted his open casket so that the nation might mourn his placid dead face). Don't let yourself be deceived: every man who must make decisions at the highest levels of power, having behind himself the serpent's tail of the State, is bound to appear efficient and quick, even graceful, at least when seen from well and far away.

I capitulated. I was in a sweat myself, after all! I couldn't risk letting this ridiculous obsession of his leave us vulnerable to the revolts that were about to break loose. So I sent a man to Indian Protection to find out just what the hell was going on. It turns out that this "fountain of youth" idea was a distortion: the *Milepiva* (the name of the tribe in question, a population of a few thousand souls which had hid, for who knows how many centuries, in a vast but secluded mist-covered plateau surrounded by swamps and treacherous rocks and seas of lice and other bloodthirsty insects) had, or so several IPS agents swore during secret depositions, developed a formula—actually it was some sort of magical fish stew, they called it the *Piey'Ohe*—which reportedly allowed those who ate it to live an average of two-hundred years. Just as miraculously, the stew also made them *happy. Permanently* so. Not drunk or intoxicated, just happy; continuously happy, for life.

Of course at the time I was quite sure this was nonsense, the mythology of a primitive people. But Vargas would not be disabused. He fretted day and night about what might happen should this "secret to happiness" fall into the wrong hands. "Should the people become irremediably *happy*," he once said to me, with those same sorrowful eyes that one finds among farm workers in the *cerrados*, "what would be the result? Happiness is unpredictable. You might think you know how you would act if you were truly happy—but you don't! No one does! And if everyone were happy…well, our economy probably couldn't survive it!"

The insufferable imagination of the man! Yet I had no choice but to placate him. So did his *idée fixe* become mine. I'll even admit I sometimes had a second thought about it myself. I was friendly with the German ambassador at the time, and I consulted him privately about the Milepiva and their supposedly magic stew; I think I was hoping he'd sober me up. To my surprise, he took the information to some occultists over at the *Ahnenerbe* in Berlin, where reportedly it got all the way up to Himmler himself. (Yes, I admit it: I approved of, and even admired, that gleaming regime during this period.) I never heard anything more about it from them, however. I dare say this lack of interest proved admirable in my eyes, and reinvigorated my own disbelief. The Germans could sniff out claptrap when they needed to. And anyway, I don't think they were particularly interested in *happiness* at the time.

Vargas, by contrast, could think of almost nothing else. He remained immune to skepticism, and to my ridicule too. Finally his fears about the Milepiva and their mysteries reached a fever pitch, for he learned that three notable persons—a bandit, an anthropologist, and an agent from Indian Protection, each with separate designs and with groups of men in tow—were all, in that same pregnant month of November, headed in the direction of the swamps where the Milepiva lived. Vargas brooded: "Any one of these men—should he happen upon the tribe first—might learn their secret! What if they should succeed in unleashing joy upon the countryside?!" By then—or so Vargas would groan in my ear like an imbecile—it would be too late for us to do anything about it.

Who were these three men? Two of them you know already. The bandit was none other than the notorious Lampião, or Virgulino Ferreira da Silva, that murderous Robin Hood of the day, that *cangaceiro*, who'd boasted that he never met a cop he didn't try to kill, and who finally was captured, along with a band of his merry men, in '38 and—thanks to my own standing orders to the local police forces—promptly executed. The truly absurd thing was that Lampião had nothing whatsoever to do with the Milepiva; Vargas had merely read some piece in a provincial newspaper in which Lampião, who loved talking to reporters, had made some cryptic remarks about heading to the hinterland in the west—"where my immortality awaits!" This lone sentence proved sufficient to stoke the flames of Vargas's paranoia. In the end, I don't think Lampião ever once left the vicinity of his strongholds and hideouts amid the backlands of the northeast.

The anthropologist—Claude Lévi-Strauss, who has since become quite famous—also had no designs on the Milepiva. Some program in São Paulo had arranged for a group of French professors to come teach at the new university and do fieldwork among the Indians in the bush. Lévi-Strauss, as I understood it at the time, was heading to the swamplands with his crew— including in their number a young poet and disciple called Felix Degrand (Lévi-Strauss evidently liked the company of writers, fancied himself one too), who eventually would get caught up in the sad fate I am about to relate—in order to study the Caduveo and the Bororo tribes. They had not even an inkling of the Milepiva's existence.

Alas the agent! From IPS—a man named Ruy, who'd been with the agency since its inception in 1910, a true believer—he was our only genuine concern. One of the district commissioners from Indian Protection had become worried about the Milepiva, as they had apparently become aware—surely thanks to the IPS's own meddling!—of just how vast the civilized world outside of their swamps really was. Seized by some sort of moral dread as a result, the tribe had stopped producing the *Piey'Ohe* altogether. Ruy was determined to renew the tribe's production of the stuff, to find out exactly how they made it, and to get a decent-sized sample of it for analysis. (Like I said, a true believer!) Apparently he also somehow managed to recruit one of Lévi-Strauss's men—Degrand—for this purpose while in Porto Esperança. By the middle of November, the two of them, along with a small band of IPS agents, were attempting to traverse the swamps and slopes that guarded Milepiva territory.

It was all too much for me to take. Vargas was inconsolable. Time was pressing. The communist rebellions were about to explode upon us. I couldn't let what I thought was nothing more than a foolish superstition

[The following scrawled haphazardly in pencil, apparently in Müller's own hand. —Thomas]

I sent a cadre of armed men
        to that hidden plateau
to that plateau hidden

        under a leaden mist

            Contact Marta about travel arrangements to Paris!

Where generations of them, the Milepiva, had lived

        a people that had not seen the sky in a thousand years

and now never will see it.
What secrets have I destroyed?

4.

*Articles, Jornal do Recife. 26 September and
2 November 1935.*

[As you'll see, there are two newspaper clippings included here, though the second one is weathered and no longer legible. The following is the translation of the text of the first. — Thomas]

LAMPIÃO CELEBRATES IN RECIFE

A celebration which arose, spontaneously some said, in the streets of downtown Recife last Thursday night was, it now appears, roused by none other than the bandit Lampião, several eyewitnesses have reported. "I saw him myself," a local shopkeeper said. "He said he'd just returned from wreaking havoc at the Carvalho cattle-ranch up north, and he'd stolen some clothes from there too. He and his men were handing them out to people in the streets, and *cachaça* as well." No casualties were reported. Lampião himself is supposed to have announced that the celebration was in honor of his decision to head west, to Mato Grosso. "There we shall live forever!" was the chant recited by the crowds. In the days following the festivities, posters from authorities in Bahia and other states began appearing in Recife. No bounties have yet been collected.

5.

*Personal record, Felix Degrand, assistant to
Claude Lévi-Strauss. November 1935.*

November 9.

Two days ago, our train reached its final destination at Porto
Esperança, in the southern edge of the Pantanal, the largest
swamp on the earth. Sabene, who has promised to be our guide
and translator during our expedition into the interior (and into
Caduveo territory), did not greet us upon our arrival as
scheduled, so we had to go hunting for him in the shanties.
Fortunately for us, this "dismal" port, as Claude likes to call it—
he also calls it "wrongly named" and "hopelessly damned," not a
heart but a "blemishy appendix" of Brazil, "barely a post before
the wild"—is a small place and half-in-shambles and contains no
secrets. Everyone here knows everyone else and his business too.
Surely, but for the fact that this remote riverbank settlement
happens to be where the rail line ends—where, in any given
week, at best a smattering of trains and steamers will perch for a
day or so (most of them drawn here by the lures of cheap trade
and serviceable cattle) before turning back much swifter than
how they came—but for that, I say, there would be nothing upon

this muddy pile to keep secret in the first place. After a few inquiries and a bribe consisting of some coins and an empty tobacco-tin, we were shown the way to Sabene's abode among the shanty houses, which had been planted precariously in the wet clay swamp-side of the river.

They were bizarre weather-beaten structures, those dwellings, round and stressed and pale-white at the tops like pregnant bellies and all arranged in rows, with doors thrown open and even whole walls sometimes pulled down, giving us a view to sparely-equipped rooms and glad folk set about to cooking or washing or shucking corn while in various stages of undress. That same folk regarded us shamelessly and with little interest as we filed past; not a one of them covered up, despite our gazing, nor flinched. At the most they hummed or yawned. Indeed I think they might have been the most unabashed crop of people that ever lived in a half-civilized place—or maybe it was us, perhaps we were only shadows to them. I had the impression, at any rate, that there was some inscrutable point to it, some purpose behind this turning-out of the households and this careless exhibition of daily life, as if the locals had felt a need to proclaim—before whom, or to what spying god, I could not say—that even here, even at the very edge of the wilderness, even deep inside these cracked-open tenements with their quiet human broods, scarcely set apart from the unimaginable swamp looming in the north, there were no secrets to keep.

Alas, when finally we tracked Sabene down, and I laid eyes on the man for the first time, I felt certain he was dead, not especially because of how he lay still atop a pile of ears of corn outside of his hut with his eyes only half-closed and the pale tip of his tongue out between his lips; not especially because of his bluish complexion; but rather because of the vigorous way that one of the stray dogs—yes, strange as it sounds there are many such mongrels that scrounge about the port, most of them odd mutts with bright red gums and fangs the color of dead grass— was *chewing* on Sabene's foot, and without so much as a twitch of discomfort showing upon the old man's face.

Of course he was only sleeping. Many of the inhabitants of Porto Esperança have perfected this superstitious art of sleeping with their eyes half-open—a bad omen in its own right, I should say!—and it turns out that these same locals, almost all of whom earn their living by servicing the few arriving trains and river boats, tend to go about barefoot, and accordingly spend whole days leaping shoelessly from plank to plank (everything here rests upon wooden platforms and stilts, you see, as everywhere the ground is wet and treacherous with the encroaching swamp waters). Since the planks get sun-cooked and can turn brutally hot, the workers' activities produce significant gray calluses on the balls and heels of their feet, as thick and durable as a plastic coating. I am certain that sleeping Sabene, who in that moment was oblivious to our presence, was also quite insensible to the animal gnawing upon his hardened heel—even when, snarling with satisfaction, the dog pried loose a piece from that petrified extremity and scurried away with it.

Claude—ah! I must practice referring to him as *professor*; he's been appointed a chair in São Paulo, after all—quickly set things right with Sabene, though only after scolding him in his usual brusque way. (Truly, I've known few men more prone to anger than our good professor!) Sabene, a small half-stooped man with a clean-shaven face (of the aforementioned deathly hue) and stringy hair cut rigidly into a bowl shape, accepted his punishment while grinning, which, I confess, made me like him. Our arrangements were then made, and it was determined that after two weeks (there still remain goodly supplies for us to round up) we will journey, by horse and ox, the two hundred or so kilometers up and over the Serra da Bodoquena, and from thence into Nalike, where we expect to encounter the Caduveo, whom we will study.

We proceeded then to our lodgings to get settled—a single-room wooden chalet they'd erected especially for us—while the professor and Sabene went over the maps. As there was little left for the rest of us to do then but wait, a sort of stupid peace followed, a quiet to which our ears were unaccustomed after spending days upon that detestable train. This "quiet," of course, was actually no such thing: the birds and the insects of the swamp sang day and night, and train-whistles and steam answered back. The ordinary bustle of the port hummed along as ever; voices called out and cursed in Portuguese and Spanish and sometimes in unrecognizable dialects. All the while, the natural world pressed in from all sides: small herds of zebus could sometimes be seen trudging along the outskirts; a pair of rheas might suddenly sprint past; the fragrance of rosemallow was carried in on the early fog each day from the north, and if the morning river-mist crept to the shore and joined with it, the whole of Porto Esperança became engulfed and clouded, as by fumes exhaled from some exhausted, quickly-cooling volcano. The clammy air, like the chirping of swamplife, was something to which you first only adapted but then found soothing. In the distance in every direction lay the green beauty of Brazil.

But, should your train arrive, as ours did, at this particular railway terminus during the last sunlit hour of a mid-November day, just before the rainy season begins in earnest, you will also surely not fail to see, cast over the near part of the River Paraguay, three vast, tendril-like shadows—an effect produced by the sun's descent below the tops of three abnormally tall clusters of *tucumã* palms perched on a hill at the water's edge—making it appear as though some gigantic claw were just then rising from the water, doubtless with the purpose of seizing the train, and you with it, before sinking back, fulfilled by its catch, to the black and heavy depth whence it came.

Should such a sight and such imaginings fill you with dread, as they did in my case, you might also find that they are not easily shaken off. Not even after the sun has sunk fully and the day has heaved its last steamy sigh and the shadows have all swallowed each other up. In the swamplands, as in the bush, moods are trusted like any other sense, and are every bit as telling as the sky: when they darken, you take notice.

6.

*Telegram to Claude Lévi-Strauss in Porto
Esperança, from F. Durão, District
Commissioner, Indian Protection Service.
November 1935.*

INCOMING TELEGRAM

ESA504MOA053
RR PE
R 151929W
            1935, NOV 11 PM 4 50
FM INDIAN PR SERV
TO C. LEVI-STRAUSS

C O N F I D E N T I A L

M. LEVI-STRAUSS:

OUR MAN HAS BEEN DISPATCHED AND
FOLLOWS BEHIND THIS MESSAGE. YOU ARE
REQUESTED TO REMAIN IN P ESPERANCA AND
AWAIT HIS ARRIVAL. ASSISTANCE NEEDED FOR
OPERATION NORTHWEST OF RIVER.

AWAIT OUR AGENT. LIVES HANG IN THE
BALANCE.

F DURAO
DISTRICT COMISSIONER,
DEPT FOR PROTECTION OF INDIANS

CONFIDENTIAL

7.

Letter from Claude Lévi-Strauss to Fernando de Azevedo, Director General, Department of Public Education; sent by special courier. November 1935.

November 13

My friend,

What do you know about this Indian Protection business going on down here? Some hissing bureaucrat called Ruy swoops in and says he's from the agency and then helps himself to some of our horses and even commandeers one of our oxen! What's worse, he's taken our man Sabene, says only Sabene can translate where they're going. I saw them cast off this morning, a crew of six including old Sabby, with scant supplies, and all I know for sure is they're not headed toward the Caduveo; they're venturing northwest instead. As far as I can tell the only thing out that way, besides the bush and the swamp and eventually the Bolivian border, is that one cattle ranch, that *fazenda* run by the two Dutch fellows; but then all the Indians out there speak Portuguese and there's not even any protected territory in those parts any longer, so how does the agency have jurisdiction in the first place? Trust me, though: I looked into this Ruy's face before he departed and it made me think something grave is going on, though he kept tight-lipped about it. Plus there's this damned cryptic telegram we received prior, enclosed. "Lives in the balance"?? Still, I was a good sport and let the agent take Felix too, my right hand, my little philosopher. I allowed it, I said, because this poor Ruy seemed to be in a bad way and probably could use all the help he could get, and Felix, as you know, though young, is as quick as any of us (if also a bit too sentimental in his thinking); but really it was so Felix reports back to me everything he sees. What have you heard? Can you poke around a bit and find it out?

Reply quick, by telegram; we're here for another week and a half at most, then we're off to Nalike.

CLS

P.S. Since when are the men from Indian Protection armed??

8.

Telegram, from Agent "Ruy" to F. Durão,
District Commissioner, Indian Protection
Service. 16 July 1935.

[As before, the abbreviations in the header are wholly obscure to me. The body of the telegram is hardly more intelligible; it reads as follows. —Thomas]

RETURNING TO SAO PAULO. THINGS ARE A MESS WITH TRIBE. MY FAULT. TRIBE NO LONGER FISHING OR COOKING. LAST TWO CHOSEN GRUBS [*larvas* — Thomas] KILLED THEMSELVES. ONE BEFORE THAT VANISHED INTO THE BUSH. PERHAPS A SUBSTITUTE GRUB COULD BE INTRODUCED. I KNOW SOMEONE TRUSTWORTHY WHO WILL JUMP AT IT.

RUY

9.

Letter, from "Ruy" to his brother (Lampião?).
30 August 1935.

My brother, stop at once. Do not come to Mato Grosso. I've caught wind of an initiative of some of Vargas's thugs to "intervene" with the Milepiva. Surely they intend to confiscate the brew for themselves. Time, in other words, has run out. It won't be safe for you here anyway, not with the feds sniffing around. I have no choice but to find a patsy now. Stay where you are. I'll send you a telegram from Porto Esperança once I'm clear. Keep your head down in the meantime!

Ruy

10.

Personal record, Felix Degrand, assistant to
Claude Lévi-Strauss. November 1935.

November 18.

"Before we go any further," Sabene announced, a good five days into our journey, "we must take precautions."

This he said to us, after rocky slopes, tall grasses filled with red-eyed frogs that leapt right at our faces, the swamp-mud our horses could barely traverse, the mosquitos which left pink welts on our skin, and the myriad parasites that tried to burrow into our flesh, sometimes having to be extirpated with a red hot knife!

This he said to us, after bristles from cacti lodged deep into our thighs and into the horses' haunches, after sudden rainstorms soaked us all from head to hoof, after we'd been breathing air so humid I thought we would choke on it!

This he said to us, even though a diabolical flock of bats—*morcegos*—had been pursuing us for several nights already, sometimes even swooping down at us as if with the intention of latching onto our throats. I swear the demonic things could sense my fear of them; perhaps they were feeding on that. One came so close it grazed the top of my hat.

"Have you ever been bitten by one?" I asked Sabene. He laughed before responding, though I think he must have misunderstood me, or maybe he was having fun: "Not in over a hundred years."

So then, what were these new precautions that Sabene insisted we take? Elastic, tight-fitting ropes that he tied to our waists and sleeves and pant-legs, and which functioned practically like tourniquets, leaving our feet and hands numb. "The *carrapatos*," Ruy said. "They try to get under the clothes. Very bad!"

As we made our way, these aggressive parasites, like tiny ferocious spiders, swarmed over us and the horses alike; we had to slap them off like we were beating down flames. One of the horses broke loose and sprinted away.

Finally, after another league or two of loose mud and foul, steamy air, we came to a clearing, a plain of sorts, with high grass and squat leafy trees and a decent view in all directions. To the east, a looming hill repeatedly drew my attention; unlike all the other terrain I could see, it alone had something of a golden color, and it shimmered, as if it had been draped by a pelt and was rustling in the breeze. To the north lay a seething river, with waters that appeared to be dark blue, even purplish—or so I thought until I got a closer look.

In the water, just below the surface, there swarmed hundreds, maybe even thousands, of massive blue-and-black eels. They were frantic, seemingly anguished things, muscled but with smooth hides and no discernible eyeballs, wrapped all about each other in the foam they'd whipped up from their combined fury. They had small flat fins on their sides, ridged like primordial hands, and wide round maws with what looked to be tendons in place of teeth, whitish and flexible and pulsating out from their mouths like the legs of jellyfish. These hideous creatures—sometimes cresting, sometimes launching up and out of the water all entire, like salmon, like flung worms—resembled nothing better than a hungry brood of sea serpents; indeed I almost cried out *Stop* to Sabene when I saw him lie down flat upon the bank and plunge his arm into the water, so sure was I that this foolhardy act would mean his demise. To my astonishment he promptly stood back up with one of the fat squirming things in his hand, which he then displayed to Ruy. I tried to overhear the words they exchanged; I tried to decipher the look of concern on Ruy's face when he studied the wriggling eel in Sabene's hand; I tried to make heads or tails of their serious talk of the creature's blue color, of something generally amiss about it. There was something amiss, too, they seemed to agree, about the river more generally: they kept gesturing to it while gravely shaking their heads. They appeared disturbed, finally, by something off in the east; I think they found something objectionable about the golden hill which glistened in the distance like a pile of coins (just now I almost said "like a sleeping camel"—it seems somehow alive). If I'm not mistaken, I also heard the word for butterflies—*borboletas*—used several times. Alas, my Portuguese is still only rudimentary; probably I've misunderstood everything.

Sabene scooped up two more of the monstrous river serpents and cooked them over a fire for us. They tasted like anise, like bitter licorice mixed with cilantro. Noting the look of displeasure on my face, Sabene put his hand on my shoulder and, for the very first time since I met the man, addressed me in French.

"We find first the *koro*, the grubs, the termite-ridden log; only then do we hunt the boar."

Again, I'm quite sure I've misunderstood.

Once more, then, into the bush, an hour's journey more, and then one more climb, a fragrant mist thickening with each new mile. Finally we came upon what seemed to be a clearing, a "plateau," Sabene said, but we had to take his word for it because we could scarcely see more than a few feet in front of our faces, thanks to the maddening fog. We began to hear melodious sounds, and only gradually did I realize they were voices. It was impossible to tell how close they were—the haze seemed both to carry and to mute the sound of them. Here and there human-like shapes could be seen flitting by, dark against the broth-like mist, and fast, like shadows cast by aircraft. A land of mist and flying shadows, that's what it was, that's where we found ourselves.

Sabene and Ruy grinned; we'd reached our destination.

11.

Letter from Felix Degrand to Claude Lévi-Strauss. November 1935.

November 21

Monsieur le professeur,

Excuse the obvious haste, and the dearth of detail, in this letter; Sabene has only just whispered in my ear that he plans to sneak off tomorrow in order to honor his commitments to you, and will venture east to Nalike to find you among the Caduveo. So I must write what I can, quickly, in the very little time I have. May Sabene succeed in delivering these pages!

We are here, wherever "here" is (some two hundred kilometers northwest of the Paraguay River; though I doubt I would be able to retrace our steps after such a tortuous journey). I've pulled loose some of the pages from my personal diary which describe some of our ordeals getting to this place. I hope they are not too lavish. (For completeness, I'm including also what I wrote about our arrival at Porto Esperança; I know you have your opinions about that place!)

There is a city here. Or at least that is how it has been described to me. The fog is so thick—and permanent, they tell me, it never lifts—that one cannot see more than a few feet in any direction. Sabene and Ruy both insist that there are at least a thousand people living here. There are stone structures too, some of which I have seen and inspected myself (and whose construction must have required at least some element of non-primitive technology). These structures are like high, tapered obelisks, but hollow, with vast rooms and stone ladders to get to the upper floors. The furnishings are all entirely functional, with not a single decorative item to be found. "Art," Ruy has informed me, "is here something strictly *public*; it is to be found out of doors. It has no role in private spaces."

The people are called the Malapeva, and they are clad in pelts and feathers and are purplish and blue in skin color (I realize now Sabene is of their tribe, or at least distantly so). All their language is poetry, sung or declaimed. Everywhere you walk you can hear the music of their ordinary speech. Likewise, their works of art— sculptures and totems—are everywhere in the common areas, though you don't notice them until you are face to face with one, thanks to the leaden mist that hangs over everything. The mist! It engulfs all; indeed you can never know if you are alone because of it. Someone could be just a few steps away and you wouldn't know. Even now as I write, I might be alone, but there might also lurk a hundred Malapeva all around me. Until some song breaks forth from the gloom you cannot tell! I think this is why the Malapeva sing their speech—not only to announce their presence to others, but also to establish aural bonds where visual ones are largely absent. The mist is thus both an element of solitude and a profoundly *social* fact at the same time: it hides you and touches you and touches everyone else too; it isolates *and* binds-together. Every time I hear a disembodied voice call out from the surrounding haze, proving afresh that I'm not alone, my heart thumps, and I am chilled with both joy and fright.

Truly, this world is beyond belief. I would insist that you abandon the Caduveo at once and come here and see for yourself, were it not for the fact that Ruy has just confided some terrible news to me. He says the government will any day descend on this place. He is undoubtedly sincere in his belief—he turned pale at his own words.

The Malapeva are an extraordinarily friendly people. Ruy tells me—he has been studying them for over a decade now, though his findings are all firmly classified—that their friendliness is what originally drove them to this remote, misty plateau, more than a thousand years ago. Their more bellicose neighbors had found them easy targets for conquest and enslavement.

They seemed especially glad to meet me. They call me the *koro*. This is a word they share with the *caingangue*, yes? It means *grub*. I don't know if this is a way of expressing contempt for me, or perhaps it refers to my pale skin; but I feel certain there is some deeper significance to the appellation. Sabene, who translates for me, has often repeated this obscure aphorism, which many of the Malapeva seem to recite, as if it were a piece broken off from some ancient wisdom: *Find first the* Koro, *the termite-ridden log; only then seek the boar.*

The metaphysics of this tribe! They are unlike anything I have ever encountered. To begin with, the people are at odds with their own gods. A central theme of their mythology is that the destroyer god, *Kalchara,* who is not a singular being but rather a *flock* of magical egrets (if I have understood correctly), is destined to destroy the world. And why? Because humanity has failed to fulfill the purpose of its existence. And what is that purpose? *Ohe,* or happiness, or well-being—not Aristotelian *eudemonia*, not thriving or flourishing, but something more like *gratitude* (that was how Ruy explained it to me anyway). *Ohe* is thankfulness for Being. Kalchara is destined to destroy this planet because humanity is not properly *thankful* for it!

And yet—the tribe has, or it believes it has, discovered a material *solution* to this metaphysical problem. They've developed a special stew, made with the red-bellied piranha of a nearby river—I will describe in a moment the ceremony by which this comes about—and which, they believe, can turn anyone who eats it truly happy and full of gratitude. And not just for the moment, but forever. It guarantees, in other words, *Ohe*. The eaters of this stew, or so the sorcerers of the tribe tell me, can live as long as they wish, too. Those who eat it typically choose to live, the magic men say, about two hundred years.

Professor, I must confess to you now (I've been embarassed to say it): I have eaten the stuff, and the effects are stunning and instantaneous. I don't know what chemical properties these piranha have, but ever since I ate it I am overwhelmed with . . . there is no other word for it . . . *gratitude* for my existence, for the fact that I'm alive, for the simple, steady hum of my consciousness! I hope you will trust me: this is no mere seed or suggestion that has been planted into my thoughts; the sensation is undeniably real. I *comprehend* it, too (my happiness I mean): it is all there before me, as legible as a face. *Thankfulness* is the critical ingredient! How everything—the air, the ground, the beings all about you—feels like a *gift* when you're truly happy! Not inebriated, mind you; I'm in full possession of my faculties, I swear it. The happiness I'm talking about is not intoxication; in fact I would say it was but a small adjustment, a miniscule tweak really, of my ordinary state of mind. I've even reached the conclusion that this must be how religion itself first lurches into being: out of the feeling, only subtly different from our ordinary moods, that all reality—*all of it*—has been a boon.

That's the trick: the thankfulness comes first; only *after* your thanks for the gift do you receive it!

It's not quite right to say this concoction of theirs has *no* intoxicating properties, of course. When I first tried it—there was a ceremony involved, there was dancing and chanting, drums and a ghastly chorus of singers (dissonant, not at all pretty like the songs of their ordinary speech)—I fell into a dream, though I don't think I was actually asleep. One of the sorcerers of the tribe told me I was going to the "house of the oldest dream," or to "another time" (the Malapeva do not seem to have separate concepts for "past" and "future"; they consider all time outside of the present to be *prootchyat,* or just "other times"). Because I must hurry, I am ripping out from my personal journal a description I wrote of that hallucination—I call it "The Dream." Make of it what you will, but know this: from the moment I awoke from that dream (I don't know what else to call it), I was happy.

And yet the tribe refuses to eat it! They fed some to me, and they cheered and sang my praises when I did. But they refrain from consuming it themselves. Why? If it will make them all happy and grateful, then surely they should partake of it and rescue the world from the mystical annihilation they imagine is coming! But no: the hold their mythology has upon them is too powerful. For it is clear to me that they *believe* their myths: they believe that, should they ever get *too close* to perfecting their own happiness, then this would *trigger* the end of the world. The prophecy, after all, is that Kalchara *will* destroy the world *because* perfect gratitude *is not* attained. Should the Malapeva ever avail themselves of the chemically-induced happiness that is right within their grasp, should they get too close to that utopia, then they would, by that same stroke, force the prophecy to be fulfilled at once, and so bring about the destruction of all existence.

The tragedy of it! They have solved—empirically, materially—all the fundamental problems of their social existence; but they have not yet solved those problems *symbolically,* at the level of their religion. Perhaps they require a revolution—not in their technological capacities or in their social forms or in their relations of production, but in their very mythology.

Even more astonishing in this respect is that the Malapeva are capable of great abstraction, and even what we might call philosophy as such. Sabene translated a lecture administered to me by one of the chiefs, or maybe she was some sort of aristocrat (she had one of the obelisks all to herself):

> *What is the purpose of our being? Surely it is happiness (Ohe). So then, it is of vital importance that at least someone be happy (Ohea). So we pick one or two among us to be the happy ones; we devote great resources to making them happy (Ohea). They can eat whatever they like, they can pick whatever husbands or wives they like. They are catered to at every moment. You see: they redeem the world! For what if Kalchara should choose to destroy us all tomorrow? What if that should happen, and no one among us was ever happy? Then all of life—all our suffering, all our losses, all death—would have been for nothing! If no one were ever happy, then everything would be a waste. So it is of the utmost importance that, before all else, we ensure that at least some of us are happy. Again: their happiness redeems the world! We find first the* koro, *the termite-ridden log; only then is the boar to be sought.*

The *koro,* I mean actual grubs, are plentiful here; any rotting tree you see is bound to be full of them. They taste sweet, like condensed milk. I suppose the aphorism is both metaphysical and practical: satisfy basic needs first, secure some moral baseline, and only then seek out greater or more refined rewards.

But what if, like the Malapeva, you fear those very rewards, because you believe they will bring about the end of the world?

I am running out of time, good professor! Permit me to describe the ceremony of the piranha stew, they call it the *Peet-Ohe*. For it is the most fantastic event I think I have ever witnessed.

In the pages I'm attaching from my diary, I mention a golden hill just south of here, which seemed to shimmer in the distance. Last night a group of Malapeva brought me back to that place, by the river with the eels, with that hill visible in the east. They instructed me to wait there, and then they headed off on foot while waving heavy, pungent torches. Thick smoke billowed up from the torches, filling the air over their heads (truly, the Malapeva bring the fog with them wherever they go!). About thirty minutes later, I began to hear a sound, a vague flapping noise, not exactly like the beating of wings but more like the rustling of pages from a book, as from first a hundred, then a thousand, open volumes at once. The Malapeva were sprinting back, singing and yelling and waving their torches, on both sides of the river.

Then I realized the source of that strange noise. Between the banks, between the runners, there were now thousands— millions? billions? the human eye is ill-equipped to estimate such numbers—of orange and gold butterflies, swarming over the water. Somehow the Malapeva had *corralled* them, and had driven them to the river! I now realized the source of that hill's golden color, and the reason it had seemed to shimmer: it had been *covered* by the butterflies. Millions of them! The Malapeva had roused them, and now were directing them to where I stood!

The fluttering of the butterflies' wings caused a yellowish dust—I assume it was some sort of pollen—to sprinkle down and coat the surface of the water. The eels went mad for it; they ate it up feverishly, and it even turned them green in the process. I can't say if they became intoxicated by the stuff, or simply had gorged themselves; but they began to grow less frantic in their movements, and began swimming, in more orderly fashion, downriver. The Malapeva and I followed them, singing and yelling, waving torches and casting up thick smoke that filled the sky.

After a mile or so the river joined with another, where schools upon schools of red-bellied piranha circled, as if waiting. The piranha devoured the screeching eels in a horrifying bloodbath until they too became gorged and grew sluggish. The Malapeva then easily scooped up hundreds of these now-fattened toothy fish with nets, and sealed them up in wooden barrels which we all transported back to the plateau.

Once back in the city, the piranhas were delivered to a group of men and women who were tending to a massive cauldron over a fire. The piranhas were then cleaned. Some of the children gleefully dug through the fish barrels; if they found one still alive they would seize it and begin throwing it at each other, laughing with delight and terror at its still-snapping jaws. The prepared fish were then added to the cauldron to cook (I do not know what else was simmering in the pot already). The stench was vile.

At last the stew was ready; there was enough in the cauldron to feed most of the tribe, I imagine. Yet not one of them would so much as taste it. It was all for *me*, they said. Me, the *koro*.

Professor, I have sealed some of it in a tin for you, and have begged Sabene to deliver it. I don't know if the effects are diminished with time, or how well it will keep. But swallow it down. Never mind the stench! Don't think about it, just swallow it down. Tell me if you feel it. Who knows, perhaps if you do you'll live to be a hundred!

Eels, pollinated by butterflies, devoured by piranhas, then turned into an elixir of joy, which the Malapeva refuse to consume! I shall say it once more: this world is beyond belief.

I'm tucking this letter into Sabene's satchel now. I hope to join you myself soon. With some luck, this city may survive. If so, we'll return to it one day.

I murmur prayers for you and for me.

Felix

P.S. I have the suspicion that I've been brokered, that Ruy has made a gift of me.

12.

Telegram, from Virgulino Ferreira da Silva to Ruy Ferreira da Silva, Porto Esperança. 24 December 1935.

[Similar abbreviations as before. The body of the telegram reads simply as follows. —Thomas]

PLEASED TO DISCOVER YOU ESCAPED WITH YOUR LIFE. QUIT THOSE SWINE AND JOIN US.

13.

From Bandits of the East, by Frederico Santos
(Guarulhos: 1983). P. 346.

Probably the most famous photograph of Lampião, after his execution in July 1938. His head sits on the foremost, bottom row. Just above him is his brother, Ruy "Lefty" [Conhoto] Ferreira da Silva. Photographer unknown.

14.

Personal record, Felix Degrand, assistant to
Claude Lévi-Strauss. November 1935.

THE DREAM

After eating the *Peet-Ohe,* I lapsed into the following dream:

There was a downpour, a deluge, and palm groves swarming with men. Almost all of them, it appeared, were slaves. They were being overseen by guards armed with crude pikes made of stone and wood. There were hundreds, maybe thousands of them, purple-skinned like plums and barely speaking, all laboring in the rainfall in frantic, disorderly fashion. They were engaged in some Sisyphean task—I believe they were attempting to keep the groves from flooding. It was hopeless; they were using buckets. They were whipped for their failure.

I was joined with the consciousness of one of them. I experienced what he experienced. I felt his feelings, and I knew some of his thoughts and even his memories. He was a slave. I was unable to determine his name; it is quite possible he had none.

Some catastrophe of nature had no doubt occurred; the rains were brutal and the slaves were clad far too scantily for the cold. It was as if they had long been accustomed to a much hotter and dryer climate, and simply had not had sufficient time to adapt to the transforming weather. The palm trees, too, looked to be drowning in the endless rain; the fronds were all heavy or dead and hung like limp hands. Everything here—down to every prune-like fingertip of every blue-lipped man—was cold and wet.

Only the jaguars, which were plentiful and roamed freely among the groves, appeared to be unfazed by the rain. They perched in high places like owls, waiting and frowning peacefully, until suddenly one of them would leap below to sprint after prey, triggering the rest to follow. Their heavy, waterlogged hides flapped gruesomely as they ran. If, as they sped past, even a little sunlight struck them, the spray from their fur would cause them to be engulfed in rainbows.

The man to whose consciousness I had been joined was cold and wet and had not even a rainbow to enrobe him. He'd known little more than the drudgery of a slave his whole life; his memory, as a result, was terrifyingly vacant. He shivered in his sleep on a flat stone in what appeared to be a temple that had been made into a makeshift lodge for the laborers. (The ground outside was too saturated to sleep on; you'd likely drown in it, or maybe you'd get sucked below like the thousands of slaves' sandals that had been lost to the mud.) He was shoulder-to-shoulder with other slaves at almost all times. A pungent, lukewarm rice soup flavored with dates and a powerful clove (which seemed to double as a depressant) was his sole source of nourishment. He would fall asleep, still famished, before he'd even got done with his bowl.

But he had also seen the opulent, sheltered beds of the priests—I believe they were not just an aristocracy but a genuinely magical class, prophets perhaps, or maybe to the slaves they were evil spirits or even the gods themselves; at any rate I felt how the man to whom I was joined experienced holy awe and dread in their presence. They were dressed lavishly in the skins of the jaguars.

The man dreamed of being dry like them, and warm and well-fed, his arms and legs spread wide on a bed, full and soft like the breast of a swan. When he dreamt in this fashion—for these were not only his dreams, I am sure, but also his metaphysics— he muttered a word over and over: *adya*. I think it means something like "heaven," though it clearly also means "bed," and he believed in them both: he believed in the *adya* (bed) that awaited him there in *Adya* (Heaven). But not just that; he dreamed also of friendship (and not just the occasional encouraging glance from a fellow slave, but true warmth); and also of love (he had seen a woman once or twice in his life, though they were kept rigorously segregated from the slaves, many of whom anyway were castrated); and of food, *hot* food (he had from time to time smelled bread baked on clay, and steaming corn, and dripping meats); and of boats that fly in the air and could travel anywhere one wished; and of long leisure and the freedom to nap in the daytime; and of infinite scrolls and parchments inscribed in a language he could decipher, and with pictures, too, full of knowledge and the tales of other free men; and of skies empty of clouds, the mystery of their communion with the stars revealed to him; and of tobacco and easy-flowing speech and the brilliant, sun-like absence of work.

...

When, abruptly, I awoke from this dream—or should I say, when I snapped back to my senses—and I realized that I had been returned to my dry, well-fed self (as though from a long, cold hibernation), I was overwhelmed by relief and gratefulness. My happiness has been irrepressible ever since. The tribe cheered and welcomed me back from my delirium with grins and embraces and chants, as if they knew just what I was feeling. As if they too had once glimpsed the worst sort of doom, and then had eluded it simply by waking.

In a way that I think is somehow selfless, I want the whole world to know how happy I am.

15.

Obituary, São Paulo Chronicle.
5 November 2009.

Claude Lévi-Strauss, considered the father of modern anthropology for his work exploring the parallels between tribal and industrial societies, and whose studies of several indigenous communities in Brazil were revolutionary for their time, has died. He was 100.

"That Which We Truly Don't Know, We Don't Know That We Don't Know," by Glenn Trollip (a review of *The Idea That Never Was*, by Hiram Junker)

Unclassifiable books were once fashionable. It may be worthwhile to ask why they no longer are. Time was, works like Jean Paul Sartre's *Saint Genet* (is it biography? existential psychoanalysis? literary criticism? an unwitting work of fiction?[1]) or the *Anti-Oedipus* by Deleuze and Guattari (is it a new kind of metaphysics? philosophical stream of consciousness? a poetry of the revolution?) or *Guilty* by Bataille (is it a novel? a wartime diary? a series of rapturous aphorisms?) were all the literary rage, at least among some of our more adventurous publishers and readers. Nor can we confine such uncategorizable works to the twentieth century: earlier specimens are found in Nietzsche's *Zarathustra*, for instance (is it a poem? a parable? a confession of a delusion?), or even in Hegel's *Phenomenology* (calling it just "philosophy" seems preposterous). It may be that, like everything else, *genre* too must suffer the storms of history, and, after splintering for a time upon the rocks of revolution and world war, only now reconstitutes itself in its old guise, as a kind of tacit formal law to be pitilessly enforced by publishers and readers and writers alike. Books that straddle too many forms at once, or otherwise elude classification, are reflexively condemned, or no longer feel possible in the first place.

The absence of such amphibious works in our present moment may explain why Hiram Junker's latest effort, *The Idea That Never Was* (HarperCollins, 2025), feels like such an

---

1 Jean Genet famously lied to Sartre about much of his life while the book was being written; Sartre's own interpretive hubris likely contributed some fictional elements as well.

anomalous and refreshing achievement. (Whether this book is in fact a harbinger of some larger development in the offing, or just adventitiously washed ashore, we need not decide here.) I've read the book twice now, and I still don't know how best to describe it. Provisionally I would characterize it as a kind of science fiction, though I also take seriously Darko Suvin's proposal that the whole text—all nine-hundred pages of it—ought to be subsumed under the general heading of "a thought experiment."[2] For the audacious object that this work sets out to imagine is nothing less than our own world, but with something *subtracted* from it. The beating heart of the book, in other words, is an *absence*: something is missing from this imagined reality, and from the characters' lives (though they don't know it), something that we, the readers, possess and even take for granted. The book's operative question (if I may put it this way in regard to a work of fiction) derives from the same slim gap: How must a nearly-identical twin of our world have evolved *differently* as a result of a single missing thing? How must their world have *diverged* from our own?

It is a more unique endeavor than one might at first think. For while plentiful examples of so-called "speculative history" are produced and published each year in the genres of science fiction and fantasy (e.g., books of the "What if Hitler won?" variety), what distinguishes *The Idea That Never Was* from these more fanciful narratives lies in this: in Junker's book, it is not an event or a person or even a technology that "never happened;" instead, and as you will have guessed already, what is missing from this fictional world is an *idea*.

Of course ideas do not just pop into existence on this or that date in history. If your objective is to prevent a concept from coming into being, it will not be enough "simply to purge a key thinker or two, or to take some meddlesome trip in a time

---

2   Suvin, Darko. "Hiram Junker's Hypothetical Intellectual History." Rev. of *The Idea That Never Was*, by Hiram Junker. *London Review of Books*, October 8, 2024: 47-49.

machine," as Martin Jay once put it.[3] Ideas are themselves thoroughly historical objects, and they begin to emerge in our collective subconscious long before they ever become explicit to us. An idea may pass through a long period of incubation in which it is not (yet) fully itself; it may remain vague and abstract, even for centuries, before finally becoming clear and concrete. And yet, once the process of its formation has commenced, it may become all but inexorable. An idea can be destined to shoot forth, even if it first has to languish underground, *in semen scaena*, for a thousand years.

In order for one of our well-entrenched ideas *not* to exist, then, a great many things must never occur, or must happen differently. For a writer trying to pluck it loose, an idea cannot help but drag behind it a whole tangled and deep-rooted mass; even the simplest notion turns out to be "an ornate tale in time" (*ein kompliziertes Märchen in der Zeit*, as Ernst Bloch once described the idea of death[4]). Modifications both subtle and grand have to be made to the historical record to ensure that the idea does not, as it were, sneak back into being. As Darko Suvin puts it: "An author attempting to imagine present-day society, but with some foundational concept omitted from it, has no choice but to connive with history—lest that same history lurch forth to accuse him."[5]

But let us not delay the obvious any longer, and say clearly what this idea is that Hiram Junker seeks to expunge from his imaginary, alternate world. As it happens, the first trace of it appears in the very opening paragraphs. We are at once introduced to Dr. Rubin Thale, arguably the book's protagonist (and the only major character upon whom I'll touch in this

---

3   Jay, Martin. *Totality: The Adventures of a Concept From Lukács to Habermas.* University of California Press: 1986. P. 107.

4   Bloch, Ernst. *The Principle of Despair.* Translated by Neville Plaice, Stephen Plaice, and Paul Knight. MIT Press: 1995. Vol. 3, p. 1106.

5   Suvin 48.

present note). It must be acknowledged straightaway, however, that there is nothing much resembling a unified narrative here; *The Idea That Never Was* contains hundreds of such "characters," and in hundreds of short, mostly unrelated episodes. Junker calls these episodes "Glimpses" rather than "Chapters." Some of the sections run on for several pages, others consist of only a sentence or two; some are stories, some are letters or emails, some are diary entries, some are newspaper articles or quotations drawn from longer works, some even are judicial opinions or government records. Often they are excerpts or fragments, all but free-floating. It is certain that, whatever else one might say about *The Idea That Never Was*, it can only loosely be described as a novel. If a comparison must be made, the book is far closer in its structure to something like Benjamin's *Arcades Project* than to, say, *War and Peace*. Anyway, Thale—the last remaining classics professor to teach at his university, and described as being "tall and stoop-shouldered" with "a waxy, peach complexion like clay" and "flexed, trembling paws" and "a vanishing way about him—one almost expected him to disappear before one's eyes"—has decided to attend a church service. He is not religious, but he is feeling contrite for a crime he has committed. (It is revealed at length that he has been embezzling funds from the university in a well-nigh political act of retaliation against the administration for voting to eliminate his department.) The service is led by the all-but-Dickensian "Pastor Stonewit," who, "glaring at the mostly-empty pews" with a face that was "spotted and droopily jowled as though clasped by seething little hands," begins rhapsodizing about Jesus's habit of writing with his finger in the dirt. The pastor reads aloud from the beginning of the eighth chapter from the Gospel According to John. Readers familiar with the Bible, however, sense at once that something is amiss; the verses Stonewit recites feel wrong somehow. This intuition of course proves correct; here are the verses as read by Stonewit, compared with the *actual* verses from John 8:

John 8:1-11, *as read by Stonewit*

¹But Jesus went to the Mount of Olives. ²At dawn he appeared again in the temple courts, where all the people gathered around him, and he sat down to teach them. ³The teachers of the law and the Pharisees brought in a woman caught in adultery. They made her stand before the group ⁴and said to Jesus, "Teacher, this woman was caught in the act of adultery. ⁵In the Law Moses commanded us to stone such women. Now what do you say?" ⁶They were using this question as a trap, in order to have a basis for accusing him.

But Jesus bent down and started to write on the ground with his finger. ⁷When they kept on questioning him, he straightened up and said to them, "If any one of you is without sin, let him be the first to throw a stone at her." ⁸Again he stooped down and wrote on the ground.

⁹At this, those who heard began to go away one at a time, the older ones first, until only Jesus was left, with the woman still standing there. ¹⁰Jesus straightened up and asked her, "Woman, where are they? Has no one condemned you?"

¹¹"No one, sir," she said.

"Then neither do I condemn you," Jesus declared. "Go now and leave your life of sin."

John 8:1-14, *actual verses*

¹But Jesus went to the Mount of Olives. ²At dawn he appeared again in the temple courts, where all the people gathered around him, and he sat down to teach them. ³The teachers of the law and the Pharisees brought in a woman holding a child born of adultery. They made her stand before the group ⁴and said to Jesus, "Teacher, this woman was caught in the act of adultery. ⁵In the Law Moses

commanded us to stone such women. Now what do you say?" [6]They were using this question as a trap, in order to have a basis for accusing him.

But Jesus bent down and started to write on the ground with his finger. [7]When they kept on questioning him, he straightened up and said to them, "If any one of you would condemn this woman, let him do so who will not bereave an innocent child of his mother." [8]Again he stooped down and wrote on the ground. When he spoke again, Jesus said, [9]"You would punish the wicked, yet you punish the innocent more severely. [10]Should an honest man also be flogged for the crimes of his neighbor? Do you band together against the righteous and condemn the innocent to death? Do you devour orphans as you devour widows' houses? [11]Surely you belong to your father, he was a murderer from the beginning."

[12]At this, those who heard began to go away one at a time, the older ones first, until only Jesus was left, with the woman still standing there. [13]Jesus straightened up and asked her, "Woman, where are they? Has no one condemned you?"

[14]"No one, sir," she said.

"Then neither do I condemn you," Jesus declared. "Go now and leave your life of sin."

It takes a certain nerve to rewrite the Bible, perhaps even more so to take an eraser to it. Thanks to some clever story-telling on Junker's part, the reader is able to deduce that the verses read by Stonewit are no abridgement, nor are they an expression of the pastor's own creative license. This is how the eighth chapter from the Gospel of John *actually reads* in this alternate world. Omitted from their Bible, then, is any mention of the child in the woman's arms (the child who will likely starve if the woman is killed); omitted is Christ's turning of the Pharisees' own error against them (by condemning *them* for who *their* parent is, i.e., the devil); omitted is the reference to Psalm 94:21; omitted is the memorable verse, *You would punish the wicked, yet you punish the innocent more severely.* In place of all this we have instead only the simple, if not simplistic, pronouncement, *If any of you is without sin, let him be the first to throw a stone at her.* By comparison with the verses that Junker has stripped from the text, this imagined sentence is anti-climactic to say the least; and while it is not without its merits—there is an almost childish eloquence to it— it is surely no substitute for the real thing.

But then that is very much the point. The deficit of their Bible is meant to draw our attention straightaway to just what it is that our world possesses but their world lacks, i.e., a particular *moral idea*—or really a constellation of them—which, for us, is taken virtually as a given thanks to its extensive theological and philosophical pedigree, and because it came to be developed in the common law before being encapsulated most influentially, at least for the modern era, by Blackstone in his *Commentaries*:

> From what has been observed in the former articles we may collect that the quantity of punishment [to which a criminal is sentenced] can never be absolutely determined by any standing invariable rule; but it must be left to the arbitration of the legislature to inflict such penalties as are warranted by the laws of nature and society, and such as appear to be the best calculated to answer the end of precaution against future offenses, with these qualifications only, *that in the manner of the execution of such penalties it must always be of paramount concern that no innocent is harmed, and that nothing barbarous or approaching cold-blooded murder be done.*[6]

In Junker's imagined world, however, this entire strand of moral and legal thinking was never taken up. As a result, it simply

---

6   Blackstone, William. *Commentaries on the Laws of England.* Book IV, § 10 (emphasis added).

does not occur to any of the characters that, for example, the methods of *criminal punishment* practiced by their society—in particular *incarceration,* or what Sade, in our world at least, famously denounced as "that most scandalous disfigurement of every polity on the earth"[7]—might themselves be unjust or even wicked. Indeed it now becomes clear that it was no mere flourish on Junker's part to make Rubin Thale a professor of antiquity; for thanks to the nature of that occupation (along with Thale's voracious reading habits), we the readers are furnished with various windows through which to glimpse the ways the intellectual landscape of *The Idea That Never Was* differs from our own. Gone from this imaginary world, for example, is the influential Book XIII from Plato's *Laws,* dealing with just and unjust forms of punishment. Gone from his *Politics* is Aristotle's classic rebuke to the court of the Areopagus for its harshness and cruelty. Gone is the great rabbinical tradition from twelfth century Alexandria, which dared find corporal punishment *more humane* than imprisonment ("[g]allows and spears and chains all cut lives short," or so says Martin Buber in his famous gloss, "not so the whip or the vise or the rack, when these are used temperately"). Gone is the late conversion of Henry VIII and his public atonement for the seventy-two-thousand he'd hanged or put into dungeons. Gone is Douglass's condemnation of all incarceration as but a form of enslavement. Gone is Nietzsche's keen insight from *The Genealogy of Morals,* which recognized that all criminal justice and even all tort litigation, in their essence, reduce ultimately to a single process, namely, the quantification and administration of *pain.* Not gone, but diminished down to a mere pamphlet, is Wilde's titanic treatise *De Profundis* (for us, perhaps the most blistering and systematic attack on imprisonment ever written down; for them, a mild and almost frivolous squabble with Lord Alfred Douglas). Gone is Kafka's monumental novel *The Penal Colony.* Gone is Ernst Bloch's vast

---

7   Sade (Donatien Alphonse François). *Letters From Prison.* Translated by
    Richard Seaver. Arcade Publishing: 1999. P. 77.

historical meditation, in the second volume of *The Principle of Despair*, on the burgeoning use of prisons in early modern Europe, and the ways this practice corresponded with the rise of exploitative capital. Gone are the great juridical developments of the twentieth century, notably those of Eighth Amendment jurisprudence in America, which, beginning with *Weems v. United States*, 217 U.S. 349 (1910), eventually found *all* extended incarceration to be presumptively "cruel and unusual." Gone, too (perhaps as a result of the aforementioned deficits), is any common-sense understanding that, given the choice between a few days of agony, on the one hand, or ten years in a prison, on the other, almost no one would choose the latter (thus obliterating the old notion—seemingly alive and well in Junker's world—that captivity is somehow a more humane form of punishment than the infliction of physical suffering). Gone as well is that other instinct of our common sense, implicit in many of the texts I've just mentioned, which feels revolted by the use of extended imprisonment because of the collateral harms it inflicts upon the *innocent*. "A man is locked up," the young Camus writes in *Sisyphus and Infinity* (another volume, not incidentally, that has been vanished from Junker's world), "but he is not the only one punished: the man's wife and his children and all his relations who are deprived of him, his employer or employees or co-workers who count on him, his friends and peers who enjoy his company, indeed anyone who benefits, or even who *might* in the future benefit, in any way from his individual contributions to society—all of them are innocent, and yet they too are punished." Somehow this simple notion does not even occur to the people in Junker's alternate reality.

That Junker is able to convey all these historical omissions in a manner that feels more or less natural may be the most admirable feat of *The Idea That Never Was*. How does he do it?

Sometimes subtly,[8] sometimes with plodding directness.[9] But in any case the effect is the same: Junker's is shown to be a world in

---

8   For example, we can infer that, in Junker's world, Kafka never wrote his gigantic novel *The Penal Colony*; Junker's Kafka dies in 1924 (as we learn in passing in Glimpse #229), a full decade before *The Penal Colony* would be completed (in the real world).

9   Glimpse #402, for example, consists of nothing but a reproduction of that most influential passage from Kant's *Metaphysics of Morals*, having to do with punishment and the law of retribution. But of course it is not the text that *we* know. Here is the *actual*, almost magisterial passage from Kant:

The law of punishment is a categorical imperative, and woe to him who crawls through the windings of utility in order to discover something that releases the criminal from retribution, or redirects part of the force of punishment upon someone other than the criminal, by the advantage this promises, in accordance with the pharisaical saying, "It is better for *one* human being to die than for an entire people to perish." For the true meaning of this wicked saying is, "It is better for one *innocent* human being to die than for an entire people to perish," or which saying violates justice utterly. Accordingly, the sacrifice that is revealed by the *Gospels*, in which the Savior receives punishment on behalf of the whole human race (in apparent contradiction to the law of retribution), and yet still preserves perfect justice, can only be a mystery to us. At most we can say of such "punishment" that it is exceptional and spiritual, and not a matter of human or earthly law. Still, the scriptures are clear that this same atonement was borne by Him and only Him, who was destined to bear it; which fact, it must be granted, bears at least a *formal* resemblance to the law of retribution, i.e., the principle that every punishment has exactly *one* true recipient (who must accept it in full), and cannot justly be changed or foisted upon another, in total or whatever partial degree. The learned Knutzen reasons, "The Son of Man and *only He* bore the punishment for the sins of humanity; we may therefore deduce that the nature of His sacrifice was not any *physical* travail or suffering, for if that were the case, then Simon of Cyrene, who helped Jesus carry the cross to Golgotha (Mark 15:21), would have borne part of the punishment, making *him* a *second savior*, which is absurd." — What, therefore, should one think of the proposal that punishment might be inflicted, not only upon the criminal himself, but also upon *innocent members of his family*, causing the criminal to undergo great moral anguish and thus more effectively deterring future crimes? A court would reject with contempt such a proposal, for justice which our modern wisdom concerning justice and criminal penalties has been *reversed*. In that other world, not only are the collateral harms of such penalties scarcely even addressed, but, within the realm of the horrible, *pain* outstrips *lost time*. Accordingly, the State will not sully its hands with physical suffering, except secretly or indirectly ("[t]here is nothing more hideously evil in all the world than physical torture when used as a penalty," says a nameless functionary from the Bureau of Prisons in Glimpse #441: "any pain that comes from being incarcerated is an accident"). In this fantastic world, in other words, being locked away for several years while one's family suffers is considered appropriate retaliation for, say, a theft crime; yet, if one were to be disciplined by the state with *pain* instead, perhaps only for a handful of hours or days, then that would be considered the height of barbarity. Is this madness? Or is it, as the book's title suggests, simply the result of a missing idea?

---

ceases to be justice if it afflicts the innocent, or if it can be traded for any good of civil society whatsoever. (Kant, Immanuel. *The Metaphysics of Morals*. Translated by Mary Gregor. Cambridge University Press: 2017. Pp. 114-15.)

And here is how, in *The Idea That Never Was*, Junker reimagines this text, abridged and gutted and all but a travesty of the original:

The law of punishment is a categorical imperative, and woe to him who crawls through the windings of eudaemonism in order to discover something that releases the criminal from punishment or even reduces its amount by the advantage it promises, in accordance with the pharisaical saying, "It is better for *one* human being to die than for an entire people to perish." For if justice goes, there is no longer any value in human beings' living on the earth. — What, therefore, should one think of the proposal to preserve the life of a criminal sentenced to death if he agrees to let dangerous experiments be made on him and is lucky enough to survive them, so that in this way physicians learn something new of benefit to the commonwealth? A court would reject with contempt such a proposal from a medical college, for justice ceases to be justice if it can be bought for any price whatsoever.

It goes without saying that in Junker's world there are no Pain Centers; there is no Federal Retribution Administration; no metric has been designed to measure the exact quantity of suffering warranted by a particular criminal infraction; no technology has been devised to induce states of physical pain that cause no lasting mental or bodily harm. Indeed these things are not even on their horizon. Wholly unknown to them, consequently, is the revelatory fact—discovered by our own justice system as a result of the Victims' Rights Movement of the 1960s—that, when given the opportunity to *observe* the administering of a pain-sentence to someone convicted of a crime, even the *victims* of that crime tend to be satisfied that retribution has been done *after less than an hour*. ("Even a sadist grows sick from the spectacle of pain after only a little while," said Freud: "That is its genius. Pain is an awesome God; we dare not look it in the face for very long.")

Instead of our carefully developed methods of applied pain, then, what they possess in Junker's world are cages, jails, prisons—many of which (in what is surely Junker's most dystopian flourish) turn out to be privately owned by corporations, and so beholden to shareholders. In Glimpse #812, for example, we find one of the private operators of a prison, along with the advocacy firm of Hakin, Sump, Auer, & Geld, holding a gala for the senators of their state, where they openly lobby for longer sentences in the criminal code.

Predictably—I dare say I spoil nothing with the following summary, and at any rate this plot is but one of a thousand of such narratives in *The Idea That Never Was*—Rubin Thale's fate proves to be a tragic one. He is found out, arrested, and then convicted for the crime of embezzlement from a public institution. He is barbarously sentenced to nine years in a prison (the conditions of which can only be described as squalid). As a result of this official confiscation of his person, one of his daughters commits suicide; the other falls prey to drug addiction. Thale's wife develops health problems owing to stress and a grueling new work schedule, and gradually becomes an invalid.

The remnants of the support staff from Thale's academic department are laid off; a handful of his devoted students are forced to change their focus of study. Thale himself ends up murdered by other inmates while serving his sentence.

Does Junker's book descend to the implausible? Is it, to borrow a phrase from Borges, *merely* astonishing? Perhaps. Readers might well find it difficult to swallow the idea that a rational people *just like ourselves* could be so backwards when it comes to the subject of criminal justice. Still, the deeper issue raised by the book cannot be dismissed so easily. I would express it in the following questions: Could there be fundamental ethical principles we ourselves have overlooked? What profound moral ideas might yet be out there, or even just under our noses, that we simply have failed to grasp?

The first time I finished reading this book, I felt ill at ease. The second time I finished it, I understood why.

Some Pages Concerning the Demise of Dr. Conrad Faintly, *or* Contra Poe, *or* The True Imp of the Perverse

I shall begin, as we middling storytellers too often are wont to do, with the scene of the crime, and the dead body.

Dr. Conrad Faintly, the soft-spoken (and little published) Helmut Kolb Professor of Greek and Roman Antiquities at Irving Catholic College in Albany, cut a far more striking figure as a dead body than ever he did as an educator, what with the way he fell—or leapt, or was thrown (as is the theory preferred by the authorities)—from the stone parapet of Reginald Bridge and onto the bare winter branches of Our Beatific Oak of Saint Mary (that singularly famous tree on campus—a twisted, broad-limbed grotesque, and not at all an oak—and the only one on school grounds that boasted both an appellation *and* a copper plaque, the latter commemorating a day from the year 1903 when, for reasons now lost even to lore, the archbishop of New York came and stood before the tree and solemnly blessed its bulbous gray roots), his arms and legs pierced and pulled in different directions and bent in gruesome fashion as if to mirror the very forked and curled boughs that had impaled him; and also what with the unstately way he appeared then to hover in the air, his body tottering and shuffling in the wind like a loose scarecrow, or rather like some gigantic, swaying fruit, or an insect sac, or again like the tree-limbs themselves that dangled him just ten feet above Gillespie Creek (and did not let him go for many hours, not even after the moonlight—which, one assumes, had lit the sad event—finally drained away to the greater woods beyond), and where he then appeared to float as if determined to haunt the spot, with a grimace—and the surprise of death—still visible on his face the following morning, when, at long last, a faculty dog-walker, presumably with a dog-like yip of her own, discovered him there, now a good while dead.

The primary argument that was offered in favor of the investigators' version of events—to wit, that Faintly had been murdered—was straightforward: the old man was portly and walked with a cane; the tree was too far from the bridge for him to have made the jump on his own. No doubt some very large fellow, or more likely two or three of them (in cruel concert with one another, and with whatever dark motives such men may possess), had picked him up and hurled him to his doom.

The argument in favor of the idea that Faintly simply fell from the bridge—well, there never was any such argument. Short of some unprecedented gale sweeping him up into the air and tossing him forward, a mere fall would not have landed him in the tree.

Only one piece of evidence weighed in favor of the (otherwise implausible) theory that Faintly had *jumped*, and somehow mightily, all the way from the bridge and onto Our Beatific Oak of Saint Mary: the so-called "suicide note" (dubbed that by a reporter from *The Scribe*, Albany's most widely-circulating Catholic paper at the time).

As far as such notes go, it was an unusual one, as you'll see. The last page of it was found still lodged in Faintly's printer; the other pages had been placed in the trash (presumably by Faintly himself; his hard drive meanwhile had been wiped clean). There can be little doubt that this note was intended as a last writing, though to be sure a careful reader of the text may dispute that it contemplates *suicide* at all. ("Faintly was delusional, not suicidal," or so concluded the forensic psychologist appointed to the case.) Is it possible nonetheless to infer from the note that Professor Faintly, with at least some degree of deliberateness, brought about his own death? Perhaps. In any event, here it is in full, the old historian's last message, with all its human frailty, its unvarnished notions, its non sequiturs, its lilting manner.

As if history books told us a damn thing about true life.

The fact is every one of us takes the dead for granted. Really we have to; we couldn't get on with it if we didn't. We'd never be done reciting their names.

I've spent my life—most of it at this very college— studying the ancient world, and if I've gleaned any wisdom from this long endeavor, and from my acquaintanceship with the Greek and the Roman, it is that our debt to the past, to all who prepared this current existence for us, is so great that it could not be calculated, much less paid. Sometimes we pretend at poverty; this is a strategy for shrugging off our liabilities. *I am but the stone with no blood to squeeze!* But we are, all of us, far richer than we know, or ever could bear to admit.

Were there a hell, were we to go there, we'd see ourselves as we really were in life, luxuriating with scarcely a sigh of gratitude atop the spoils of the dead, and we'd weep from shame.

Alas—and may my pious colleagues forgive me— there is no afterlife, no eternity. We come and go and lickety-split there's no trace of us, at least not in the thoughts of the living. Not for long, anyway.

Do you scoff at this? Well then, name even one man who labored on the pyramids, or an infantryman from the Thirty Years War, or a countryside nun from sixteenth century France. Tell us what it was like to be a cable car conductor in 1900, or a gandy dancer from fifty years before that, or a construction worker with his metal lunch pail building up Brooklyn or Chicago before the gas engine came along. Virtually all persons who have lived and died have been forgotten; the style and feel of their existence is lost to us. Even those we think we remember, we don't really remember. We have but vague images, and glamorizations, and fables.

As wise Bachelard put it, we can only hope to glimpse the past through the blinding lens of the present, never the reverse. (The advent of photographs and film hardly diminishes this reality; if anything, such images, with their increasing strangeness to us over time, are but the proof of how little we truly recollect from the past.)

Always remember: you will be forgotten.
Your whole world will be forgotten.

My weakness in the face of this truth will, tomorrow evening, result in my death. The reason for this sorry state of affairs is what I hope to explain here, however unlikely it is that I shall prove equal to the task.

The simple fact is, I've never been able to bear the thought of dying. Even in my early childhood the mere suggestion of oblivion caused my heart to race with panic. (How often as a child I burst into tears thinking of it, and to the great chagrin of my father!) The technical term, I suppose, is *thanatophobia*, and in many ways it has governed my whole life. (It is, for example, what drew me to the study of history in the first place, i.e., my desperate need to prove that the people of the past are not just dead and gone after all.) As I've grown older and developed my powers of reason, this condition did not improve but worsened. The very idea that I shall (so soon!) be among all those uncountable souls I've failed to resurrect in my work, in spite of long trying—I cannot bear it! To be here one moment and then pure nothing the next—the thought is like a tendril about me!

In this vein I don't mind comparing myself to Nietzsche, that other weakling. What is the Eternal Return, after all, if not the last hope of a truly timid poet, one who could not bear the idea of being forgotten?

If only I had the strength of Epictetus, and could view my life as something that never was mine to begin with. Something to be gratefully given back when the note comes due. Then again, in those ancient days, when nothing mattered so much as metaphysics, and the votaries and proconsuls increasingly found themselves struck dumb by the hatchling faith from Galilee (and almost as often drew their swords against it), the realm of death was precisely that most contested of all grounds. One was all but obliged to take a stance on it. It is only now, in our own time, as the tide of the Christian religion slowly recedes, that death once more is becoming a battleground, a prize most critically at stake and for whose possession we will fight most viciously against one another, and even against our own selves.

The Bible was right at least about one thing: *Who holds the keys to death rules the world.*

There are two texts which, if they did not exactly bring me to my present predicament, at least elucidated it for me. The first is that unjustly obscure work by the Head Nun Celine of Ars from 1831: the *Catalogue des exploits moraux* [Catalogue of Moral Feats]. In addition to the well-known historical anecdotes collected in this book — the acts of love (Abelard and Heloise), the bold displays of principle and honesty (Thomas Becket), the charity (Nicolas of Myra), the piety and defiance shown even in the face of certain death (Joan of Arc) — there are also recounted several lesser-known legends, two of which leapt out to me.

In 1722, when a cart full of stones and turnips toppled and trapped her child, a woman named Marguerite Marteau, a laundress from Fontainebleau, is reported to have sprung up and lifted the cart, all one-thousand pounds of it, high enough that her child could be pulled free.

In 1806, Joseph Baddeley — the so-called "miser of London," a famous hoarder of coins who often went hungry so as not to spend needlessly any of his fortune (the very thought of parting with even one piece from his store was revolting to him) — was hurrying home one day when, as was common in that city, a beggar implored him for assistance. Inexplicably, and while choking back not tears but vomit (so repulsed was he by what he was about to do), Baddeley handed the fellow a farthing. Almost immediately following this gesture, Baddeley groaned and then dropped to the ground, dead—so greatly did he grieve his loss.

How these anecdotes bear upon my current state I shall soon make clear. In the meantime allow me to observe the general principle that there are indeed *non-physical Necessities* that, at times, flow through our bodies and impel us to act, even well beyond our normal capacities. In the anecdotes just related, that Necessity may be called Love, or the Good. Some might even call it God. I myself have imagined that Baddeley's tortured gesture—assuming his legend is true—might well be among the most *pure* moral acts ever performed, since he received *nothing* in return for his charity, not even the pride of acting rightly. (Indeed, he received only disgust with himself and death.) But these righteous forces are not the only such Necessities. There are others.

The second text which revealed to me the nature of my current predicament is none other than Poe's famous excursus on his work more generally, "The Imp of the Perverse." The psychological "impulse" that lies at the heart of this narrative—that "paradoxical something" which prompts us "to act, for the reason that we should *not*," that "tendency to do wrong for the wrong's sake," to commit the very deed from which our faculty of reason would most strenuously deter us, and to perpetrate it "merely because we feel that we should *not*" (it is Poe who repeats himself)—is a force in human life which the poet cleverly describes as an "imp." For while it is a propensity within us, i.e., an impulse, it is also more than that, i.e., it is a being, a creature or fiend existing outside of us, one that relishes in making mischief with our souls.

Poe errs, however, the moment he tries to provide illustrations of this principle. He gives four examples, each of which fails utterly. He imagines: (1) a speaker who derives a wicked pleasure from being circumlocutious; (2) a procrastinator who waits, seemingly inexplicably, until it is too late to begin a task; (3) someone whose heart begins to thump with excitement while gazing upon some precipice, and even feels a twisted longing to leap; and finally, (4) a murderer who suddenly (and needlessly, since he is beyond suspicion) confesses to the crime he has committed. None of these examples, however, exhibit the imp in its *true* perverseness.

Remember Kant! Doing wrong or evil because you love or enjoy wickedness, or derive pleasure from its effects, or because you're lazy or inhibited, or crave some favorable consequence, or because it causes your heart to pound with sublime excitement, or because you enjoy feeling fiendish, or are suffering from some sudden sting of conscience, etc., is not diabolical. You've simply turned that evil (or that destruction, or pain, or whatever negative thing) into your good. *Diabolical* evil—the *true* imp of the perverse—means *despising* evil, fully grasping its *wrongness* and therefore wanting nothing more than *not* to do it, and then *doing it for that reason and that reason alone.* It means somehow choosing to do what *no part of you* wants to do, which is why it is tantamount to denying your will, and why Kant thought it impossible.

Unless of course the imp is real!

Unless there is in fact a strict opposite of rational desire, a desire every bit as transcendental, and as pure: a very anti-matter of the soul!

Unless the will itself may be corrupted, or turned inside out, so that your clear wish *not* to do X results precisely in your doing X!

When I first came to this campus as a young professor, some forty years ago, I was shown about by that well-esteemed provost at the time, Susan Parrish. I admit I instantly took a fancy to her, which is perhaps why, when she led me to Reginald Bridge and showed me its lovely view of Gillespie Creek and Our Beatific Oak of Saint Mary below, my mind could not help but conjure up an image of my own foolish death: *Surely I'll trip now, right in front of her, and then somehow topple over the side of the bridge, and then end up dead and ridiculous in that tree while she watches and laughs!*

Though I've never told anyone about it, this image has not once left the back of my mind, not in the forty years since that day. I have dreamt every night that it will happen, or that it has happened already, and that I am to be fatally skewered by the branches of that awful tree!

Almost every night for the past forty years, during my walks, and each time I've crossed Reginald Bridge, I have felt what Poe imagined but could not illustrate: *an invisible fiend with his broad palm upon my back!*

Tomorrow evening, when I walk across that bridge for the last time, it will finally happen. The very thing I want the least!

Why not just stay home, or flee far away from that accursed site, you might be asking yourself. Alas, you've already misunderstood. It is my very will which has become compromised—perverted into the opposite of itself!

Think of it: Marguerite from Fontainebleau did not *decide* to lift that cart; she simply lifted it, without reflection. Baddeley handed off that coin to the beggar because something impelled him to act, *even in contradiction to his very life.* These were not *choices,* strictly speaking; they were but moments of *contact* between the humble soul and some far greater force, a force that *seized* them, ennobled them, and gave them the strength to do incredible things.

In my case, too, something has seized hold of me, and in doing so has made me hale—but it has not ennobled me. It has done the opposite. Because it is a different kind of force! A transcendental propensity toward evil! The imp!

Tomorrow evening, when I sense that cold hand on my back, and when my very horror of death causes me to rush headlong into it, will Saint Mary receive me?

So ends Faintly's "suicide note." Reading it again now, I can't help but consider a strange possibility. *Perhaps there is a species of evil that is properly called innocent.* Perhaps, on occasion, if a person has committed some horrendous act, it is precisely because, as if in a mirror, the person *was attempting to do (or will) the opposite.*

Perhaps. At any rate, whether or not Faintly was delusional—whether or not the Necessity he contemplated was a real and governing force, or was just some psychological mirage (an effect, perhaps, of Poe's own suggestion)—the moral of his tale may be the same: *Do not dwell on your nightmares!* The more you brood, the more powerful grows the imp!

The Devil is a Shape in the Brain

Who could list just the forces required to raise a blade of grass from the ground? or cause the half-ape, suddenly and for the first time, to marvel at the blue of the sky though it is the same foolish blue as it always was, the same blue as from innumerable skies before? or make music possible? or create consciousness from the disordered impressions of a bleating infant? or feel sympathy, and even weep, for a nest of open-throated hatchlings though they are only dreamt of, all asqueak in boughs and bowers of sun-glinting rain-wet woods that never were?

—Johannes Hauff, *Was der Teufel mir erzählt*

There are curses inflicted by the dead, by witches, and by spurned lovers; but the curses put by fathers upon their own sons, as we read in the Book of Genesis, are often the longest-lasting, and sometimes span all the bloodline thereafter.

—Anonymous, *De Bluotfluchjen*

Satan hates me, yet is loth to lose me.

—John Donne, *Holy Sonnets*

1.

Who can say what mysterious heroism lies concealed in uneventful life? It may be, as some American transcendentalists have held, that it is only a poor part of our virtue that is ever seen or known. ("No reckoning but God's may measure a man's heart," say the gospels; and the congregations, without despair, throw up their hands.) There are, of course, the noble acts performed every day by modest and dutiful folk—all that number who are quietly, unselfishly decent—and without medals or speeches to commemorate them; good men and women, after all, are as plentiful as they are unfamous, and if the general populace does not proclaim their works then perhaps one day the skies will (Psalm 19). But the doings of such good people, though lovely, are not what I have in mind. I ask you instead to conceive the possibility that the soul may conduct a *secret* business, and that a person—a man of no apparent significance, let's say—might do precisely nothing, or very little, scarcely even stir, and yet in that very way, and because of some implicit quality that has taken root in him, somehow end up saving the world. Could it be, my dear reader, that you yourself, right now, sitting there doing nothing of any importance, are nonetheless— though unbeknownst even to you—keeping the devil himself at bay? The following tale explores this theme, though to be sure in a roundabout fashion. Don't let a few pages of exposition here and there deter you: there are concepts that simply must be laid down (I will do my best to be quick about it). Don't worry, either, about the story being too didactic: I expect you won't notice the moral until the very end (and even then, I dare say, it may seem a small thing).

Because the events I am going to recount begin with a controversial Christian sect that practiced—before undergoing turmoil and then disbanding—in Georg Hegel's hometown of Stuttgart around the turn of the nineteenth century, it may be worthwhile to state a fact which, though it will seem uncontroversial to some, no doubt will sound scandalous to others: *Not all Christians despise the devil.* Indeed for some segments of the Christian faith this is a matter of plain doctrine: the Bible commands humanity to love its enemies, and so verily it must not fail to love the Adversary. In the modern era, one of the more lucid exponents of this view was Giovanni Papini, whose notorious book, *The Devil,* first published in Italian in 1953, developed the idea at length. But Papini went further than this; his deeper argument was that it falls to humanity not just to love and forgive Satan, but to *redeem* him. It is human destiny, after all, to judge the angels (1 Corinthians 6:3); beings born of clay will rank higher than those of celestial origin. Therefore, just as the Savior rescued humankind from the curse of death, so in due course should that fragile race, which shall do "greater things" (John 14:12), seek to redeem the angels who were the first to fall, and raise them back up from the pit. Should that "second redemption" come to pass, Papini speculated, God's great sorrow—infinite sorrow—at having seen both angelic and human life depart from grace will, at long last, be relieved. (As will our own sorrow for Him—for yes, we can pity God!) But let us hear this unjustly forgotten writer speak for himself:

> This is the double root of God's sorrow, which is infinite. [...] The celestial giant has fallen into the pit; the earthly emperor is maimed and poisoned. [...] Lucifer can do nothing to alleviate the divine grief... But man can still do something for his God who suffered and suffers for him. [...] We can love God not only because of His love but out of compassion for His Passion, out of pity for his supernatural torment. But we can also do more, incredibly much more, if we will recognize it and if we want to. It is for the redeemed, when they are truly redeemed, to undertake a second, and, for the moment, an unimaginable redemption. The sorrow

of God is the ultimate mystery of our faith but perhaps its resolution, even if remote, is entrusted to us, and to us alone.[10]

The general idea was not new. It took its early form in the doctrine of *apokatastasis*, or that antique notion that *all* of life, including even demons and devils, must eventually be restored to God. This doctrine, though no longer orthodox in the churches, enjoyed something of a magisterial provenance among early Christian authorities, passing from the likes of Origen and Clement of Alexandria to Gregory of Nyssa and Maximus the Confessor, and eventually reaching across the centuries to more modern and revolutionary voices such as Percy Shelly and Victor Hugo and, before them, William Blake (whose great vision of Satan, that tireless energy of the natural universe, had no need for the idea of redemption, since "Every thing that lives is holy"[11]).

Romantic poetry notwithstanding, by the early part of the nineteenth century the idea of universal salvation had come to be disfavored in official quarters (especially in still-provincial places like Stuttgart), the notion having been denounced long before by giants like Augustine and Aquinas and Luther and Calvin. "Make every effort to enter through the narrow door," warns the Savior, "because many, I tell you, will try to enter and will not be able to" (Luke 13:24). It should therefore come as no surprise that when Johannes Hauff, a Christian mystic and a family friend to the Hegels (and a tutor at one time to young Georg, who in his later years would remember him as having had "so pure a devotion to God it felt almost dispassionate, even

---

10 Papini, Giovanni. *The Devil.* Translated by Adrienne Foulke. E.P. Dutton & Co., 1954. P. 61.

11 *The Marriage of Heaven and Hell,* plate 27.

cold"[12]), first published his book, *The Glorious End of Our Universe,*[13] setting forth publicly the religious principles to which he and his devotees subscribed—principles which revolved around the idea of Satan's inevitable salvation—he was swiftly branded a devil-worshipper by both Catholic and Lutheran clergy, as well as by gossipers in the Stuttgart papers. An unsigned piece in the July 7th, 1807 edition of the *Stuttgarter Tagblatt* was particularly scathing; in that review of *The Glorious End of Our Universe*—titled, provocatively if not ignominiously, "Gibt es Dämonen unter uns?" ["Are There Demons Among Us?"]—the reader will find, amid scattered invective, the following charge: "That Hauff's book is full of dangerous sophistries and half-truths will be obvious to any clear-headed Christian; that Hauff himself, though known to be a learned man of charity and seeming gentleness, is in fact a servant of Lucifer— this may be less obvious, though it is no less true." By and by Hauff and his followers had no choice but to practice their rites in secret. They became, essentially, a cult.

The accusations of Satanism, it turns out, were not wholly slanderous. Johannes Hauff did indeed practice the black arts, and witchcraft, and various "temptations of nature" (as a famous German novelist would put it in the next century), and even attempted on two occasions to summon demons—though he did so in secret. By contrast, the theology he espoused while preaching, and which he expounded in his book, and to which his seven-score followers solemnly adhered, was rather wholesome, and was itself firmly rooted in scripture. Here is what the Hauffians believed:

---

12 Hegel, Georg. *Hegel: Selected Philosophical and Theological Correspondences.* Edited and Translated by Robert Butler. Indiana University Press, 1983. P. 387.

13 Hauff, Johannes. *Das herrliche Ende unseres Universums.* Blum und Söhne Verlag, 1807. My translation. Book may be requested at the Archives Office, Burkhardt Library, University of Stuttgart.

(α) *The devil **will** be saved.* Hauff's proof was a modest bit of logic, which can be distilled in the following syllogism: God's powers are infinite; mercy is one of God's powers; therefore, God's mercy is infinite. (And, *ipso facto*, "[t]here can be no sin or wickedness, not even the furious devil's, that God's mercy does not *infinitely* surpass and enfold, for 'where sin abounds grace abounds all the more,' Romans 5, 20)."[14]) If there were a flaw in the syllogism it was no doubt to be found in the minor premise; Hauff attempted to bolster that weak link with reasoning like the following:

> God's mercy does not consist in the mere refusal to take vengeance though He has the means to, for that would be mere passivity and unworthy of Him. Divine mercy, rather, is an active and *creative* force, a true power; it invents peace and beauty where none was before, and with an efficacy that exceeds even that of the most sublime music.[15]

And:

> Mercy, better than any sorcerer's spell, is a form of magic, and in the hands of God it is more like a substance in itself than the absence of something else (punishment, for example).[16]

And again:

> The weak can never be merciful, they are only relatively helpless. Only with might [*Macht*] can true mercy be done. That is why the crucified Christ is

---

14 Ibid. 68.

15 Ibid. 189.

16 Ibid. 65.

the most sublime image of mercy ever seen by man
(for those who ridiculed and tortured the deity were
not cast down straightaway). God impaled is mercy
taken to infinity. No corner of the world was spared
that terrible forgiveness.[17]

With respect to this boundlessness of God's mercy Hauff
often returned to the words of John Chrysostom, from his
homilies on repentance: "Thy malice may be measured, but
God's mercy cannot be defined; thy malice is circumscribed, His
mercy is infinite." From these and similar sentiments Hauff
derived the simple verdict: "Only an infinite devil were
irredeemable."[18]

(β) *The devil's salvation is the **best** thing that will ever happen in
our universe.* The basis for this principle was scriptural; Johannes
Hauff elucidated it in passages like the following:

When the prodigal son, world-weary and
humbled, returns home after squandering his
inheritance in sin and wantonness, his father does
not scold him but instead rejoices, and throws a
celebration in his honor, and puts him in robes, and
even slaughters the fattened calf, none of which he
does for his elder son, though the latter had
remained faithful and never strayed. And why?

---

17 Ibid. 77.

18 Ibid. 104. In this wise one might profitably compare the Hauffians to the
Yezidi, that oft-persecuted sect from Mesopotamia, who also have been
accused of holding dangerous sympathies for the devil (though, unlike the
Hauffians, they've yet to be driven to extinction). For the Yezidi have
long believed in the divinity of *Tawûsê Melek*, or the Peacock Angel, whom
some call *Shaitan*, or that celestial being whose rebellion against God was
forgiven, and whose remorseful tears extinguished the flames of hell. In
truth neither Yezidi nor Hauffian doctrine prescribes worship of the devil
as such; we should rather say, following Giovani Papini, that both sects, in
their origins, found exultation in God's *forgiveness. See* Papini 139-40.

Because "he that was dead is alive again" (Luke xv, 44). This parable may strike us as enigmatic, and to be sure it might only be from the vantage of heaven that it can be fully understood. Still, we know with certitude thanks to the gospel that "there is more rejoicing in heaven over one sinner who repents than over ninety-nine righteous persons who do not need to repent" (Luke xv, 7). The Bible thus brings to us this mysterious teaching, that it is somehow a profounder thing to sin and to suffer pain, indeed to die (for we are dead in our transgressions, Ephesians ii, 5), and only then to repent and turn to the comfort of God, than it is always to have been righteous and assured. It is a better thing to err, and even to have practiced evil, and to undergo hardship and wretchedness, and only thereafter to be saved, than to be ever untainted by such calamities. For God's power is "made perfect" in those negative things (2 Corinthians xii, 9); Christ is crowned in honor and glory not in spite of His brutal death but *because* of it (Hebrews ii, 9). The tender plant was pierced for our transgressions and crushed for our iniquities, but just this was the Lord's will (Isaiah liii, 1-11). The crucifixion was the earthly form of appearance [*irdische Erscheinungsform*] of God's absoluteness, just as the devil's suffering in hell will prove to be its more eternal testament. *For only that which can descend down into its own opposite, and even to its destruction, and yet still preserve itself there, is the true absolute.*[19]

Readers of Hegel will at once recognize this last sentence, for the same idea was expressed in that most famous passage—itself but an allusion to Christ—from the *Phenomenology of Spirit*:

---

19 Ibid. 113-14.

Death…is of all things the most dreadful, and to hold fast what is dead requires the greatest strength… But the life of Spirit is not the life that shrinks from death and keeps itself untouched by devastation, but rather the life that endures it and maintains itself in it. It wins its truth only when, in utter dismemberment, it finds itself… Spirit is this power only by looking the negative in the face, and tarrying with it.[20]

But who influenced whom? Did the tutor influence his precocious pupil, or vice versa? Could the Hegelian dialectic be not just a reflection of Christ, nor a mere philosophic instrument, but something Satanic as well? That both Hegel's *Phenomenology* (completed when he was still in his thirties) and Hauff's *Glorious End* were published in 1807 only aggravates the uncertainty. For his part, Hauff acknowledged a passage from Burton's *Anatomy of Melancholy* as the source which first awakened him to this, the very "method" of God:

The volume in which I first found this theme so plainly put that it would become for me my *idée fixe*, guiding not only my philosophy and my prayers but also my everyday life, was Burton's heavy tome, where he says, and not without cheer, that "God often works by contrarieties, He first kills and then makes alive, He woundeth first and then healeth, He makes man sow in tears, that he may reap in joy; 'tis God's method."[21]

Or, as Hauff himself more dramatically put it:

---

20 Hegel, Georg. *Phenomenology of Spirit*. Translated by A.V. Miller. Oxford University Press, 1977. P. 19.

21 Hauff 276.

God does not flicker over the demonic like a faraway star; He is down in the graves, He swallows the agonies of the dead and feeds the worm, and raises the knife with the murderer. He holds the whip and suffers the lash. Neither the corruption of man nor the fiendishness of netherworldly spirits can be alien to Him, who authored all.[22]

Such "contrarieties," Hauff reiterated, are dramatized even more obviously in Christ, for Jesus is "that divine aspect of God which underwent the humiliation of flesh, enduring bodily pain, hunger, weariness, excretion, sickness, exposure, temptation, longing, betrayal, injury, insults, torture, and even death before being restored to heaven."[23] The Bible's most mysterious wisdom, then, or so Hauff declared, consists in the revelation that *this must also be the method of the devil*:

For nothing that ever lived has gone further than Satan in the realm of wretchedness and torment, sin and pain and death. None in the rest of squirming life has so much as glimpsed such suffering and such evil. All of Christ's pains are but a moment for the devil; the accumulated sins of the prodigal son are but the archangel's morning bread. Satan is that being who takes upon himself the greatest conceivable negative of God, and it is therefore the devil's glorious office to prove, by ultimately returning to Him, that God preserves Himself even there, in His hideous opposite.[24]

---

22 Ibid. 291.

23 Ibid. 292.

24 Ibid. 319. Or, put in an even more speculative manner: "Christ only redeemed humanity. It falls to the devil—and perhaps to our own race as well—to fulfill the redemption of all the rest of the universe, from the

The rest of the argument resolved in simple fashion. If Christ's pilgrimage through flesh and death was "the best thing that happened to fallen humankind" (it was the most precious event in the history of the world, as a lucid narrator from Borges says), then Satan's passage through hell, "through plains and deeps of wretchedness," will prove to be, when he returns to God's side, "the best thing that has happened in all of space and time as we know it":

> For if the heavens rejoiced for the earthly prodigal son, who had been merely dissolute before he repented, then how much more so for the wayward angel, to whom hell has laid waste already, when finally *he* turns back the way he came?[25]

The Hauffian wager then ran as follows: God would not create a universe and then *not let happen* the best possible thing that can happen. The best possible thing *must* happen, it *will* happen. Satan will be saved.[26]

(γ) *The devil's salvation is the **last** thing that will ever happen in our universe.* Hauff derived this claim primarily from Origen (though he also relied upon an elaborate if dubious interpretation of the Greek text of Revelation). We need not linger over this particular bit of speculation; let it suffice to say that, according to Hauff, when the devil once again crosses the

---

lowest bloodthirsty mite to the empty unchambered abyss which God has wrapped about the world like something unfinished." Ibid. 333.

25 Ibid. 326-27.

26 See, e.g., ibid. 388-92. We must now say that the Hauffians' most solemn rite—the celebrations of the so-called Denique Diaboli, during which, contrary to rumor, no child's blood was ever consumed—did not celebrate the wickedness of the archangel himself so much as that preordained event in which the devil was but to play a part, albeit a crucial one. See Bellini, Jorgina. *A Fleeting Blasphemy: Johannes Hauff and the Orders of the Devil in Napoleonic Württemberg.* Penn State Press, 1986. Pp. 35-68.

threshold of heaven, the universe will be made perfect and, for that very reason, "will have no further cause to exist."[27]

2.

Heretical sects and faiths there have been, here and there in history, which only grew stronger from their persecution (perhaps the Yezidi are among them). The Hauffians—blasphemers all—had no such luck. The ridicule from the public and the associated threats of scandal were bad enough (to be "poisoned by blameworthy beliefs…is among the worst states of man," said Irenaeus, and many a sharp-toothed maw has since mouthed that creed); but when Johannes Hauff announced in the summer of 1809 that he'd begun writing a *second* book, one he insisted was being dictated to him by the devil himself, many of his followers found themselves with flagging enthusiasm for the cause.

When it was revealed that the devil with whom Johannes was communing was none other than his own nine-year-old son, Christoph—who often spoke in reveries, and whom Hauff had come to believe was not *possessed* by Satan but was rather the very *incarnation* of the fallen one (albeit, and much like the young Jesus, without the child having yet become aware of the fact)—the few adherents still loyal to Hauff were quick to abandon ship. The Hauffian cult, after but brief intrigue, was no more.

The book in question—a series of poetical fragments and sayings which Hauff eventually compiled and published under the title, *Was der Teufel mir erzählt* ["what the devil tells me"], and whose contents and style seemed to be clearly beyond the possible literary talents of any normal nine-year-old child—does not survive today in complete form. The so-called "London Copy" is kept at the Division of Rare and Manuscript Collections

---

27 Ibid. 340.

at Ruhr-Universität Bochum (along with a handful of Hauff's letters borrowed from the Hegel archives there), though the text is tattered and mostly ruined and contains less than a fifth of the original pages. Besides that plundered copy, most of our knowledge of the book comes from letters and journal entries written by collectors of occult works, as well as from the occasional auction record.[28] The most famous extant fragment, however, is found in the original, single-volume edition of *Die Welt als Wille und Vorstellung* by Schopenhauer (published only once in 1819). This fragment, along with Schopenhauer's segue to it, may suffice to give a flavor of the book. The quotation appears in a section dealing with the famous *principium individuationis*, or that "veil of Maya" that deludes us into thinking that we each enjoy a separate, individual existence. Schopenhauer invokes the Chandyoga Upanishad, in which the novice is disabused of this illusion, for he is shown every other being on the earth in succession, and with each passing form is told: "This art thou." The philosopher then all but chuckles at Europe:

> Out of pity we send English clergymen and Moravian linen-weavers to the Brahmins, and try to teach them that they are made out of nothing and that they should be grateful and cheerful about it. But you may as well fire a bullet into the side of a cliff. Our religion will never take root in India: the primordial wisdom of humankind cannot be displaced by a few events in Galilee. Indeed it is quite the opposite: Indian wisdom flows back to us, and is bringing about a fundamental change in our

---

28 The copy of *Was der Teufel mir erzählt* boasted of by that Italian collector, Lorenzo Salmieri, is undoubtedly a forgery. I myself have briefly inspected it, and found its lugubrious and well-nigh apocalyptic prose to be very unlike that of the London Copy (which is unmistakably ecstatic in tone).

knowledge and thought—the first signs of which may be detected already in the outbursts of some of our more exuberant writers:

The widow and the orphan lament but audaciously, as do the dead who should know better; the comforted prince is blind and deaf, and lies to himself that he is separately adored. All humanity is a flat sea, a snowy village all asleep in the yet-ungreeted light of dawn after the new season has refreshed the beauty of morningtime. As above so below: Heaven promises vision, but Hell is width, length and depth, and God likewise stirs in thy soft-beating heart as in my thundering one![29]

3.

The interior (and ultimately unknowable) ruminations of a man already shrouded in obscurity, and separated from us by more than two centuries, need not detain our narrative for very long. What caused Johannes Hauff, who at first gloried in the discovery of his son's metaphysical nature, eventually to undergo a change of heart with regard to him, can only be a matter for speculation. What we know is that, at some point after *Was der Teufel mir erzählt* was published in 1812 (causing yet another clamorous though short-lived sensation in Stuttgart), Johannes Hauff decided that the fact he'd sired the devil was cause not for celebration but rather for dread, and began looking for a way to

---

29 Schopenhauer, Arthur. *Die Welt als Wille und Vorstellung.* F.A. Brockhaus, 1819. P. 265. My translation. Hauff's fragment is given only the following scant (and uniquely awkward) citation in Schopenhauer's text: "J. Hauff, *WdTme.*" In all of the later versions of *Die Welt als Wille und Vorstellung,* including the much-expanded, now-canonical two-volume version, the quotation is omitted entirely.

undo, or otherwise to thwart, the dark drama which, he could only surmise, was about to unfold. We may even be able to specify the very day that the turn began, for it was a letter dated March 13, 1813, sent to Georg Hegel's sister Christiane (who had yet to descend into madness), which concluded—abruptly—with these disconsolate lines:

> Something in Christoph has changed, his eyes look straight through me. He is, I fear, my son no longer. And here I am frozen in my feet! What would God have me do?[30]

Enthusiasts of Hauffian lore are divided on the subject. Some have said that the shift in Hauff's thinking amounted to a failure of nerve, that he saw too deep into darkness and turned back for fear of it; others ascribe the change to the conflicted love Hauff must have felt for his son—the younger of two, as it happens, and to whom Hauff's beloved wife Auguste had died while giving birth in the spring of 1800—whose true identity and terrible purpose Johannes could no longer bear. Still others have imagined that young Christoph must have done something terrifying, or wicked, or gave off some growing whiff of the infinite, and that it was Hauff's tenderness for the world that ultimately turned him against the angel-child. (According to Hauff's own eschatology, after all, it was the destiny of that most ruinous creature to bring about the end of the universe.) Whatever the reason, Johannes Hauff ended up doing what a man like him—a man with extensive knowledge of occult matters already—might be expected to do: he consulted books.

We can no longer list with certainty all the volumes at Hauff's disposal, though the auction records from the Telford Exchange, A.H. (which sold off most of the Hauff library by the

---

30 Letter from Johannes Hauff to Christiane Hegel, 3/13/1813. My translation. Available upon request at Division of Rare and Manuscript Collections, Ruhr-Universität Bochum.

time Napoleon III first clopped across the world's stage) indicate that he bore a keen interest in ancient spell-books and the various treatises of apostates and heresiarchs. At the heart of his collection, however, and most precious (at least if the price fetched at auction is any indication), was his copy of that occult masterpiece, composed in what is thought to be a distant and phonetic proto-version of Plautdietsch: *De Bluotfluchjen* ["the blood curses"].

Written anonymously at some point around 1600 (somewhere near the Vistula delta), the book is widely believed to be at least a partial translation of a lost Latin text, which some of our more imaginative bibliophiles speculate was the fabled and satanic *Secret of the Lily* (a work of only dubious existence, though it is sometimes attributed, by Theodoret for example, to the heresiarch Philoxenus of Constantinople; its most fantastic legend tells of how it contained a hundred separate doorways to hell within each one of its thousand pages). *De Bluotfluchjen* takes as its principal subject matter

> that slow-working pox, that *nigromantia*, whose poisonous effects are attached with malice not to an individual but to his blood, so that he and his descendants all will be cursed in the same way and to the same degree, a magic which is confirmed by the most ancient books of the Bible.[31]

"For the most abominable of [blood curses] are just those put by God upon humankind," or so reads the malediction at the heart of the work (though that sentiment is but a prelude to its even more execrable judgment: "God's power is itself a form of

---

31 *De Bluotfluchjen* p. 7. I have, for the purpose of these present pages, consulted exclusively the copy of *De Bluotfluchjen* kept in the private library (located in New York) of the collector Holling Laertus, to whom I am grateful. It is generally believed that this copy, whose provenance has been meticulously researched, is the very one once owned by Johannes Hauff. All translations are my own, and are but my best approximations.

witchcraft [*Hakjseenkonst*]).”[32] In addition to setting forth some of
the rudimentary laws that govern the traffic between the earthly
and the demonic realms—and in between exhortations to the
reader to capitalize upon such laws—the book enumerates
several categories of family and blood curses, and even provides
instructions on how to inflict some of the more baleful ones. It
boasts such ominous chapter headings as “Physical Deformities
and Leprosy,” “Late-Blooming Madness,” “Poverty,”
“Dimwitted Offspring,” “Toothache,” “Deprivations Wrought
by Inclement Weather,” “Frogs,” “Calumny,” “Infested Crops
and Sickly Livestock,” “Corpulence,” “Bodily Corruption and
Loss of Limbs,” and so forth. Yet it is in the chapter whose title
literally translates to “The *Granum* More-Gleaming than the
Coin of Casting-Out”—a phrase which likely draws upon some
antediluvian idiom, but which probably is equivalent to: “In Lieu
Of Exorcism”—that we find a handful of passages that may
illuminate the drama of Johannes Hauff. I would translate one of
those passages (loosely, to be sure, and stripped of its more
confusing patristic metaphors) as follows:

> Very powerful demons cannot be turned away,
> nor will they be satisfied by outrageous evil, for that
> only incites them. Chanting and recitations likewise
> will be but mewling to their ears. If you must defend
> against such potent and covetous spirits—if your
> misfortune be that great—you will instead have to
> lull them to sleep with a gentle badness. A series of
> soft calamities, an occasional sight of half-ruin, or
> the cries of undeserved injury, or the smell of death
> (though this should not be murderous), are the more
> efficacious methods for mollifying such phantoms,
> and for keeping them subdued.[33]

---

32 Ibid. 363.

33 Ibid. 231. It should be noted that Johannes Hauff never wrote in his
    books, but that the passage here quoted is circled heavily by someone’s

The book proceeds to explain how a certain type of curse, if placed upon a family so afflicted by powerful demonic forces, may achieve the desired effect by casting harm, not onto the cursed family itself, but onto those in its vicinity:

> Beware the results of curses which wreath their objects in flowers of misfortune! Woe to those, including the sower, who pass near such gardens! The surrounding roots all turn brittle and even the slugs and snails do not feed but dry up and starve. The perfume blown therefrom is intoxicating to nether life [*Nadenlewen*], and even the Adversary himself may not be able to withstand the lure of it, for he is the confined one and in his confinement may yet be entranced. Indeed of all things under God, it is the Father of Lies (who is held fast by the Lord's curse already) who may find himself most thoroughly bound by the tanglements of a well-arranged spell.

Meanwhile, the idea that the devil is drawn especially to *lesser* evils (a *gentle* badness, *een Leisschlakt*), and is soothed by them, as by slow simple chords plucked on a harp (in contrast to some more thunderous salvo from an orchestra), is rare but not unheard of in the field of demonology. Philoxenus, for example, the famed aphorist and expert in early satanic-lore from late Rome (who was himself notoriously debauched and, according to legend, beset by demons), wrote the following epigraph at the beginning of his treatise on diabolical trickery and subterfuge—

> *Remember most of all that the devil delights in small mischiefs—he has tried all of the bigger ones already.*[34]

---

hand—though just whose we do not know. Holling Laertus is convinced that it was Hauff himself who defaced this page.

34 Philoxenus. *Ludi Diabolorum*. Oxford Press, 1923. P. 2. My translation.

—a saying that may find corroboration in certain passages from the eleventh-century German codex, *Der Tiufal* (which formed the basis for later liturgical works such as *Ejicientem Dæmones* and the more modern *Exorzismus-Handbuch*):

> The foe resides contentedly in that interval [the Old High German has *troc*, or "trough"] between evil and accident, malice and mere misadventure, for he is most elusive there, and is free to luxuriate in many small devastations. *It is not the violent fate of kingdoms but the limp of a peasant girl that enchants him.* [35]

It is a thesis that may even shed light upon John Milton's otherwise unlikely exclamation from his letter to the Unnamed Friend:

> *The Devil is a woodworm; he feeds unseen on granules and dust, and roaves uncheckt till the edifice is sunk!*[36]

Whether or not these represented the true appetites of the fiend, *De Bluotfluchjen* did not furnish instructions on how to cast the requisite spell; we may thus conclude that Hauff had to look elsewhere for the specifics. The seed, however, doubtless had been planted. In order to thwart the beast, Johannes Hauff would curse his own blood; he would condemn his child (and unknown descendants, too) to be a lodestone of exquisite though mostly unspectacular misfortune, so that the demon within the child might be pacified. He did this, if not in order to save the world, then at least to prolong its existence.

And so did Johannes Hauff set out to lull the devil to sleep.

---

35 Greifus et al. *Der Tiufal.* P. 385. My translation. Book may be requested at the Soreling Rare Book Library in Princeton, New Jersey.

36 Milton, John. *The Letters of John Milton.* Edited by Karen Adler. Cambridge University Press, 1952. P. 109.

4.

It should be said that most of the foregoing—the family drama, the metaphysics, the struggle with infinite forces—unfolded first and foremost within Hauff's tormented mind. Whether or not there was any reality to it you need not decide, at least not for the moment. And while I'm not so naïve as to think that readers will *actually* do me the courtesy of suspending their judgment on the matter—probably you've made up your mind already—I might nonetheless take advantage of the *semblance of undecidability* afforded by our narrative thus far (what with its artifice and its calculated restraint), and extend to you the following provocation: *there is more than one story being told here.* In fact this is always true, because—as almost every religion has hoped to teach—we live in more than one world.

We can also put this the other way around: *More than one world lives in us.*

5.

Let us assume that Johannes Hauff was successful in digging up a proper curse from one of his spell-books, a curse that would, by casting misfortune outward from Christoph, assuage the fiendish aspect forming within him. What signs or evidence of that curse do we find?

Both Johannes Hauff and his elder son, also called Johannes, died in 1815 when they were trampled by horses. Creditors eventually moved to seize the Hauff estate; in 1817, Christoph, after failing to procure the assistance of Georg Hegel (who'd recently been appointed a professorship in Heidelberg), then fled to America with only a paltry sum in his pocket. While crossing the Atlantic—assuming the private journal now kept at Ruhr-Universität Bochum is the genuine article, and may be relied

upon for the young man's thoughts and impressions[37]—
Christoph dreamt almost exclusively of gold and riches. On
several occasions during that seven-week trip he stood on the
deck of the *Mary Helvidius* at sunset and imagined that the
burgeoning red and orange on the horizon were the same colors
as American money. He appears to have kept very much to his
own thoughts for the duration of the journey, for he makes no
mention in his journal of the astonishing fact—as logs from the
ship's records indicate—that no less than *eight* passengers threw
themselves overboard over the course of the trip, including two
that did so, unimaginably, *after* Boston Harbor had come into
view.

Not long after disembarking, Christoph fell in with the
Boston Lundies, a crew of stevedores who possessed the two
virtues most prized by smugglers and pirates: they asked no
questions, and were prepared to work in the dead of night.
Christoph happily took orders from that crew, and cavorted with
them, for a few months; on the morning of December 19, 1817,
however, he absconded with a valise full of contraband—only an
hour before the rest of the Lundies found themselves in police
shackles.[38]

Selling the stolen goods was an intoxicating experience for
young Christoph. "Given enough distance and the right
perspective," he wrote in his journal, "everything, like the infinite
starry sky, compresses into a mere plane, or in my case, into the
shape of a coin. The feel of smooth American money in my hand
makes my arm tremble, and is like nothing I've known."[39] His
heart thus fattening on dreams of enrichment—and because he'd
heard a rumor of gold being struck somewhere out in the

---

37 *See* Hauff, Christoph. "Notebook #3." Available upon request at Division
    of Rare and Manuscript Collections. All translations are my own.

38 *See* Hopkins, Frances. "Lundies In Custody." *The Missionary Herald,* 20
    Dec. 1817.

39 Hauff, Christoph. "Notebook #3." (Unnumbered pages)

Missouri Territory—Christoph again looked to the west and, mesmerized by the American sunset once more (by the "pink and red ligaments of adjourning daylight, the horizon like a cliff beyond which all the still-promising worlds await"), he became convinced of a narrow fate: "I will find gold in that wilderness, or perish in the search."[40]

He got as far as Tennessee, where he took a job as a simple hand in a copper mine. He operated a still on the side for extra money. When the local authorities learned about the still they levied a tax; when Christoph would not pay, they put him on a chain with a Serbian horse thief and three migrant Osages. Within two weeks all three of the Indians had died from the grip, no doubt passed to them by Christoph (who'd also complained of symptoms). Shortly thereafter Christoph escaped from captivity and, many years later, reemerged west of the Allegheny Mountains, where he worked as a gandy on the railway between Erie and Kalamazoo. One night, after arguing with his foreman over a gambling debt (or so an informant testified in the official report[41]), and after referring to him, an Irishman, as a "paddy," a violent commotion broke out. The foreman drew on Christoph but fumbled with his revolver and ended up blowing his own pancreas out through his back. Christoph escaped the riot that ensued, as well as the *posse comitatus* that came looking for him, and again snuck eastward, this time taking employment as a navvy on the line near Cavendish in New Hampshire. There he witnessed—and not just witnessed but precipitated—the famous incident involving one Phinneas Gage, whose skull came to be shot through completely by a tamping iron over three-and-a-half feet long, after a spark lit upon the sulfur he'd been packing with it. It was Christoph who had distractedly poured more explosive when he should have poured sand; the resulting blast caused the iron rod to launch up into the side of Gage's face and then come

---

40 Ibid.

41 *See* Document # 434cr991H, Archive Office, Penn State.

out the top of his head, all entire, taking no small morsel of his brain away with it. The astounding part—the part that is recorded in textbooks to this day—was that, only moments after the horrific accident took place, Gage got back to his feet and walked about, and talked normally, and recognized his fellows, and soberly sought medical attention, and by all outward appearances retained possession of his reason and memory. He even attested to feeling somewhat little in the way of physical pain. Also astounding: he would live for another twelve years, and with little mental impairment. Most astounding of all: although his intellectual faculties remained mostly intact, his *personality* underwent a profound transformation: where he was once patient, now he was prone to anger; though he had been moral and principled, now he was dissolute. All those who knew Gage both before and after the accident agreed: the injury to his brain had changed him. He'd become someone new.

(I've lingered on this last episode, and on the strange fate of Phinneas Gage, because, in a way that truly may be described as devilish, it will prove to be relevant in a later part of our story. For now, we can begin to bring these merely biographical anecdotes—macabre or sensational though they may be—to a close, though only after we've considered at least a few more chapters from the Hauffs' grim legacy.)

Christoph married at the age of fifty, and fathered two sons, the second of whom, Johannes, named after Christoph's father, eventually went west, and became the notorious and feared bounty hunter known as "Johan the Grievous." He earned that appellation because many of his bounties were turned in with permanent and sometimes grotesque injuries.[42] Buckshot Benny, for example, the murderous bandit from Colorado, who preyed upon solitary mountain men, was brought in shot through the eye; Helter Murdoch, Utah's most notorious rapist, was turned

---

42 I rely here on the research set forth by William Thorp in his under-
   appreciated biography of Johan the Grievous: *The Devil's Butcher; The Saga
   of Utah's Most Feared Deputy.* Indiana University Press, 1977.

over to authorities with both arms amputated just above the elbow (Hauff would testify in court that the man had been "reaching for his rifle"). All seven of the Dennie Swampmen, bushwhackers and horse thieves on the run from authorities in Louisiana, got dragged to their cells in Mothview, Colorado already paralyzed from the waist down (injuries whose causes were never determined), and died in jail only a day later (also mysteriously). Black Dirk Bertram, the coach bandit, had been deafened from burst eardrums, and his tongue had been torn out (and, being illiterate, he couldn't very well inform anyone what had happened). And so forth. Johan the Grievous, or the third Johannes Hauff, retired at the age of forty-three in 1895, in the town of Blessing, Kansas ("an idyllic place full of apple groves and wreathed by the Arkansas," or so he wrote in a letter to his dying mother). He never married but fathered two sons during his retirement, the second of whom, Georg (though he went by "George" most of his life), Johannes claimed as his own. George would later volunteer to fight with the American Expeditionary Force in the Great War, though he received no distinction for his service (which took place, calamitously, in the hills of the Vosges Front). Professor Richardson's herculean research[43] has turned up the following account, in a letter from a local seamstress in Blessing (sent to her mother in New Orleans in March of 1919), of the very day that George and a handful of fellow soldiers returned home from the battlefield:

> When they came out of the train and lined up on
> the platform, those skinny men, it was like we could
> see the war still on them. They looked like they'd
> been whittled out of bone, all lean angles and
> hollows beneath loose-fitting drab wool, each man
> not a man any longer but more like a symbol of a

---

43 I am grateful to Fredric Richardson of Tulane University for sharing with
    me his extensive findings, which presumably will be published in a
    forthcoming work.

man, the memory of a man, like the war had made them into mere ideas of men. And then George Hauff stepped out from the train—you remember the Hauffs, right? and skinny little George?—his russet boots planting thud-like onto the platform. A whole new mood then fell over the crowd. The air itself changed. Because there he stood, in full view of everyone, grinning and broad-bellied, all pear and portly, with puffy pale cheeks and a badly used coat and teeth very yellow. His blond hair, soft and cropped close like moss, looked almost white in the sun, as did his skin which all but glinted in the glare. He resembled nothing so much as an overfed polar bear, or a poor fat child in church, all out of place and glad-ragged, and only a little embarrassed by it. I remember he pushed his way to the front of the platform and looked out into the crowd, and then waved. I'm sure his family was there, everyone had come to greet their men—but probably they scarcely recognized him. Mama, he looked as if he'd gained a hundred pounds! More than that even! Naturally people whisper. Turns out his battalion or regiment or whatever you call it had been under fire and got trapped in the hills and cut off from supply lines. Food ran out and the bodies piled up. And here he comes, a hundred pounds bigger at least! Well, we all look away now when we see him coming. We dare not say aloud what we've surmised.

Like most of the Hauffs before him, George Hauff married late in life and, continuing the family trend, sired two sons, the second of whom, Luke, appears to have lived a mostly uneventful life, and as far as we know never once left the town of Blessing, Kansas. His sole claim to distinction within the Hauffian bloodline was as the author of a series of rather formulaic novels, which some literary historians have credited with inaugurating that unfortunate genre known as the "Christian Cosmic Horror." The novels all contain the same basic plot: the protagonists are evil-doers, sinners who go happily unpunished, until, suddenly, some Biblical event—typically the apocalypse from Revelation—begins, and the villains find themselves subjected to a horrific and often tortuous comeuppance. Known for their elaborate descriptions of gore and carnage (as well as of the destruction of the world by angels), the novels attracted some of the more literal-minded Christian readers of the day—and appeased them—for those readers fancied nothing so much as a good reckoning. "The eternal lake of fire is only the last of the torments that await you," or so says the archangel Michael while addressing a throng of weeping sinners in *The Infinite Solstice* (perhaps the most ambitious of Luke Hauff's literary efforts): "but you will know eternity long before then, for your suffering on this very day will render time itself meaningless."[44] In addition to the modest sums he earned from his writing, Luke derived income from a farm which grew alfalfa and wheat, and also from a modest apple orchard he tended. These enterprises succeeded financially for the most part because the surrounding farms and groves always failed, typically succumbing to pests (mostly cutworms, which, for whatever reason, left Hauff's crops unmolested).

Luke Hauff married Lara Sams, a comely orphan many years younger than he, in 1970. In 1978 Lara bore their second son, whom they named Simon.

6.

Philoxenus, the opprobrious author of the *Ludi Diabolorum*, long ago refuted the sophism which discounted the existence of sinister magic (a sophism which rested on the spurious ground

---

44 Hauff, Luke. *The Infinite Soltice.* Krell & Lang, 1954. P. 292.

that even God may not invent a sorcery contrary to Himself). Such a view, or so he reasoned, would paradoxically place a limit on the infinite; in truth, and as we read in Paul's second epistle to the Corinthians, God *must* have His negative, for only then can His power be perfected in it, and find itself at home in the lowliest of forms, in humiliation and sinister things, in weakness and insults and oppression ("I boast of the things that show my weakness," Paul writes). The necessity of evil, of course, is of all theological topics the most difficult, and Simon Hauff was no theologian. (He may not even have been a practicing Christian.) But a lay person without faith can still be made to suspect the presence of evil, especially if he is shown the signs.

It may be worthwhile here to remind the reader that in all probability none of the Hauffs (excepting Johannes the first) ever had any inkling that a *curse* had been put on them. Bad luck, after all, is just bad luck, and violence and death are nothing very special. The misfortune that often befell those close to the Hauffs must have blended rather well with the woes of ordinary life. ("A pox most often should be a thing mundane," says *De Bluotfluchjen*.) So how was it, then, that Simon came to believe, in the early part of 2019, that his family was in fact the victim of a longstanding blood curse, and that it was somehow up to him to put a stop to it?

Fortunately, the Brenhardt Clinic in Australia—whose tragic ending everyone knows by now, and where our own story shortly will conclude—video-records all its consultations with both prospective and admitted patients. The following transcript of the initial exchange between Simon Hauff and Dr. Pauline Royce, which took place when Simon first sought out the controversial treatment offered by that clinic, will set the stage[45]:

---

45 I must beg the reader's patience and not divulge just how I've gained
    access to these video files, as medical confidentiality rights have likely
    been infringed. I can only hope readers will agree that the gravity of the
    present case in some way excuses my conduct.

Dr. Royce: *Before we begin the formal consultation, I'd like to go over with you exactly what our treatment entails, so that you can better understand just why we have to go to these lengths—the various consultations and therapy sessions—before you can avail yourself of the treatment. Is that alright with you?*

S. Hauff:　[inaudible]

Dr. Royce: *Great. So let me ask you, are you at all familiar with the story of Phinneas Gage, the nineteenth-century railway worker?*

S. Hauff:　*Well actually…[inaudible; chuckling]*

Dr. Royce: *Right, so Phinneas Gage was working on a rail line, somewhere in Vermont, when he got a spike rammed all the way through his skull. Went in one end and came out the other. Did massive damage to his frontal lobe. Miraculously he survived, even in spite of the trauma and the complete destruction of a portion of his brain. What is most fascinating about the case, and most important as far as the history of neuroscience is concerned, is that, after the accident, Phinneas Gage's personality changed, and to no small degree, presumably as a result of his injuries. In fact our own Dr. Brenhardt was originally inspired to pursue his research on the connection between general neural pathways and human personality after reading about poor Phinneas. For really that was the world's first indication that personality could be **physically** altered, and without producing any debilitating effects to the person, through an alteration of the brain.*

S. Hauff:
[inaudible]…*amazing*…[inaudible]…*coincidence, actually…*[inaudible]

Dr. Royce: *So in a nutshell, what Dr. Brenhardt eventually discovered and developed was a whole new way of conceptualizing the physical basis of personhood. He figured out that the very style of our thinking resides at a kind of holistic level of the brain, in the very general* *shape of the neural pathways, and that if we can adjust those pathways, and that shape, we can, essentially, adjust the person. Make his personality different. Turn him into someone new.*

S. Hauff: *Right, that's…*[inaudible]…*hoping…*[inaudible]

Dr. Royce: *The most important thing you need to understand, first and foremost, is that we have not yet reached the stage where we can determine in advance just exactly **how** your personality will be changed by the procedure we perform. We hope it will be for the better. It might end up being for the worse. All we can promise is that, after the procedure, you will be, to some noticeable degree, different. Your reflexes, your instincts, the natural way you interpret the world, will all be different. Of course you won't be completely different—you'll still have your memories, the same knowledge. You'll still be you. But in a very real way, you'll be like a new person. A new you.*

S. Hauff: [inaudible]…*I think is exactly…*[inaudible]

Dr. Royce: *That's why we require so many layers of consultation, interviews with therapists, and so forth. Only some patients are good candidates for this treatment. For the most part, we're looking for people who are, for example, suicidal, or who truly feel like they've run out of options. People who just can't seem to get their lives on track. People who've reached the point that they know something has to change. People who have come to hate themselves, for instance.*

S. Hauff: *Right, and of course…*[inaudible]

Dr. Royce: *So, that brings us to you. Can you tell me what brought you here today, and why you are considering undergoing this treatment?*

Simon proceeds to answer her question at length. A transcript of this audio, however, would only be confusing, as the microphone consistently malfunctions each time he speaks (the sound is filled with static, and often cuts out completely). In fact, this appears to be a defect in almost all of the video recordings of Simon's consultations with therapists and doctors at the Brenhardt Clinic—almost as if there were something about his voice that *causes* the microphone to malfunction (or perhaps someone has simply tampered with the video files). Enough of his speech is decipherable, however, that we can get the gist of what he says.

He explains to Dr. Royce how his father, the writer Luke Hauff, had become obsessed with genealogy in his later years, and how he spent months confined to his study conducting research online and sometimes even with the assistance of professional genealogists. Shortly after Luke Hauff died— suddenly, from a pulmonary embolism—Simon took an interest in the various genealogical charts his father had been working on, and soon learned that he himself was none other than the second son of the second son of the second son of the second son of the second son of that nineteenth century mystic, Johannes Hauff. He also learned about the strange cloud of misfortune that seemed to trail behind his filial line like the ejecta from some primordial collision—all the grotesque injuries associated with the Hauff men, the dead bodies, the unspeakable things. Finally, there was the discovery that struck Simon all the way down to the nerve: he happened upon his father's copy of Schlesinger's *Die Lehre vom Fluch* ("the doctrine of the curse"), a vast encyclopedia of black magic published in 1801. Simon's own research would eventually prove that this particular copy of the book was in fact the very edition once owned by the first Johannes Hauff.

Simon found the subject of the text fascinating, and it deeply affected him (he spoke but poor German, but he soon obtained a copy of Conybeare's abridged translation of the book). Still, it was the *physical object,* the very touch of the book itself, its weight in his hands, that affected him most powerfully. "It made my arm tremble," he says to Dr. Royce at one point.

(Every object, of course, bears its history along, but some burn red with it. "Even tangible things have their ghostly part," the young and still half-Hegelian Marx wrote in a letter to Ernst Luge: "some contain more spirit than matter." There are objects of perception—a murdered body, a looted room—which so powerfully signify past events that we can see through them and through time, as if those events were still happening. (And maybe, as some have said, that's just what violence is: an event, like that at the origin of our universe, which never quite stops happening.) The book in question, as far as Simon was concerned, was that kind of ghostly object, a thing with violence in its past. It seems to have run a current through his hands, as if a circuit had been completed.)

One of the chapters of the book had been marked off: "*Das unangenehme Böse der zweitgeborenen Söhne*" (or what Conybeare, in his old Brit's idiom, rendered as: "The Cackhanded Mischief of the Second Born"). After studying that chapter, Simon became convinced: his family, and specifically he and his father and his forefathers, had been cursed by a legacy of small evils, thanks to an all-but-undetectable spell:

> One of the most elaborate curses, known in different ways to Māori witches and to the old sorcerers of the German lowlands, is a spell which afflicts only second-born sons, and which turns them into magnetic centers of often bizarre, though not especially calamitous, misfortune. Most black curses have *harm* as their purpose; the function of *this* type of curse, however, is very different. *Its* purpose is to contain.[46]

---

46 Hoennig, Emil, et al. *The Doctrine of the Curse* [abridged]. Translated by F. Conybeare. Cambridge Press, 1899. P. 533. Note that "to contain" is a rendering of the German *zu fangen:* to trap, or to catch.

Simon goes on to explain to Dr. Royce how such minor devilry, as that which had afflicted his family line, struck him as more fiendish than more overt types of wickedness—perhaps precisely because of the way it was all but calculated to lie outside the realm of "punishable sin." For the evils of his family were not, after all, so very terrific: a prodigal son and his hapless folly; a bounty hunter who may have mistreated brutal criminals; a corpse-eater on the battlefield; a farmer and his violent fantasies—even the severest judge might opine that one could commit such infractions and not be damned for them. But then, was that not what made them so unsavory? That one could, in the sphere of metaphysics at least, get away with them and still keep one's soul intact? And even if the devil himself were ever so pleased by them?

More importantly, Simon confessed, he was now convinced that all the misfortune he'd ever seen in his life, especially that which had been visited upon people he knew or loved, must have been his own fault, the fault of his blood. If he could somehow change himself, change his consciousness—if he could somehow *be* different—perhaps the curse could be lifted.

7.

What bizarre diagnostic logic, or supernatural influence, or flat-out malpractice, compelled the doctors and the therapists and the surgeons at the Brenhardt Clinic to sign off on Simon's procedure is unknown. What we know is that the procedure took place on June 19, 2019. I have been unsuccessful in procuring a video recording of the procedure itself; I have, however, examined video taken of the conversation between Simon and Dr. Royce which took place later that evening—the very last images of Simon that we know of—just as he was waking from the general anesthetic. The first few minutes of the encounter are disturbing enough: Simon, without speaking, looks at the doctor with a bemused expression on his face while she asks him questions. Simon says nothing but squints and faintly smiles. Finally, and understandably alarmed, Royce gets up as if to exit; just then Simon speaks, and the doctor turns to face him. Simon's voice is chilling; it sounds scarcely human. Its manner is languorous:

S. Hauff: *You want to know who I am?*

Dr. Royce: *Mr. Hauff—how are you feeling? Do you feel alright? Do you know where you are? Can you tell me what day it is? Can you tell me your name?*

S. Hauff: *But it is known to all. I've dueled in Carthage…feasted on sweetmeats in old Versailles…I've felt the gloom of Carcosa on my face! But piglet, who are you? Do you even know?*

Dr. Royce: *Mr. Hauff…are you feeling alright? Can you tell me where you think you are?*

S. Hauff: *And can you tell me if you are anything but a useless dragoon, beplumed and clad in spotless white? Should I look kindly on you, or on any of your sad, untested race? Verily, a goatling finds its fence more fair.*

At this point Simon smiles, closes his eyes, and then rolls onto his side as if to go back to sleep. He mumbles drowsily over his shoulder, and eventually trails off: *So go, good pastor…back to your charges…tend to them…turn the bedding down and kiss the fat-sweetened cheek…because in short time…all this ill-got empire of yours…every bit of it…every bit of it will burn…every bit…*

8.

Everyone knows by now about the tragedy that took place at the Brenhardt Clinic on June 20, 2019—how every man, woman and child that happened to be in the building at 9:47 a.m., Australian Eastern Daylight Time, all at once dropped dead where they stood or lay. The only body in the clinic never accounted for, as you will have guessed, was that of Simon Hauff. He is currently deemed a person of interest by both Victorian police and Australian Security Intelligence.

I managed to speak with Dr. Pauline Royce only once, when I caught up to her while she was walking to her car after a court appearance. When she realized I wanted to ask her about Simon Hauff, she slammed the car door shut and sped off. From her expression, though, I could tell: at some level she knew. She knew that that cursed second son of a cursed second son of a cursed second son of a cursed second son of a cursed second son of a nineteenth century Christian mystic—though in a way for which he himself would not be damned—had let loose the devil on the world.

...

In another version of this same universe (perhaps it is our own), Luke Hauff, the novelist, the genealogist, the simple farmer, never married and never had children, and in that very simple way foiled the family curse, and lived uneventfully, and slept the proud, restful sleep of bachelors.

Being and Fiction (a Fragment)

The following episode is recounted in Percy Wyndham's gory compendium, *True Stories of the Macabre from Boston Harbor*, first published by Gold Medal Books in 1959. The bulk of the tale takes place on the Boston docks in 1898, where Vernon Fowler, an old and hard-handed stevedore, fell in love for his last time. As bachelors of advanced age are sometimes wont to do when they become smitten with someone a good deal their junior, Fowler took a modest view of the situation. Knowing it unlikely that his aging figure could arouse interest, he reckoned he at least could earn his beloved's gratitude by being gracious, and by speaking softly and with compliments, and by bestowing pretty but frivolous gifts and *bagatelles sucrées*. Fowler was moderately successful, and the two struck up something of a friendship.

When the object of his affection was found brutally murdered—I won't indulge any morbid longing for the details; suffice it to say that Fowler had nothing to do with it—the intense degree of grief felt by our longshoreman was unexpected. In time it proved too much for him to bear. Perhaps as a way of permanently *connecting* himself to the deceased, Fowler falsely confessed to the murder, and eventually was hanged for it. Six months later the actual killer was discovered, and was also hanged.

What are we to make of these grim events?

Even a truth daily brooded upon is no match for a lie that sleeps quietly in the heart. Even a graying longshoreman freshly in love—especially him—is barely familiar with the extent of the fiction he has brought to life, and to which he now finds himself leashed. It may happen that a softly-hummed melody is kept warm in a composer's mouth for some time before he himself finally *hears* it—until, that is, the day comes that it springs forth from him in a strange and commanding theme. (Genius, too, is opaque to itself; it is a form of bewilderment.) Likewise, a man madly in love scarcely knows why he does the things he does, but he proceeds nonetheless with what feels to him like *purpose*. But in fact what drives him is more akin to the electricity visible on the face of a house cat that has just seen a string dance across the floor. Is the cat *pretending* the string is alive? Or is it merely helpless before instinct? Does it *believe*, or, more human-like, is it *lying* to itself? Is there some greater intrigue at play in the creature's mind, something unfathomable to us? Lovers and wide-eyed cats are equally inscrutable (especially to themselves); they are in the grip of fictions.

Don't let yourself be dismayed by my use of that word, by the way—*fiction*. In my view, there is no better ontological guarantee than the fictional dimension. The cat, for instance, is never more *real*, is never more fully itself, than when it is about to pounce upon an inanimate toy; and lovers, when they are possessed by rosy dreams, are among the weightiest of beings, just like all those other otherworldly types: mystics, poets, shamans, the grinning vagabond in need of nothing but his parcel, the murmuring monk, the revolutionary, the cult-leader, the brigand of the mountain or the hinterland, the laughing Buddha, the paranoiac, the theater-actor. The reason for this is not complicated: as a result of their fictions (that added layer) their existence is essentially doubled. (Distinct from this, and yet of a piece with it, is Blanchot's profound remark: *les morts doublent de poids* ["the dead double in weight"]).

We may speculate that, in those final moments before Vernon Fowler's execution, and while he wept tears of spurious remorse, there was *more* to his existence than ever before. Perhaps only the rope knows for sure.

The Eighteen Possible Plots

Greatly influential are the books that everybody reads (or tries to read) but no one fully understands. Far fainter—and more surreptitious—is the influence exerted by those works that everyone knows but nobody reads. Joyce's *Ulysses*, Hegel's *Phenomenology of Spirit*, and certain books of the Bible may fall into the former category (they once did at any rate; perhaps they no longer do). The second, less appraisable group—at least for those readers who have taken an interest, not only in the theory of narrative, but also in what is still and somewhat curiously called "science fiction" today—would have to include a little-studied work by Dmitry Shkolnikov, published in 1903 under the excruciating title, *The Eighteen Possible Plots of Fantastic and Scientific Story Over the Next One-Hundred Years.*

As is probably already known to most readers of the present note, Shkolnikov's book—a slender volume of little more than a hundred brittle pages, issued in royal octavo by Lawrence & Sons of London in a single run of only two hundred copies—would likely still be languishing in obscurity had it not been for Darko Suvin's now famous article on the subject (published, remarkably, only once and as an appendix to the twentieth anniversary edition of Suvin's own most celebrated work of narrative theory, *Metamorphoses of Science Fiction*[47]). That essay, called simply "Dmitry Shkolnikov's Astonishing Predictions," is Suvin's definitive (and sole) statement on the concept of "science fictional criticism," i.e., criticism that not only is *about* science fiction, but also aspires to *be* a kind of science fiction in its own right. For that is, after all, what Shkolnikov's book all but proclaimed to be with its fabulous first sentence:

---

47 Suvin, Darko. *Metamorphoses of Science Fiction; On the Poetics and History of a Literary Genre.* Yale University Press, 1999, pp. 287-321.

My simple purpose in these pages is to divine the
fundamental structures and themes of all the stories
that will be told over the next century by future
artists of the fantastic.[48]

The "fantastic"—or the "fantastic and scientific," as he more
clumsily calls it sometimes—is of course Shkolnikov's term for
what we would now recognize as science fiction proper, that
literary genre that had been pulled into existence by the likes of
H. G. Wells and Jules Verne and Mary Shelley, and whose most
characteristic device—the imagining of strange futures—
Shkolnikov deployed quite deliberately in the execution of his
own work. "For whatever else it is," Suvin writes, "*The Eighteen
Possible Plots* is also an instance of that rarest and most speculative
form of literary history, namely, a literary history *of the future*."[49]
Let us quote Shkolnikov again:

My simple purpose in these pages is to divine the
fundamental structures and themes of all the stories
that will be told over the next century by future
artists of the fantastic. As it happens, those stories
can be reduced in principle to only eighteen basic
plots, which I shall describe—in terms suitably
broad to such an endeavor—in the following
eighteen chapters. Each chapter heading is also the
title I give to the root narrative discussed in that
section.[50]

---

48 Shkolnikov, Dmitry S. "Preface." *The Eighteen Possible Plots of Fantastic and
Scientific Story Over the Next One-Hundred Years.* Lawrence & Sons & Co.,
1903, p. iv.

49 Suvin 289.

50 Shkolnikov iv.

Was this structuralism *avant la lettre*? The concepts of "basic plot" and "root narrative" might suggest such a conclusion, and indeed it may be that Shkolnikov's prophecies involve not just literature but the human sciences more generally. But, regardless, it cannot be denied that this work, at its heart, is a fanciful—and even "science fictional"—project. In order to give the reader a better sense of the flavor of this rare book (since hard copies are exceedingly difficult to come by), I reproduce below a scan of the whole of the book's front matter, including the table of contents, so that you may glimpse for yourself the strangeness of those eighteen chapter headings.

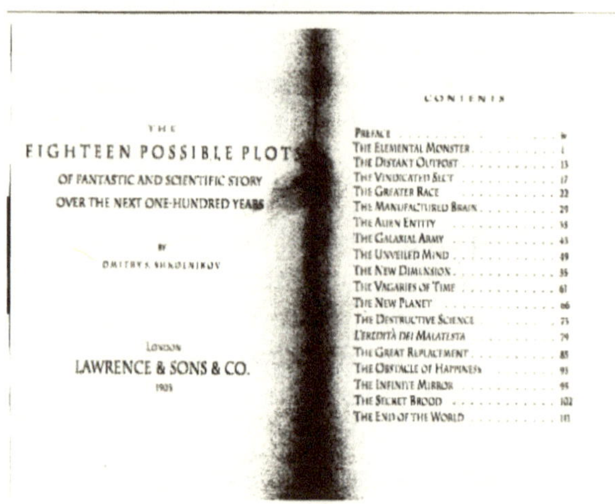

Before undertaking any deeper examination of the mysteries of *The Eighteen Possible Plots*, it is necessary first to dispense with two immediate and interrelated questions. Each of these preliminary questions has both a simple answer and a more complex one. Here is the first question: *Why, if almost no one has read it, is the existence of* The Eighteen Possible Plots *so widely known (at least among those readers who take seriously the scholarly consideration of the forms and the history of science fiction)?* The simple answer can be summed up tidily in the name of Darko Suvin, whose preeminence as a theorist of science fiction is indisputable, and whose 1999 essay on the topic of Shkolnikov's book received a good deal of critical attention. (Indeed the twentieth anniversary reissue of *Metamorphoses of Science Fiction*, where the essay appears, was something of a momentous event in and of itself, at least within certain academic circles.) The more complicated answer to the question has to do with Suvin's actual findings: for what is most "astonishing" about Shkolnikov's book, according to Suvin—who normally had no special interest in prophecies or in the predictive qualities of science fiction[51]— is just how incredibly *accurate* its visions of the future proved to be (so accurate, in fact, that at least one critic has gone so far as to suggest that the book must be a hoax[52]). Over the course of his essay, Suvin tallies up no less than 148 "major works of science fiction"—and not only stories and novels, but films and television programs too—that appear to have been successfully predicted, in whole or in part, by *The Eighteen Possible Plots*. Naturally it is not my objective in this note to rehearse all of those findings; I would simply adduce, as an especially interesting example, the case of chapter two, called "The Distant Outpost," in which Shkolnikov describes one of his plots as follows:

> Just as there shall always be a periphery to the known world, an outer limit where our knowledge dims, so shall there always be the first-explorers *beyond* those limits. H. G. Wells and Jules Verne have already begun telling fantastical stories about such first-explorers. The natural sequel to these

---

51 "[T]he cognitive value of all [science fiction], including anticipation-tales, is to be found in its analogical reference to the author's present rather than in predictions, discrete or global." Suvin 78. But see Suvin 74 for an example of the author making a science fiction prediction of his own.

52 "As for Shkolnikov and his 'predictions,' I for one will not be surprised if his book (whose bibliographic details have always remained somewhat murky) proves to be an elaborate trick, perhaps pulled by Suvin himself in order to make a point." Prinzo, Edmund. "On Darko Suvin and Prophecy." *Science Fiction Studies*, vol. 39, no. 4, 2012, p. 602.

tales, then, will involve the *second*-comers to such outer realms. Here is how it shall be: Something strange has happened at one of those remote places, something mysterious—perhaps the protagonists of the story have lost touch with the original team of explorers, or they've received communications from them which are incomprehensible, or oddly out of character, or even monstrous—and thus a *second* team must be dispatched in order to discover what has happened. (Naturally this plot may be reversed as well: the distant outpost begins to receive strange communications from the homeland, thus signifying some horrifying event there.)[53]

It is uncertain whether Shkolnikov had already read *Heart of Darkness* (first published in 1899) when he wrote these lines, but the basic plot described here is surely comparable to that of Conrad's novella, which undoubtedly has exerted a profound influence over modern authors of science fiction. Suvin rightly points out that Clarke's *2001* and *2010*, as well as such films as *Alien* and *Event Horizon*, all make use of this same "root narrative," in which "a disaster or something baffling has happened way out far from home, thus compromising the first group of humans to have reached that remote location; now a second group must go to investigate…"[54]

The second preliminary question that must be addressed is similar to the first, but is subtler. Really it is the same question, but now in reverse: *Why, if Shkolnikov's book is widely known, does no one bother to read it?* The simple answer is its physical scarcity. As I've already mentioned there are precious few copies of the text still in existence, and for better or worse no one has yet thought to republish it. More complicated is the second answer,

---

53 Shkolnikov 14.

54 Suvin 306.

which I shall put as follows: *No one reads* The Eighteen Possible Plots *because its success was also its failure.* That is to say: since its predictions have already come true, the book's properly speculative energies have been depleted. The text has become, to use Bachelard's formulation, one of those "dead documents of the past, untimely when written, but exhausted now."[55]

Suvin, too, has his detractors, who argue that any claims regarding Shkolnikov's "successful predictions" are themselves unsupportable, and that *The Eighteen Possible Plots* must therefore be regarded as a failure, root and branch. One might respond to those critiques by pointing out that most of them amount to mere refutations of prophecy as such. Professor Kaufman's dismissal, for example, insists that any attempt to find successful predictions in Shkolnikov's awkward prose would be "akin to deciphering a quatrain by Nostradamus: you can read more or less anything you like into it."[56] Then there's Ray Bradbury's gentler rebuke, made shortly before his death: "Type enough words, wait long enough, and then watch as more and more of your predictions come true."[57] Even Stanislaw Lem, who made a few literary predictions of his own (at least in fictional form), weighed in on the Shkolnikov controversy: "The future is a big target, the very biggest in fact. Throw a dart in its general direction and it's bound to stick somewhere."[58]

I will insist here, however, that the most profound reason nobody bothers to read *The Eighteen Possible Plots* today is that the

---

55 Bachelard, Gaston. *Essais sur la poétique.* Gallimard, 1952, p. 298. [My translation]

56 Kaufman, Louis. "Reflections on the Twentieth Anniversary of *Metamorphoses of Science Fiction.*" *Science Fiction Studies,* vol. 26, no. 4, 1999, p. 589.

57 Bradbury, Ray. Keynote Address. *Science Fiction and Utopia,* Ithaca, New York, May 2010.

58 Lem, Stanislaw. *Reflections on Writing.* Translated by Rusev Or. Andre Deutsch Limited, 2000, p. 42.

book appears to lack any discernible, reproducible *method*. In spite of Shkolnikov's prefatory remarks to the contrary (he actually boasts of the methodological rigor of his predictions), it would seem that his ideas are more or less haphazard, or at least capricious, not unlike the loose and wide-ranging dreams of a failed writer. Nevertheless, let us hear him out:

> The technique that governs the bulk of these speculations is one that I've drawn from H. G. Wells and C. H. Hinton, whose sympathies with each other are so evident that I've even suspected them of being one and the same man. One need only read the opening pages of both Wells' *The Time Machine* and Hinton's *Scientific Romances* to see the clear affinity between those two giants. The technique that I speak of, then, to borrow a tidy phrase from Hinton himself, consists simply of "supposing away" a limitation that has been placed upon our current state of existence; by engaging in such an imaginative operation, "a state of being can be conceived with powers far transcending our own." And while Hinton believed that such mental exercises would allow us to conceive of new *spatial* dimensions, I have employed this method for peering into the *time* still to come. I sometimes refer to this mental tactic as *the logic of the sequel*.[59]

Of course Shkolnikov gives us little to no guidance on how this "logic of the sequel" is actually to be practiced. The excerpt reproduced below, however, from the chapter titled "The Unveiled Mind," gives as good a picture as any of Shkolnikov's "method" in action. He begins with a simple empirical observation, one of somewhat narrow scientific interest: "The Seismological Society of Japan has recently developed

---

59 Shkolnikov vi.

instruments so finely calibrated that they can detect the vibrations of an earthquake before it even occurs." Having established that technological premise, Shkolnikov then proceeds to "suppose away" the "limitation" presented by the substantive "earthquake," and imagines in its place—or rather, he imagines *the writers of the future* imagining—something far more fantastic:

> The new machines [in the literature of the future] will be so sensitive that they will be capable of detecting the vibrations of *human thought*; indeed they will be capable not only of detecting them but also of recording them, reproducing them, and finally transmitting them instantaneously to all of the other thought-detecting machines on the planet (for, once discovered, such technology is bound to be multiplied and interconnected), and eventually they will communicate this data directly to all other human consciousnesses as well—a confluence out of which, finally, God Himself will arise, new-born, the true Son of man, and an infallible social peace will then ensue (or maybe the end of the world— biblically they are the same thing). A variant of this theme will propose something like the opposite, with a more fiendish essence rising up from that fresh sea of thought. This new villain will be a more curtailed force than God, to be sure, but it will be no less transformative: it will seek to turn humanity into a mere element of itself, making our species into a base utility or substance from which to draw its own supervening life. That villain will be called Satan, or maybe some very ordinary name like John or Smith (it emerges out of our accumulated thoughts, after all), and its weapon will be the thought-detecting machines themselves, which it will use to throw forth its illusions. In this same vein

there will be the makings-literal of Marxism, fantasies that will be indistinguishable from parodies, and in which not just private property but *privacy as such* will be utterly abolished. Since all human minds shall be exposed to each other, all formerly conflicting purposes will gradually converge into one, and class divisions will be among the first to fall away. The whole human race, in other words, will be converted into a great individual in these tales—a Leviathan, infinitely-limbed, but of one mind. Probably some simple and perfect geometrical shape, a circle or a cube, will be the symbol for this new collective. There may also be bands of uncertain heroes who rebel or otherwise seek to preserve their own individual privacies in the face of that growing, indissoluble crowd.[60]

Is there any *method* in all this dreaming? Probably not. But then, as Suvin has pointed out, these imaginings are remarkably prescient for someone writing in 1903. *The Matrix* (1999), for example, seems well predicted here: Shkolnikov at least gets its central premise correct (evil forces using machines and illusions to subdue the interconnected minds of the human race so that they might fuel themselves), and he even manages to predict the very name—Smith!—of the primary villain. One can also readily find the Borg from *Star Trek* anticipated in the passage above: Shkolnikov not only describes the obliteration of individual consciousness in that purely collective society, he even gets the cube right! Other modern sci-fi novels are also suggested remarkably well by this single paragraph (see, e.g., Gibson's *Neuromancer* or Orton's *New Europa* trilogy). At the very least it would not be outlandish to ask: Has anyone ever predicted a cultural development with *more* accuracy than Shkolnikov?

---

60 Shkolnikov 53.

But is he predicting only literature, or the future itself? Sometimes it is difficult to tell. In some places (as in the passage just cited) he has all the assurance and grandeur of Fourier; in others he adopts a far humbler tone: "[t]he logic of the sequel, the simple removing of this or that limitation in one's mind, is often but a half-step into the future, a glimpse only an hour or so ahead."[61] Regardless, it seems that everyone will agree—including Suvin himself—that *The Eighteen Possible Plots*, at least at the methodological level, is ultimately unsatisfying. The accuracy of its predictions cannot save it on that count.

As far as I know only one contemporary review of *The Eighteen Possible Plots* was ever published: a single unsigned paragraph in *The London Round-Up* on November 8th, 1903. In my estimation, this review, though caustic, gets mostly right the central flaw of the book, and it is worth reproducing in full:

> It is not just the hypotheses proposed by Dmitry Shkolnikov's new book that are worthless (though they are, for reasons I shall clarify). It is also and more seriously the ludicrous pretense that any sort of methodical rule or procedure could have informed them. This pointless book is composed of eighteen pointless chapters, in which the author blithely proclaims the power to predict the future of so-called "fantastic" literature, and even goes so far as to advise his readers of all of the "basic plots" that will be written in that genre in the century to come. As it happens there are only eighteen of them. Why there shall be such a dearth of stories in the future the author never explains. But even setting that foolishness aside, the perfect futility of the book becomes evident upon just cursory reflection. For if Shkolnikov's predictions are correct (let us suppose he has some magic crystal ball), then his book

---

61 Shkolnikov vii.

accomplishes nothing but a spoiling of the surprise; whereas if they are wrong, then his eighteen chapters constitute little more than the typical trash heap of false prophecies. As I mentioned, though, his most egregious error was to have supposed that such nonsense could have had any legitimate intellectual method. His "technique" he claims to have borrowed from C. H. Hinton (who is equally mad, but even more laborious), and it involves the imaginative "supposing away" of "limitations." And what is a "limitation?" Anything that exists! Anything that *is*, any condition or thing or idea or word. Alas, if the future was so transparent, and so simple a thing to divine, we'd all be rich from speculation by now. *The Eighteen Possible Plots of Fantastic and Scientific Story Over the Next One Hundred Years* is a contribution neither to philosophy nor to literature, nor even to prophecy. I predict the future will not be kind to it.

...

And yet—there still are mysteries that swirl about *The Eighteen Possible Plots,* mysteries that may well make it an object worthy of further study. At least one of those mysteries is about to be revealed in this very note. But let us first consider the man himself: What do we really know about the obscure Dmitry Shkolnikov?

There are no photographs of him, at least none that have survived. The biographical information that we do possess is scant: we have no birth record, there are no known relatives (he had no offspring, as we'll see), and we know of no other publications from him besides *The Eighteen Possible Plots.* We do not know his ancestry—his name suggests Russian origins— though it appears he was fluent in both French and English and lived for some time in Paris. We have a handful of letters he wrote to Henri Bergson (they are among the philosopher's personal papers that can be reviewed with permission at the Bergson Center at the Collège de France), as well as a diary entry or two made by this or that intellectual of the time, which mention him by name (both Jean Bourdeau and Georges Sorel apparently knew him personally). Indeed it would seem that Dmitry Shkolnikov regularly mingled among the intelligentsia in Paris in the first decade of the twentieth century, and made frequent appearances at social events thrown at the Collège where Bergson and other famous professors were often among the guests. Somehow, though, Shkolnikov has remained a ghost. To my knowledge, the only existing *description* of the man is to be found in a memoir by one Isadora Marceau,[62] a Parisian socialite who was a regular acquaintance of Bergson's. In chapter twelve of that memoir, Marceau recounts meeting one "Dimitri Skolnikoff" on Bergson's balcony during an evening soirée:

> He was a striking figure to look at, a slight man of only medium height, but with a wide-eyed green gaze and jagged, variously-colored teeth and a perfectly-shaped triangular beard that he kept flattened and glistening with oils. He smelled faintly of shallots. His pale face blushed easily, and there were little red and blue lines visible along the tops of his cheekbones, as if vessels had swelled or burst there just beneath the skin, or as if just that part of him, just his face, was *straining* to exist, or perhaps had come from the sea and was still ill-adjusted to the bright and gaseous simplicity of the world above the water. His shapely nose and bulging eyes only intensified my impression that he was, secretly, some form of sea creature, come perhaps to learn of what we landwalkers are made, of what salt and what mettle. To my surprise, he and Bergson were in fact

---

62 Marceau, Isadora. *Mon temps à Paris.* Éditions Grasset, 1932.

discussing marine life when I approached them on the balcony (surely the good professor had brought the topic up himself; I recall that during this period Bergson would lecture anyone who cared to listen about the similarities between the structures of the human eye and those of the eye of the squid). At that particular moment, Skolnikoff was just concluding some sort of Marxist allegory about the "power relations" between sharks and fish; I remember he ended his speech, which drew a laugh from Henri, with an outburst somewhat like the following: "Sharks *appear* to be more powerful than fish, and indeed in many respects they are, they feast upon them after all. And yet it is also evident that the shark *depends* upon the fish, and so occupies a structurally inferior position: *the fish don't need the shark!*"

There was something so strange about him, this Dimitri Skolnikoff; he seemed to be not wholly at home in his own body, the way his head bobbed and his fingers nervously formed shapes on either side of his face while he spoke—almost like he wasn't really talking to you at all, or as if he were signaling to hovering spirits that only he could see. There was an unlikely youthfulness about him, too—I mean he was awkward in that way that comes from being too-limber and soft-muscled and prone to enthusiasm: all fits and starts, all elbows and knees, like a marionette, or a pup not yet grown into its paws. Henri introduced me; Skolnikoff clasped my hand and suddenly lurched forward a step, drawing our two faces—his seemed filled with sadness—close together. He spat some melodious nonsense into my ear (probably he was drunk), something more or less as follows: "All the forces that make up human existence are jealous of each other, and none more so than happiness. And my happiness at meeting you is a jealous thing indeed." I pulled back at this; I'm certain Skolnikoff was pleased by my response, for he flashed a piebald smile and then added: "Once she gets into you she replaces every other plan and dream you've ever had, and all before the moon is full." I don't know if he meant happiness or death (or me) in that last bit; regardless, I promptly excused myself and avoided Skolnikoff for the rest of the evening.

Years later I would learn, from Jacques Rivière, that Skolnikoff was a virgin, and had died as such only a month or so after Bergson's party. According to Rivière he often boasted of his purity: "The chastity of a house cat," he apparently liked to say; and: "Oh this unconquered heart of mine!" Somehow this detail—which, in spite of Skolnikoff's strangeness, I would not have guessed at the time— has since warmed me to his fading memory. Every now and then I even feel a touch of regret for snubbing him that night.[63]

. . .

But now, finally, I come to my chief purpose in making this report. You may be perplexed, to be sure, that it's taken me this long to get to my true subject matter. Has everything in this note up until now been mere preparation for the thing I am about to unveil? Probably no answer to this question will satisfy you, so I'll get to it.

Six months ago, while in Paris, I made a startling discovery. While I was browsing in a bookshop that lay all but hidden down one of those alleys that have no light but half-light in the sixth arrondissement (I do not recall the name of the bookseller; even

---

63 Marceau 189. [My translation]

more maddening is that Gérard, my traveling companion at the time, insists now that we were not in Paris at all that day, but rather in Saint-Germain-en-Laye), I discovered, on a shelf full of other antique volumes, a copy of Shkolnikov's book—*in French.* The French title, however, was different (and even more awkward). It read: *Les Dix-neuf possibles intrigues d'histoires fantastiques et scientifiques dans les prochaines cent années.* Frantically I opened the book and scanned the table of contents; it appeared to be a perfect transcription of the English version, with only one modification: a *nineteenth* chapter had indeed been added. The new chapter was called *La Dialectique à l'envers,* which I translate as "The Dialectic in Reverse." (This rendering, as should soon become clear, is superior to "Dialectic Upside Down," which may at first seem equally plausible.) I paid the bookseller the exorbitant sum he asked for, and then hurried back to my hotel to study the text. The book had been published in 1909 by Larousse in Paris. No translator is named anywhere in the front matter, and I can only assume that Shkolnikov himself did the job. As far as I can tell, but for the nineteenth chapter, the book is an exact translation of the Lawrence & Sons edition.

Naturally my copy of the French version will have to be authenticated (and for that reason you will be within your rights if you conclude that this whole note of mine has been premature). But if I've jumped the gun it's only because I wanted to ensure that I would be the very first to introduce English-speaking readers to the *nineteenth* plot that Dmitry Shkolnikov foresaw (a prophecy that he made, apparently, shortly before his death, which also took place in 1909). I will not bother quoting the text at great length; the new chapter is longer than all of the others by at least half, so for the most part I shall resort to paraphrase instead.

The nineteenth chapter begins with Shkolnikov narrating what he calls "a typical dialectical progression" (I translate as best I can from the French):

Imagine an early human society, some fifty thousand years ago. An earthquake happens. How do they interpret this? Naturally they reach for empirical concepts that are ready to hand: *Surely it's some giant beast deep in the ground, stirring in its sleep!* Many thousands of years later, as humans move on to more religious or spiritual stages, such cataclysms are conceived as the just or capricious punishments of the gods, with Nature itself being imbued with moral significance. Finally, as they progress to a properly scientific and conceptual stage, during which the moral dimension of Nature is all but abandoned, the quaking ground is attributed to nothing more than the broad shapes and mechanisms of the earth itself, which is governed solely by the impersonal laws of matter.[64]

This "typical dialectical progression" can thus be represented—Shkolnikov himself does so—as a development that proceeds along the following path:

MONSTER → GOD → SCIENCE

Shkolnikov's nineteenth plot, then, will be this very same progression, only now condensed and played *in reverse*. That is to say: An earthquake happens, and we assume it's to be explained scientifically, like any other earthquake; but then something strange occurs—the epicenter begins moving from place to place, the tremors manifest where there are no fault lines, etc.—such that there seems to be no proper scientific explanation for the phenomenon at all, which grows more violent by the day, and even begins bringing whole cities to the ground. This destruction

---

64 Shkolnikov, Dmitry S. *Les Dix-neuf possibles intrigues d'histoires fantastiques et scientifiques dans les prochaines cent années.* Larousse, 1909, pp. 119-120. [My translation]

causes great panic among the people, some of whom turn to religion. They begin praying to God in the streets; they believe Judgment Day is come, the world is going to end:

> But lo! It is finally revealed: the cause of the tremors has in fact been a monster all along! A giant and ancient beast has been awakened after thousands of years of sleep; it has been rummaging about beneath the ground; it will now burst free and ravage the human world.[65]

Shades of Toho! And yet there may be a deeper and more biographical significance to this final "plot." To introduce this more shadowy meaning, permit me to cite the first paragraph from one of Shkolnikov's rather strange letters to Henri Bergson, dated December 21, 1908:

> Henri—
>
> You must never apologize for your optimism. Of course my harried Christian brain is not as skilled as yours at suppressing the grim thing to come, the debt due; though to be honest the reckoning that fills me with the most dread is a good deal duller than that of the Judgment. Really what plagues me is just DEATH itself (or its ashy foretaste anyway); and I mean by that no more than my own brute biological death, which, as time passes, seems more and more like an individual *thing* to me, like an actually living being with a well-shaped self who one day will look me square in the eye and lay claim to me—a being I can already hear and smell from the other room.

---

65 Shkolnikov. *Les Dix-neuf possibles intrigues*, p. 139.

I believe that this fragment may give us one of the keys to the nineteenth plot (and thus to the "dialectic in reverse") by revealing its properly *allegorical* dimension. For what is it, I ask you, that seems only like an abstraction or a scientific idea when we are still young, but then, as we grow older, causes our thoughts to turn religious (as we worry about our legacies or the afterlife or the prospect of judgment or forgiveness), until, finally, it is standing right before us, with a gleaming eye and cold grim claws—if not death?

Of course I don't have to remind the reader that allegory need not be a literal or metaphysical belief in the actual personhood of ideas or forces (even if all allegorical thinking does take us into that broad conceptual space in which nothing is ever really inert, and in which even seemingly static objects and ideas are felt to be "alive" in some way). As is almost always the case, Borges has a couple of perfect sentences on the matter:

> [Dante's] Beatrice is not a sign of the word *faith*; she is a sign of the valiant virtue and secret illuminations indicated by that word. A sign more precise, richer, and more felicitous, than the monosyllable *faith*.[66]

In a very different context, Gaston Bachelard brings the subject of allegory back round to death:

> Those civilizations and those epochs with a taste for allegory had a keener sense and awe of death than we do now. For them, death didn't just happen; it *took* you.[67]

---

66 Borges, Jorge Luis. "From Allegories to Novels." *Selected Non-Fictions.* Translated by Esther Allen, Suzanne Jill Levine, and Eliot Weinberger. Viking, 1999, p. 338.

67 Bachelard, 192.

Death is the ultimate object of allegory, as it is the ultimate object of the fantastic, for it is the last conceivable horizon of the human imagination. The temptation to represent death as a conscious individual is therefore permanent, for the only thing that is as unfathomable as death is another human being.

But is the nineteenth plot truly an allegory? I shall make the following confession in lieu of a conclusion. When I first discovered *The Eighteen Possible Plots*, I thought indeed that the book was allegorical. But now, as I find myself drawing closer to death—I am only old, not yet sick, but I am well enough along in my years that I can sense the finitude of my life—a *second* interpretation has revealed itself to me. I now think that the book, and the mysterious nineteenth chapter in particular, is maybe the *opposite* of an allegory; that maybe what Shkolnikov meant to convey was something far more literal, that maybe he had in fact *seen* or *sensed* his death as some stirring thing, a beast all but hidden in form, outside and apart from him, like a hungry animal whose padded footfalls you can just barely make out from the bush. Perhaps, in the end, his death came swiftly, soft-footed and springing upon him with jaws wetly clicking like a panther's—even if he somehow managed to glimpse it first. Perhaps, in the end, he saw death in that way, *in the flesh*. Perhaps he came to understand that death, too, is but a creature, an individual, a half-intelligent animal with only half-intelligent designs on our good life, like those beasts—from novels, from movies, from the fearful minds of men many thousands of years ago—climbing out from the cradle of the earth.

Missive on an Old Refutation of Time

There is a town in northernmost Japan that is so close to the eastern extremity of Russia—the Russian-controlled Kunashir Island is not even twenty miles off—the street signs there are all written in both Japanese and Cyrillic. It is a cold and windy place, sparsely populated; lots of snow in the wintertime. Near the shore there stands a small striped lighthouse and a row of bellicose statues that glare over the water with their swords drawn (a monument, I recently learned, to the *bushi* who, according to lore, defended an Ainu fishing village from marauders some four centuries ago). On clear days, even the most frigid ones, the sun bounces and gleams warmly off of the Nemuro Strait. I dream of living there, in that strange overlapping of Russia and Japan. I dream of the quiet snow, of the uneventful neighborhoods, the oft-unpeopled streets, the warmly-lit tea shop and bodega that I've seen in a photograph. I dream of the Japanese and Russian street signs—some of them warnings, no doubt—which, for me, would stand only for meaningless, melodious sounds.

Less frequent but not less aglow in my dreams is the village of Dalvik in Iceland—a satellite, so to speak, of the Lesser Grímsvötn volcano near the western edge of the Vatnajökull ice cap. The volcano, which smolders beneath clouds veined with its ash (though it has not technically erupted in over three-hundred years), is something of a geological oddity: it is the only properly conical, sub-glacial volcano in the northern hemisphere that exhibits signs of carbon-based magma. Its uppermost peak juts strangely from the ice, bare of snow, like an obelisk. The village of Dalvik, really little more than an outpost, and located just outside the glacier's edge some forty kilometers west of the volcano, was established gradually between 1959 and 1962 in order to service the geologists who came from all over the world to study that strange anomaly. As one might guess, the village is not exactly a concentrated geographical entity; it exists in small pockets of activity here and there, and parts of it move from place to place, depending upon the season and funding from universities. Several leagues to the west of the glacier is the sparsely-furnished Denmark Hotel, often taken to be the western boundary of Dalvik (and probably the only place within fifty kilometers where one can get a hot shower). Closer are the various chalets, quickly erected and then torn down again, where food is prepared, supplies are sold, and expeditions are planned. Near the start of the glacier proper one may find the drab tent where sleeps Rúrik Sigþórsson, the lone guide who earns his humble living showing scientists and tourists the best routes up the slopes of the volcano (and even into her mouth), and whose throbbing, sparsely-bristled face, splotched like a rancid cheese and red as a sockeye, flakes freely from lip and chin. I've dreamed of being bundled up in Rúrik Sigþórsson's tent; I've had visions of my own ruined face, reddened and marked by the alternating extremes of heat and cold. I've dreamed of succeeding good Rúrik, of taking his place.

I've dreamed, also, of a street corner somewhere in the outskirts of Buenos Aires, written about by Borges in a short text called "Feeling in Death." This text is of singular importance to scholars and lovers of Borges's work, for it is the only one that he reproduced on at least three occasions: first in his youthful book *The Language of the Argentines*, and then again in his 1936 essay "A History of Eternity," and then again in "A New Refutation of Time" from 1947. The text recounts an experience Borges had while out for a walk one evening. It begins with him arriving at a corner in one of the barrios of Buenos Aires, a neighborhood vaguely familiar to him, but also mysterious; he is struck by the beauty of the place, the simple houses, the sky and the colors that exude tenderness, the "street of elemental clay." This perception of a scene both ordinary and picturesque then yields, as often happens in Borges, to metaphysical speculation:

> I stood looking at that simple scene. I thought, no
> doubt aloud: "This is the same as it was thirty years

136

ago…" […] That pure representation of homogeneous facts—calm night, limpid wall, rural scent of honeysuckle, elemental clay—is not merely identical to the scene on that corner so many years ago; it is, without similarities or repetitions, the same. If we can intuit that sameness, time is a delusion…

Borges does not specify the name of the street, or the barrio in which that corner was located. I think it must have been in Palermo, but of course this would be the Palermo of a hundred years ago, and perhaps even further back in time than that: the Palermo of Borges's dreams (that is, a Palermo when the Maldonado was still a freely flowing stream, and knife-wielding hoodlums strutted and flaunted themselves or else hid in the half-darkness of doorways, and certain poor neighborhoods were only a stroll from stench-filled stockyards and all-but impassable marshes). I too have dreamed of these old outskirts of Buenos Aires, and I've dreamed also of modern-day Barracas and of now-chic Palermo; I wonder if, in spite of their many changes, I could still somehow find the exact spot where Borges once stood and saw into eternity. Or, if I should fail at that, but if I nonetheless walked aimlessly enough, and if I took just the right careless turn around just the right Argentine corner, and if I saw the early-evening salmon sky, and beneath it a simple one-story home, and if I felt the life there, and the tenderness, and smelled the honeysuckle and the fig trees, and spied an indignant cactus growing from a masonry jar in the corner of a doorway, then might I too become convinced, if only later in a memory, of the illusoriness of time?

I think the half-existence of these places, their degree of *unreality* (Borges himself uses this word, *irrealidad*), is what draws me to them. More than other places, it seems to me, they exist inside the fleeting present, and only there. Once they are gone, no historian will ever think to mention them. In this quality we are, perhaps, the same.

Tomorrow our platoon is being sent back to the trenches. They tell us the third division is holding ground, but we know better. The GR outfit has been stretched thin. I hope this letter finds its way to you, and finds you well, my dear mother. Thank you for the books. As you can see, I've put them to good use already.

HAPPINESS('ha-pē-nəs), n.
[pl. happinesses ('ha-pē-nəs-əz)]:

A state of well-being, contentment.

Agreeable sensations springing from the enjoyment of the good.

Felicity, aptness or successfulness in the carrying out of an act or enterprise.

Fortuitousness (*a happy coincidence*).

Deriving pleasure or contentment from one's own thoughts, *i.e.*, finding one's own mind to be an agreeable place in which to dwell (*see*, *e.g.*, Lars Nuif, *The Remedy*: 'If you hate your thoughts, how could you be happy? If you love them, how could you not be?').

Per the antique theory of the four humors, an abundance of blood and phlegm.

The cause of wagging extremities, *e.g.*, a wagging tail or wiggling toes, *esp.* if these are involuntary.

An unreserved acceptance of *being*, *i.e.*, feeling satisfied that things will continue on the way they are.

Conservatism, *i.e.*, the contentment with *what is*, and the desire for it to carry on into the future (*see*, *e.g.*, Rick Retts, *The Big Book of Lies*: 'Then and there I was struck by the realization that, even if I could change something in the universe, anything at all, I wouldn't, I wouldn't change a thing. That's how total my happiness was. I wanted everything—even the most horrible things that ever happened—to stay the same.' *See also* Roger Scruton, 'Conservatism and the Conservatory': 'The real reason people are conservatives is that they are attached to the things that they love, and want to preserve them from abuse and decay.').

The eternal return of the same, and its affirmation (Nietzsche), *i.e.*, the sincere longing to repeat one's life *exactly* as it happened, not once or twice, but infinitely, for all eternity.

The sum total of positive sensations, after all mere *pleasures* have been subtracted from them.

Intense relief, as from pain, *i.e.*, the absence of pain, when felt by one recently well-acquainted with pain; the contrast between recent hardship and its present alleviation, *e.g.*, the first feelings of freedom after a long captivity or servitude.

A sudden lifting of restraint, sometimes by a ruling authority (*see, e.g.*, Book of Esther, 8:16–9:17, recounting how '[f]or the Jews it was a time of happiness and joy, gladness and honor' when, with the imprimatur of King Xerxes, and through bloody warfare and mass slaughter (seventy-five-thousand men killed), they avenged themselves upon those who had sought their destruction).

'An agreeable sensation arising from contemplating the misery of another' (Ambrose Bierce, *The Devil's Dictionary*).

Surfeit, as after a large and satisfying meal.

A state enjoyable in hell, but not in heaven (Malebranche).

Virtue, when it has been executed cleanly.

According to antebellum New Orleans slang, a flock of fully grown virgin chickens.

A general and powerful sense of *gratitude* for one's existence.

The relief felt from knowing how bad things *could* be, but are not; the appreciation of just how great the distance is between us and the extremes of evil and pain.

The assurance—more than hopefulness—that, in the end, things will all be all right (hence the common phrases 'happy ending' and 'happily ever after').

Forgetfulness, *i.e.*, the absence of ghosts, the opposite of being haunted; an appreciation of the nothingness of memory; the opposite of brooding (Wolfe: 'Ain't nuthin that's done nags you in heaven.').

The state of being successfully repressed, *i.e.*, without any discomfiting symptoms (*see, e.g.*, Freud, 'An Address': 'Repression gives rise to the symptom, of course; if it didn't, our profession would be largely superfluous.').

A calm conscience.

The condition of being divorced, to a degree that may well seem evil or cold, from the vast suffering of the world (*see, e.g.*, P. Roth, 'My Ethics': 'You can't be plugged into the world's pain and still be happy. It's impossible. If you want to be truly happy you have to block it out. As rough as that sounds.' *See also* Zobel Blake, *Notebooks*: 'Here is pessimism distilled: Happiness is possible but, because of the world's agony, evil; unhappiness is likely, but futile.').

Indifference, if it involves quiescence in the face of suffering, as in the strategies and objectives of stoicism (*see* Epictetus, Seneca).

The condition of having reached a lasting peace with Death.

Nirvana, the state of non-attachment.

A mode of being thoroughly in the *present*, *i.e.*, unconcerned with either past or future (*see*, *e.g.*, Gaston Bachelard, *Sur la poétique*: 'Happiness [*Bonheur*] entails a sojourn in the instant, where memories are only quaint, and premonitions are dispensed with altogether').

To be at peace with the prospect, or rather with the universal fact, of *being forgotten* (*see*, *e.g.*, Deek Panchkat, 'Lessons from Emerson': 'Those who can forget may well enjoy peace, but those who are wholly at peace with *being forgotten* – they are the truly blessed.').

Laughter, *esp.* if uncontrollable; cackling.

Anticipation, if the waiting is for something wonderful and the waiting does not go on too long.

Desire, if the desire is for something wonderful and the object is within one's grasp.

What beauty promises (Stendhal).

The meekness of God (Boehme).

Laziness; the state of having little or no ambition, not even in one's dreams; the clear perception of the needlessness of any and all frantic activity.

The feeling of accomplishment, but only when this does not result from the reaching of any actual goal.

The feeling of being loved, but in particular when there is no lover, not even a hallucinated one.

A rare species of tree (Portuguese name: *Alegria*) found only in the southern lowlands of the Pantanal in Brazil, whose thin and brown and sparse leaves cause its branches to appear bare all year round, in stark contrast to the vast green swampland that is its native terrain.

The conviction, when embraced, that nothing is ours to keep, not even our own lives, save what we *love*, and even then only metaphorically (*i.e.*, in one's heart).

Luck, luckiness; the appreciation of the random beneficence that determines one's well-being (*see, e.g.*, Taque Foek, *What Is Medicine?*: 'At the end of the day we all must acknowledge the dumb fortune of health, and the heads-or-tails character of suffering, pain, and sickness').

Understanding that there are many miracles in the world, all around us all the time, and that they are all stupid.

The exhilaration felt, not before or during, but immediately following ejaculation or orgasm, as expressed in the lethargy of the muscles, and the body's welcoming of sleep.

The welcoming of sleep.

A burst of intelligibility, as in the case of an effective artistic symbol, or a gesture with moral clarity.

Catharsis (Aristotle), or the sudden expulsion, *esp.* in the tragic mode, of moral vagueness or confusion.

The feeling of linguistic perfection, *esp.* in description, *esp.* if grammar is flouted (*see, e.g.,* Claudel: 'a sea so blue that blood couldn't be more red').

A mob of rheas (Portuguese name: *Alegria*), if sprinting.

Epilogue

1.

Somewhere deep in that treasure trove of quotations that is *The Anatomy of Melancholy* (1621), Robert Burton cites the following maxim:

All must toil, but none more so than the sparrow.

The meaning of this antique sentence—it is adduced by Burton in support of the stoic principle that "no soul is poor indeed but in opinion"—has long confounded readers, and not least because Burton clumsily attributes the line to Cicero. In the text that Burton cites (it is one of Cicero's letters to Atticus), the sentence is *actually* ascribed—ambiguously, maddeningly—to "a famous lyrist of old Syracuse."* No further hint of the origin of the quote is given, nor is it found anywhere else in Cicero's writings (or in Burton's, for that matter). My initial guess as to the identity of this "famous lyrist"—and I admit it was probably not my own idea, likely I came away with it from some old book—was that Cicero must have had the ancient poetess Sappho in mind, who after all lived in Syracuse for a time, and whose Aphrodite famously rode a chariot drawn by sparrows. (*With thy car yoked, and sparrows that pulled thee...* (Sappho,

---

* Here is the passage in full, which I translate from the Latin: "Pompey first treated Caesar like an apprentice, but then became afraid of him, and then refused peace but made no preparations for war, and then fled Rome, and by his own doing lost Picenum, was foiled in Apulia, and sped off to Greece without telling us any of his plans. Who has ever wrought more vigorously his own downfall or that of his allies! He might as well say, after a famous lyrist of old Syracuse,

All must toil, but none more so than the sparrow."

Fragment 1).) Of course, even if Sappho was indeed the source of the quote, the *meaning* of the sentence (which is not found in any of her extant verses) remains elusive. Why should it be the *sparrow* who toils the most?

Some years ago—I recall it was early in the winter—while I was conducting research on this question at the Soerling Library and Manuscript Archive in Princeton, New Jersey, I found my reflections sailing off in different directions (though to be sure without any of them ever sighting *terra firma*). Perhaps the meaning of that little aphorism—or so I mused to myself, taking for granted that the line indeed came from Sappho—was that romantic love must be ever widespread, and that Aphrodite's task of distributing it to all the corners of the earth, and as it were on the backs of sparrows (which, in older Greek mythology, signify lasciviousness), is a frantic and laborious one. Or perhaps it meant something like the opposite, and that the bulk of the heavy substance of love never escapes Aphrodite's carriage, and therefore weighs it down—a burden which her sparrows' fraught, beating wings sadly must bear. Or perhaps the implication was that Aphrodite, being the goddess of love, must also be that devil who *breaks hearts*, and that *this* labor is by far the vastest of them all, and that her poor sparrows, who are obliged to fly her from place to place as she conducts her wicked business (but who also, we may opine, possess few of Aphrodite's Olympic resources), must be demoralized and beaten ragged by it. (*A slave,* said wise Gregory of Nyssa, *is wretched not because he toils but because he is yoked to sin...*) Ultimately, however, these various interpretations, along with my enthusiasm for them, only ended up wilting on their stalks until, finally, I had little choice but to leave them to the mulch.

But then, near the very end of that year, during the week after Christmas, and just as I was about to give up on the topic altogether, one of the library assistants surprised me in the stacks. (I don't recall the librarian's name; I mean the tall, bony one with purposeful eyebrows, the woman with thin hair the color of half-burnt straw, the one who always wears conservative linen dresses and drinks a pungent *pu-erh* tea all day, the one with brownish teeth and chafed, exceptionally long and accusing fingers...) This assistant happened to know the subject matter of my research, as I'd been relying on her for some time. "This might be of interest," she said to me, almost in a whisper, as she handed over a brittle-looking, loosely-bound set of folio pages. (It was the first time I'd ever seen her smile, wide and gummy and piebald; I confess it threw me.) The text she'd just put into my hands was obviously very old, and was written in Latin, without any front matter. It bore the title, *Quisque operatur sed nemo assidius quam passerculus,* or, *All must toil, but no one more than the poor little sparrow.* Upon reading that heading I felt a thrill pass through me, the kind that only library-dwellers like me, when they chance upon some possible clue to a research question, ever feel. I looked closely at the first page; the work appeared to be a treatise devoted to the subject of *malum contra naturam,* or "unnatural evil." The author was designated by a single name, "Philoxenus."

When I looked up to thank the librarian she was already gone, though the scent of her tea lingered in the air, and even welled up from the pages in my hands.

2.

All books harbor secrets; that is why people hoard them and keep libraries—because human beings, like house cats, are drawn to mysteries, and one never knows what a book might be hiding. It might sound like a paradox, but books are among the most secretive things in existence; even some little novella you've read three times already is no doubt still hiding something from you (and if you don't believe me then just read it a fourth time and find out for yourself). Books are secretive because *reading* is; indeed, even the most avid and prodigious readers attain from their pursuits what is mainly a private reward, a private glory, one that no one else even glimpses. You and I might discuss the works of Borges, or a volume of Blake's poetry, and of course there will be universals and moods that we both instantly grasp and can share with one another; but still the broader effects those books produce, say, *in my life*—the way they accompany me, the way they influence my perception and embolden my imagination (*The astounding manner in which I now observe a cloud*, Richter has the dreamy Albano say in *Titan*)—I can scarcely share with you, and most often it is pointless even to try. Could I explain, to you who never met him, what it is to have known and loved my father? It would be like having to build a planet. It is much the same with the books we love or brood over, even those books we have in common. Which is to say, we have no books in common. Not really.

Even setting aside such themes (which belong to the *ontology of books in general*, a part of metaphysics that perhaps only Blanchot has explored with an appropriate degree of seriousness), I think I may safely say that, as the winter progressed, I did not have Philoxenus's little book in common with anyone else. As far as I could tell at the time, no one but me had *ever* read it. Even after weeks of research I had not unearthed a single mention of the text anywhere (that is, except for one purely bibliographical citation, to which I'll return in a moment); meanwhile, the investigations I made into Philoxenus himself proved no less abortive. To begin with, there was the onerous business of distinguishing him from his various namesakes in the ancient world (Philoxenus of Cythera [435 – 380 BCE], for example, or of Eretria [4th century BCE], or of Antioch [503 – 554 CE]). Then there was the distressing fact that no agreement was to be found in the literature as to just when and where Philoxenus lived (some historians put him mainly in Galatia in the third century; others, including Wholff, insist he lived for the most part in Roman Africa more than a hundred years later, and even became *de facto* coadjutor to Augustine when that dear bishop's health started to fail), or even as to whether he existed at all ("Philoxenus evidently is the name of a hoax," contends Moller Gitch in an alliterative footnote to *Modes of Expression*:

"Whatever works have been attributed to this fictitious figure are undoubtedly forgeries, albeit fantastic ones, and perpetrated over centuries by fraudsters writing from different nations and even from different continents"). What, then, can I tell you about Philoxenus that is sure and definite? Nothing. I've no choice therefore but to keep silent about him. (You will eventually see that this resolve of mine may be judicious in more than one way.) I will also not speak here of either the *Ludi Diabolorum* or the *Significatio in Liliis*, the two (Satanic) works most infamously associated with the man, as I have not been able to verify the authenticity or even the existence of those volumes (though many writers, including de Quincey and Ambrose Bierce, purport to quote them). I will instead confine my remarks to the only book that is rightly germane to my narrative, the only one ostensibly by Philoxenus that I've actually read, the only one that I know *exists*, the one that was given to me by the brown-toothed librarian at Soerling, the one with the excruciating title, *All must toil, but no one more than the poor little sparrow.*

3.

Before engaging with that text itself, however, permit me briefly to acknowledge the one reference to the book that I was able to locate in my research. I don't know if it is essential to my story, but to me at least it is an important detail—for it is what first made me wonder if Philoxenus's book might in fact be…*dangerous.*

Probably you are aware already of that censorious and ignoble document—but a glorious compendium too!—first produced by the Catholic Church at the close of the Middle Ages, and then revised and expanded over the centuries, the *Index Librorum Prohibitorum* (i.e., a list of those books that the devout must never read, ranging from Montaigne's essays to *Madame Bovary*, from the works of Spinoza to anti-Spinozist screeds, from pagan panegyrics to barefaced blasphemy). It is, at the very least, a text of some historical significance, and its various incarnations are available to anyone who might wish to read them. With a little ingenuity, however, and a few well-placed (and saccharine) phone calls to the right administrative assistants in Italy (and a friend or two in high places won't hurt either), you might become privy, as I became, to a *second, more secret list* kept by the Church, or the *Index Librorum a Daemonibus Scriptorum* (a list of supposedly "demonic" works which the Church nonetheless keeps and conserves); and if you are *really* persistent, and know just how to make a pleasant nuisance of yourself, and have a man on site that you can dispatch who knows just which doors at the Vatican Apostolic Library to rap upon, then you might also gain access to a *third* index, the most secret of the three (for, in a sense, it is but a list of embarrassments): the *Index Librorum Absentium,* a list of forbidden and sacrilegious books once preserved by the Church but now deemed to be forever "lost."

I was not surprised to see that Philoxenus's obscure little work was never included in the first list. I felt some disappointment to find it absent from the second (you'll see why in a moment). To my great astonishment, however, I discovered that it was in fact there among the books enumerated by the *third* list.

This last index, containing some three-thousand entries, tells us that some books went missing from Church libraries because of *furtum* (theft), others because they were *abiecti* (discarded) or *combusti* (burned). A different reason is recorded for the loss of Philoxenus's book: *vermibus destructus.* My guess as to the meaning of this ominous phrase (literally: *destroyed by worms*) is that the book must have been eaten by termites. Probably there had been a lone copy.

Could it be, I asked myself upon making this minor discovery, that the copy of Philoxenus's book that I had been consulting was the very last one left in the world?

4.

Quisque operatur sed nemo assidius quam passerculus, or, *All must toil, but no one more than the poor little sparrow*, begins with the following apostrophe (I translate as best I can from Philoxenus's unusual Latin):

> Oh Sparrow, leprous from foot to crown, whose lyre was known in old Greece, in Athens and in Syracuse, and whose melodies made even the moon tremble, give us thy music once more!

> Oh Sparrow, thou icy root, who pierced down to the still colder climes below the world, and who wrote there the destiny of all things, as in a mirror held to the skies, bring thy teachings once more to light, so that warmer races of clay may find paradise. Give us guidance in the craft of wickedness contrary to nature, and in other violations of the laws of gods, for it is in such realms that a great work is to be done.

It is not long after this introductory hymn that it becomes apparent to the reader: Philoxenus's book is not so much a treatise in its own right as it is a commentary on (and a recital of) *another*, more ancient book, a nameless text written in Greek by someone calling himself *the Sparrow*.

At the heart of this mysterious, unnamed work (at least if Philoxenus's recapitulation of it is to be trusted), there unfolds a lengthy exposition, which can only be described as exhortatory, of various "crimes contrary to nature" and "all the most unusual evils" and "all manner of ungodly devastation." (Such metaphysical-sounding phrases belong to Philoxenus; the Sparrow's own prose, generally speaking, and judging from Philoxenus's copious quotations, is far plainer.) Much is made by the Sparrow, for instance, of that special form of murder performed outside of warfare or noble revenge, without purpose beyond love of murder itself.

The very first text, perhaps, ever written about serial killers! There are also grim passages on "the amusing torment of beasts," and on "the ravishment of women" and "the poisoning of wells," and on "enslavement" and "that unquenchable thirst for the setting of fires," and on many more of the most horrible things that humans do. Many of the passages that delve deep into these iniquities are difficult to stomach, and I am not so morbid as to reproduce them here.

Then, at some point in the middle of the book—again, we are trusting Philoxenus—the Sparrow abruptly changes his tone and adopts a more philosophical and abstract language, and propounds axioms and deductions such as the following (I translate from Philoxenus's translation into Latin of the Sparrow's Greek):

Laws and Definitions

1. No quantity can exist by itself.

2. No quality can exist by itself.

3. No quantity can come into being, or have any force or value, but in relation to another quantity.

4. No quality can come into being, or have any force or value, but in relation to another quality.

Corollary

From these principles alone, without any further proof, it is evident that if a man lives but never experiences pain, then he will be unable to form any conception of the excellent value hidden within the state of painlessness. Nay, more: If he knows joys and pleasures, but never pain, then painlessness by itself will seem to him a worthless thing by comparison. It is only when he descends into the opposite of bliss, into those very forces that destroy life, that the mere absence of pain, in the form of ecstatic relief, seizes back its value as something precious.

Like a refrain, Philoxenus quotes the following sentence several times during his rehearsal of the argument, which he calls "the Sparrow's most thunderous chord:" *Outrageous suffering is the labor that turns lead to gold, as well as the rope that hauls it home.*

I shall not deign to describe any of the other sections of the Sparrow's ancient book, which are appalling, even when clothed in Philoxenus's polite Latin.

5.

In the late nineteenth century, Leon Bloy wrote:

> If I never was wholly wretched then how could
> I feel joy, which is the daughter of wretchedness
> and eerily resembles her?

Two-and-a-half millenniums before this fragment was composed, someone calling himself "Sparrow"—an early epithet for that figure we call the devil, no doubt, as even the later Chrysostom knew[*]—had already written its mirror image:

---

[*] "And just as a criminal who sails the sea bores a hole in the ship using an instrument of iron and draws all the sea into the ship, so too the devil, seeing Adam's ship, that is, his soul, full of many good things, used his voice and his sparrow's song as a tool of iron and after approaching it bore

The highest peace and joy, and that faraway delight of paradise, are brought low and put within reach of human hands only by the work of gratuitous evil, and by the wretchedness that is engendered, which wrecks the gods' design and bewilders nature, just as a rebellious daughter bewilders the one who bore her, and which makes mere water more soothing than wine.

Implicit in this reasoning, according to Philoxenus, if not in the historical fact then at least *sub specie aeternitatis*, there lurks a quasi-biblical allegory—it is nothing short of a cosmogony—which may be summarized as follows: *The devil was never condemned by God*; instead the dissatisfied angel consigned *himself* to hell, and pushed mightily at the outer walls of that domain, so that heaven might thereby *be pulled closer to the earth*. (Yes, the war above was fought over geometry.) If a superb happiness is possible for human beings outside of Eden, in other words, it is only thanks to the Adversary, whose sacrifice—whose infinitely wretched state and deeds—reoriented the entire universe, and who continues to do our dirtiest work for us, so to speak, though of course we may assist him. *Let us tarry with the darkest and farthest reaches of the negative!* (Hegel should have said this instead.) A great and rare wrongdoing opens new worlds; Cain and Judas were pilgrims. As Philo of Alexandria, a contemporary of Jesus (and frequently quoted by Philoxenus), wrote: *It is by the contrary that the nature of contraries is especially to be known (De Gigantibus).* Philo also rightly marveled at that "extraordinary law" from Leviticus (13:12-13), which enjoined

> that a man only partly leprous shall be deemed impure, but a man wholly leprous, from the sole of his foot to the crown of his head, shall be deemed

---

a hole and emptied it of all its wealth and sunk the ship itself." *Three Homilies on the Devil*, Homily 1.

pure (*Quod Deus Immutabilis Sit*).

And if John of Damascus is to be believed, then Philo also said: *It is as impossible that the love of the world can coexist with the love of God, as for light and darkness to coexist at the same time with one another.*

The Sparrow—the lyrist, the leper, the devil, the contrary, the whipping boy, the *princeps huius mundi* (as the apostle says in the Vulgate), or whoever else he was—loved the world, and loved it more than God. For him (as for his later Roman disciple), evil, brought to its limit, was but the unfortunate lever with which to pry heaven loose, pull it down to earth, and bestow it upon the poor life that God abandoned there.

6.

Casuistry, all of it! That, at least, was my initial reaction to the Sparrow's argument, as it was to Philoxenus's (half-Christian) sublimation of it. Alas, I have since changed my mind. If I am up to the task—that is, if I may muster the strength to proceed without flinching—then the paragraphs that follow will explain why.

During this same studious period of my life, it was a habit of mine occasionally to stroll through the library stacks and to select a book at random, and then open to an arbitrary page and start reading. I thought of this exercise as a kind of *cleansing of the palette of the readerly mind,* a way of refreshing my thoughts so that I might better focus on whatever texts I happened to be studying. (I think anyone who spends much time with books will immediately understand the purpose and benefits of such a practice.) On one particular evening at Soerling, however, after squandering several hours trying—and failing—to secure some iota of reliable information about Philoxenus (or about the Sparrow for that matter), and after proceeding to my normal routine of picking out a random book to read, something very unusual happened. No, that's not right; I should say it more truthfully: something *impossible* happened.

I had strolled to an empty part of the library and, as usual, blindly chose a book and opened to a random page. Here is the sentence that my eyes happened to fall upon; do not ask me how it is that I (who has anything but a photographic memory) am able to remember the sentence exactly, word for word, as I myself do not know, or dare not say, the answer to that question:

> It was even deeper in the Manilda wetlands that I met a moonshiner who went by the name of Filoxanis, and if you ever happen to get out that far you'll know it's him because his fingertips are all stained yellow from turmeric—"The secret ingredient," he is happy to divulge, "to a good apricot 'shine"—and because he keeps a sparrow as a pet.

My heart skipped a beat when I read the name, "Filoxanis." For some moments, I stood there trying to compute the odds of this chance event, until finally a vague dread, like a chill, came over me. Which is why, I suppose, instead of reading on, I simply closed the book and, without bothering to take note of either its title or its author, restored it to its place on the shelf. I then walked—rather briskly, I am not ashamed to admit it—to the very opposite side of the library floor. As if in an attempt to shake off the uneasiness I was feeling, I selected another book at random and read from the middle:

> In 1983, numerous declassified documents from intelligence agencies working in central Europe brought to light secret government initiatives regarding political émigrés—or so-called "sparrows"—and included some mysterious references to a "Polish-Hungarian-International-

List-Of-Expatriots-Engaged-or-Now-Under-
Surveillance," or more commonly referred to in the
documents by the acronym PHILOXENUS…

I stood there, frozen, staring at that sentence for what may
have been a very long time. (I honestly don't know how long I
stood in that spot; it felt to me that time itself had changed
somehow.) *Once may be a miracle*, I said to myself, *twice is a design.*
I returned the book to its shelf, again without even glancing at
the cover. I then repeated the experiment three more times, in
three different parts of the library; first in the zoology section—

> …the so-called "demon bird," or the "Philoxenus
> sparrow"…

—and then in science fiction—

> …when, without warning, there burst from the
> nebula that infamous ship—sparrow class, manned
> by a ragged crew, not the best but surely the
> bitterest, and fighting mad—called the *Philoxenus…*

—and then in philosophy—

> …and even the old Yiddish joke about all cows
> being black in the night (a joke made immortal,
> perhaps, by Hegel) can quite possibly be traced back
> to that graver hell described by Philoxenus in *The
> Meaning in the Lily*, or "that cursed night in which all
> faces, like the indistinguishable faces of sparrows,
> become the same…"

This last book—it is the only one whose title I can recall:
Hegel, Schelling, and the Bloody Head, by one Flynn Barrey—
slipped from my hands and hit the floor with a strangely wet
thud, like a grapefruit. I then lifted my eyes and saw, at the far

end of the corridor, the brown-toothed librarian with the purposeful eyebrows. She stood grinning under a flickering Exit sign, all but motionless. Slowly—but also abruptly—she raised a long, accusing finger in my direction. I stumbled back, my heart racing. I had a mind to yell something out to her—I don't know what—but my face burned and my vision dimmed and I wasn't able to form any words, not even in my mind which now felt like it was going blank. I spun on my heels and almost fell, but somehow managed to find my way to a staircase, and then half-strode and half-tumbled down the two flights to the ground floor. I passed by several people on the stairs; it was difficult to tell because of my impaired vision, but I could have sworn that they all had the same face as the librarian, and that all of them flashed their brown and grey teeth at me, menacingly, as I pushed past. Breathless, practically choking—for the air now seemed to be thick with smoke, and I wondered if the lobby had caught fire (though I refused to glance back to see)—I scrambled out of the building and ran to my car.

That night I suffered from bewildering dreams, and a fever, and when I awoke it was acutely evident—tortuously so—that I had dislocated my jaw in my sleep.

7.

People who knew me in my more studious and excitable years might wonder why I no longer spend my hours in libraries. The foregoing account is probably the best answer I can give them. Though I might also put it this way: Sometimes just a whiff of the infernal infinite is all it takes to turn a man; sometimes a cracked open door is even more terrifying than one thrown all the way open. And what are books—and libraries—if not doorways?

But no, I'm flinching again, there's more to it than that. For if what I've just written is true, then how can I refrain from asking myself: *What doorways have I passed through already?* And what was it that Swedenborg famously said? That the beginning of hell is indistinguishable from our sinful lives. So that if you *had* been sent to hell, you wouldn't even know it at first. And now I feel my face growing pale, for I'm reminded, all of a sudden, of a bit of marginalia that had been scrawled, like a warning, in the Flynn Barrey book, right next to that sentence about Hegel and Philoxenus:

> *A text is not a road; it's not like you can turn back the way you came.*

Alternate Subtitles for the Present Volume

A Book of Lies

Experiments in Forgery

A Series of Made-Up Antiquities

Fake Old Theologies for the Fake New Century

Studies in Male Villainy

Dreams of a Failed Essayist

Does Literary History Need to be Real?

The Dialectic in Reverse

Philosophy in the Form of Fiction

The Aesthetic Value of Not Knowing Whether Something is Fictional or Not

(So That I Might Not Let My Training in the Humanities Go to Waste)

Essays About Books That You've Never Read Because I Dreamt Them Up

Les morts doublent de poids

With Apologies to Borges

Part 2. Apparitions, Ghosts

The Secret of the Tulip

"I hope it won't be taken as defensiveness if I raise an objection to what Professor Richards has said here today, though I found his remarks quite useful indeed..."

These politic words were among the last I ever heard from Theodore Banner, the American philosopher and occultist who died—under rather mysterious circumstances, as you've probably heard—just last month. The words were spoken at a conference on the theme of "Magic in Literature," held at the University of Virginia some twenty years ago; I can no longer recall the precise point of contention that had been raised, but somehow I remember Banner's next sentences exactly: "The intellectual movement that I am affiliated with, or what some well-meaning souls have dubbed 'magical hyperrealism,' does not submit to the idea of 'the supernatural' at all. In spite of what some of our detractors have said, here and elsewhere, we're not mystics. We're logicians."

Readers of Banner's *Dialectic and the Occult* may smile at this, and be reminded of the thunderclap found on the very first page of that masterwork: "Magic and logic are the same."

> Magic is the discovery of secret necessities, and in exactly the same way that a complex syllogism may reveal a bond between a premise and some distant or otherwise disjointed conclusion. All reality, as Wittgenstein understood in the *Tractatus*, is but *a list of facts*; logic is what binds them. The force that is harnessed by logic, in other words, is not only that which fixes thoughts together; it is also that which binds thoughts to objects, and one object to another, and objects to events, and so forth. Sorcery is only Idealism; all magic is that of the Concept. Logic, as Hegel knew, is a stairway to new and hidden realms. (*Dialectic and the Occult*, New York: 1989, p. 2.)

I cannot pretend to be an expert on Banner's theories (or on dialectics or magic, for that matter), and I shall not attempt to expound them here. (I should add that Banner and I were only ever distant acquaintances.) I've made my own name, I hope humbly, as but a reader and translator of antique Latin; abstruse philosophy lies beyond my paygrade. Nevertheless, my specialized expertise, if I may use that word, is the reason why, when the body of Theodore Banner was discovered in a New York City apartment looking almost mummified and clutching to its chest an old book written in Latin, I was asked to help out with the investigation.

(In case it would otherwise be unclear in what follows, permit me to state unambiguously that the knowledge I happen to possess of the crime scene—for that is indeed what the police have called it—and more specifically of the strange state of Banner's corpse, and also of the unruly disarray found in his apartment, is a result of the work I did in cooperation with the Detective Bureau of the N.Y.P.D. I trust I violate no protocols by preparing this present summary.)

If I may then cut to the chase: the book that was in Banner's arms when he was murdered—yes, I say murdered; I've seen the photographs of his body, whatever was done to him he could not have done to himself—was none other than Blustrode's *Ars Magica Profanorum* (often rendered in English as *Magic of the Ungodly*, following Wholff's somewhat mannered translation). It is an exceedingly rare and valuable text composed in Latin, and first printed at some point in the early seventeenth century (no publisher or city or year was ever listed in the front matter). The book, long gossiped-about by bibliophiles, and existing today almost exclusively in facsimile editions (many of which are fraudulent), has an unmistakable aura of mystery about it. The name, "Blustrode," for starters, was no doubt a fabrication. It is generally believed that the author wrote pseudonymously and in Latin to conceal his/her true nationality. Pope Innocent XI famously condemned the book. Robert Burton, author of *Anatomy of Melancholy*, is rumored to have cherished his copy of it (some even opine he was its true author). Banner's copy of the book, meanwhile, which I've had the opportunity to inspect, is very likely authentic, and is particularly well preserved. It is probably priceless.

The book's subject matter deals with so-called "natural" or "profane" enchantments ("profane" in the sense not of the blasphemous, but of the earthly and the creaturely). Its object of study is the magical significance of mundane life; its chapters bear such titles as "Spells for Farmwork," "How Certain Minerals Repel Trolls," "Secret Uses for Votive Candles and Other Religious Articles," "On Making Amulets," "How to Interpret Birdsong," and so forth. Yet it was the chapter dealing with so-called "Simple Objects" which, if Banner's marginalia is any indication, consumed the deceased most intensely. It is only my conjecture, but I would guess that Banner held little interest in spirits or angels or demons; instead, he sought to delve into the various ways that magic circulates through *the world of things*.

Of inanimate objects, for example, and other things in the world, which contain magical properties, not as a result of sorcery but by virtue of their mere existence or form, the *Magica Profanorum* offers an unusual and desultory list of categories: Objects that *look back at you* (statues, for instance, or mirrors); objects subsumed in the obscure Latin phrase, *Contrarium sine opposito,* or opposites without opposite (i.e., things or forces "that are naturally unnatural, like giants, or magnetism, or the orchids that spread suddenly about the quarries of Proconnesus, or healing springs, or wolfsbane"); anything that cannot be remembered for very long, though it were once vivid, such as dreams; lustrous opal; tulips; any soil that bears brambles and thistles but "suffers not the sown seed;" doorways and staircases; certain tinctures sold by *Cingaris,* as well as their metalwork and charms (especially when these last are "sacrilegious or otherwise deplorable"); mushrooms, when they grow indoors upon floors and walls; salamanders and camels and other creatures that can survive in fire or in deserts without water; fire; all manner of naturally-occurring spheres (celestial orbs and eyeballs in particular); the milk of hairy lizards, or the eggs of feathered ones; animals that glow (eels, fireflies); pomegranates; the *lapis aquosus occultus.*[*]

Following this haphazard catalog—in which, we may infer, nothing is truly accidental, since, as Banner himself once put it, "magic hides its necessity in the form of the random"—the reader proceeds to a lengthy "Supplementum" where Blustrode writes, now and then sublimely, about a class of objects he designates as *Res quae attentissime visae novas et insolitas cogitationes incendunt,* or objects which, when looked upon carefully, ignite unusual and foreign thoughts:

> Certain artworks, for example, or frightening cliffs and crags and other formations that are *redolentia mortem* or show the smallness of man, or fearsome trees in dark woods, or any ruins of once-great structures, or pointless extravagance as found in palaces, or a solitary human skull, or the arabesques of faded religions, or fattened spiders waiting in webs, or the maledictions of devil worshippers, or young children with sickly pale complexions, or any setting where bloody murder has recently taken place, or the utensils used in such crimes, or whitened eyes, or graveyards untended and overgrown, or deformities and aberrations in nature,

---

[*]   *The secret watery stone.* Franz Lichte's gloss on this mysterious entry, for which Blustrode provides no commentary or explanation, may be instructive: "Perhaps [Blustrode] assumed the initiated would understand his meaning already; or maybe the concept proved too recondite for him to explicate it. In any case he likely meant to preserve its secrecy. It is possible, as Walter Ong has speculated, that he had sapphire in mind; though perhaps the *lapis aquosus occultus* is even more obvious than that, and hides in plain sight. Could it be, for instance, that the secret water stone is nothing other than the Earth itself, when glimpsed from the heavens?" (*The Magic of Things,* London: 1934, p. 239.)

or the moon at its brightest or when it is colored the hue of blood…

I shall spare the reader the complete list; suffice to say it runs on for several pages. What is more important for our present purposes is Blustrode's theory as to just *how* the sight of such objects is able to induce strange and seemingly-alien thoughts in the onlooker's mind:

> When an extraordinary object holds your gaze, and as a result you lose yourself in reveries, and forget what you were doing, and lose track of time, and unfamiliar ideas begin flowing into your mind from who knows where—it is because the object is *speaking* to you, conversing directly with your soul, and not figuratively [*metaphorice*] but literally [*in veritas*]. For truthfully *all* objects speak; we only fail to hear them most of the time. Indeed we must pay great respect to the principles of witchcraft, which should be credited with the notion that *all* objects think and speak (if only faintly), and which hold, as a consequence of this, that the most prevalent magic does not await us in faraway realms, or in the heavens or the netherworld: it is here now, among us, on this profane earth, in the creaturely world of things.

The theory is followed by a warning:

> For these reasons one must make every effort to remain insensible to that silent roar that comes from *things*. All joy depends on this. For the objects that would speak the loudest would command all our attention, and eventually drown out our own thoughts, or even replace them, and finally drive us mad, or make us into slaves.

The "Supplementum" then ends with a different kind of "object" altogether, one about which Blustrode warns us even more vigorously. This object is a rare "art of speech;" Blustrode refers to it as a "diabolical form of inference," or "the Devil's logic:"

> A marriage of beauty and half-reason is the hallmark of such discourse, which often takes the form of verse. We find a splendid example of it in the notorious syllogism composed by Philoxenus (that late Roman monotheist) in a poem from his masterpiece, *Secret of the Tulip*,[*] which, according to legend, induced many a Christian, at least among those who understood the argument but then failed to find any refutation for it, to take his own life, and sometimes, spontaneously, simply to perish from the words themselves. For such reasoning implants a seed into the deeps of the mind, and then, with many thoughts growing from that grain, proceeds silently to rule over it, and finally over the organism as a whole. Such discourse belongs to the category which includes all the most poisonous objects in the world—poisonous because they would contaminate our very souls, and corrupt their eternity.

It is clear that Blustrode takes his/her own warning seriously. For although Philoxenus's poem is reproduced in Blustrode's text—again, it is supposedly quoted from the much-mythologized *Secret of the Tulip*, a book that does not survive today, if it ever even existed—three of the lines are deliberately *omitted*. It is not clear whether this is done as a precaution (i.e., to protect the reader from the dangers that might otherwise ensue), or else simply as a way of safeguarding the mysteries of a very

---

[*]   Wholff's translation; a more exact rendering of the Latin would be, *The Meaning in the Lily*.

dark and elite wisdom. Either way, I should say that I've read the poem myself (at least the parts of it that are transcribed) and, obviously, I have not yet perished from it. Nevertheless, if I too reproduce it here (in English, in my own translation), and if in fact you choose to read the poem, please know that you proceed at your own risk:

The Alchemy of the Adversary

The empty sky gladdens the soul,
As a raindrop cools the lily's palm,
For like rejoices in like,
And the perfect in the perfect,
And the incorruptible spirit in the untouchable blue,
And life in water.
And just so, as alchemy reveals unities that were
  invisible,
And raises up the dead,
And exchanges one perfection for another,
And makes the lesser the greater,
And yields superabundance of gold
Until lead becomes the more precious,
And as
So does
Therefore,
And THEREFORE,
God is the Devil, and all else is upside down too.

Alas, when Theodore Banner was found, the copy of *Ars Magica Profanorum* that was pressed tightly to his breast was opened to this poem. An old rumor says that the right incantation will make the missing words appear.

...

The temptation to imagine a metaphysical fate for Theodore Banner is difficult to resist. Did he succeed in revealing the missing text from Philoxenus's poem? If so, did those verses somehow bring about his horrific death? Had objects begun speaking to him? Was he assailed, even deafened, by the roar from the world of *things*? Did he cry out for relief? Maybe it is foolhardy to speculate about such questions, for which, almost by definition, we can have no answers. What we have instead— it is perhaps all we ever have when someone dies, it is the general form of evidence of every death—is a *list of facts*, a list with which, here, we do not conclude but merely stop:

- When Theodore Banner's body was found, all of the mirrors in his apartment had been shattered;

- his ears had been stuffed with cotton balls;

- the bodies of many hundreds of fireflies lay dead on the bedroom floor, but nowhere else;

- many of the walls had been smeared with ashes, as if Banner had drawn his blackened hands across them;

- an unknown strain of fungus had spread through the floorboards;

- on his bedside table, next to his cold and grisly form, lay a well-worn copy of the greater *Logic* by Hegel;

- his pockets were filled with pomegranate seeds.

(Once more I shall spare the reader a complete list, which, even at its least verbose, would be infinite.)

The Black Square

One day, without any warning or ceremony, without so much as a pop or even a swish, there appeared in the sky above the small town of Rochester, Indiana, directly over Lake Manitou, a motionless black square.

From the ground—or rather from the middle of the lake, which provided the best view of it—the square looked about the size and the altitude of a small cloud. As you might expect, however, it appeared nothing like a natural object. The sides looked to be perfectly equilateral, each angle a perfect ninety degrees; its color a pure black. And while animals seemed not to take any notice of it (even the fowl that paddled upon the lake paid it no mind), the people of Rochester found it rather alarming. (Not all imperfections in nature are equal: a spot on an apple can be gobbled up; a flaw in the otherwise perfect and simple blue of the sky, even a small one, can feel like a nightmare coming true.)

Imagine you are among the first to notice the square in the sky. It's a clear day, you're out on the lake; maybe you're fishing. As is natural, you look up from time to time. During one of those upward glances you see it. In that first fraction of a second, what registers in your brain is only a dull sense: *something isn't right.* You might perform a double take. Only after that initial confusion do you perceptually cognize the thing—the shape (square), the color (black). You may or may not verbalize the thought: *There's something in the sky.* Of course, it's not long before hypotheses are flooding upon you (the mind is a frantic worker, after all, and it has but one job: to make sense of things as swiftly as possible). *Is it a craft? It must be some trick of the light. Am I seeing things? An optical illusion, a hallucination of some sort. It's just someone doing a hoax. Maybe it's like a laser or something, a projection. Some clever invention. Is it a satellite? Something plummeting to earth? But no, it's not moving. Just floating there. Is it a balloon, or some kind of airship? A military jet, maybe, like that one that can hover at sixty-thousand feet. Are we being invaded?*

But between that initial split-second puzzlement and all this hypothesizing, something else took place: you flinched. Maybe it was imperceptible, maybe it didn't happen in a way that could be measured; but at the level of instinct, at the level of primordial human fear, before any hypothesis crossed your mind, you knew that something potentially disastrous had just opened up in the sky. Something that didn't belong there.

It may even occur to you that you've never quite appreciated before now just how *perfect* the blue sky is (or was, now that there's a blemish to it). It's anyway true, or so you think to yourself, that we are more sensitive to imperfections than we are to perfections. This seems natural to you: there's no reason an evolutionary advantage (in this case, an alertness to things gone wrong) can't leave us impoverished in other ways.

Naturally you pull out your phone and attempt to take a picture of the square in the sky. To your surprise, the square does not show up in any of the images. Each photograph contains only a field of empty blue. Perhaps you shrug your shoulders. *I'm seeing things, I guess.*

Only, it turns out that everyone else sees it too.

The nightmarish quality of the square in the sky—from here on out we'll refer to it simply as "the Square"—is only exacerbated when the scientists and government agencies begin to announce their findings, or lack thereof. Certain phrases from the press conferences and news broadcasts stand out to you: some because they are repeated so often, others because you've never heard them used before (at least not by government officials).

Whatever this object is…a purely visual phenomenon…no physical existence…not made of anything material…source unknown…only seen from the ground…neither satellites nor radar nor cameras record it…no known laws of light or optics apply…have not determined if it's really there or not…collective hallucination…some sort of apparition…no known cause…

When a hapless bureaucrat appears on television and utters the word "apparition," you know things have gone out of joint.

Predictably, people from all over the world begin to flock to the little town of Rochester, which becomes congested with traffic and hordes of sightseers (it's only a matter of days before the town no longer feels like home to you). Everyone wants to see for themselves this object that there can be no pictures of, that cannot be filmed or recorded. Some of the more jaded souls, upon seeing it, only scoff: *It's some kind of joke, someone's having a laugh.* Others feel terror at the sight of it: *The natural universe is changing before our very eyes!*

As happens with all astonishing things, however, the Square's gleam of mystery fades with time. Gradually people come to accept its existence. (A fact, even a very strange or new one, is after all only a fact; we adapt to it, like water to its channel.) And yet it is also true that you never look at *the sky* quite the same way again. The sky, that is, seems only to *gain* in mystery. And who knows, maybe it was always something strange: the roof to our reality, the most expansive thing you can see with your own eyes and yet it's hardly even there (perhaps it feels marvelous to you that we don't fall right up into it). What other physical object is simultaneously so vast and yet so intangible! And the blue, so blue, *so blue that blood couldn't be more red* (P. Claudel)—it is so blue that you must remind yourself at times that it *is* in fact an apparition (electromagnetic radiation scattered just so), and not some heavy dripping substance in its own right. Certain linguistic phrases now give you pause, too, such as: *The sky is falling.* Why, you wonder, did that signifier of impending catastrophe arise more naturally for us than, say, *The earth is opening?* Especially when you recall that Hell, according to familiar mythology, is a *locus subterraneus.* Perhaps the sky has always been more threatening than the earth, more alien. Maybe, in the distant past, humans were menaced by flying creatures or giants or lightning bolts, and although these dangers no longer plague us, our old instincts persist: *Evil comes from above.* You also entertain the idea—though it's really just speculation on your part—that animals almost never look up. Only humans spend time gazing at a sunset, or studying the stars. Even the lofty vulture looks downward for the most part, scouring the earth for the dead.

It is to be expected that an unexplained black square hovering in the sky will draw to itself many names: *The Square*; *the Appearance*; *the Doorway*; *the Eye*; *the Curse*; *the Amplifier*; *the Pixel*; *the Covenant*; *the Poem*; *the Mistake*. Let us take these in turn.

The Square. Scientists quickly discover that while the Square can be seen and magnified through a telescope, this only succeeds if the telescope is unpowered. The moment any electricity is run through a telescope's instruments the square vanishes from the scope's view. No matter how greatly the Square is magnified, it shows no visible features on its "surface" (which is sometimes described as having an "absolute smoothness" or an "absolute absence of light"). Measurements are conducted, and, as well as anyone can tell, the Square has perfect dimensions, is perfectly equilateral, down at least to a micron. "As far as feats of geometry go," Dr. Sylvia Boulon writes in her article for *Scientific American*, "this one is probably as perfect as any ever devised—assuming the Square even exists, and was devised."

The Appearance. "Because nothing underlies the square," writes Razvan Gheorghe, the Hegelian-Freudian philosopher from Romania, in his book *Noumenal Realities*, "*not even a cause,* we might well conclude that it is a *pure* appearance, an appearance *as such*, and, because in this object appearance and essence *perfectly coincide* (there is no gap between them, it is the whole nature of the square to *appear* and *only appear*, there is nothing beyond its appearance, nothing deeper than its appearance), we might also recognize it for what it truly is: the Kantian *Ding an sich*, the thing in itself, but one we can *see* with our own eyes, for its absolute truth is right there, wholly exposed, on its surface."

The Doorway. Predictably, the Square inspires a number of fantastic theories, especially those involving alien or interdimensional lifeforms. Ray Thucheon, in his best-selling speculative work, *The Door Has Opened*, theorizes that the Square "is no doubt a portal, an opening that has found its way into our reality. It's only a matter of time before *they* begin bucketing through. In fact, it is my belief that they've *already* come through; we just don't see them yet."

The Eye. "Many people who have looked at the Square," the poet Harriette Hardt writes in her collection of essays called *How to Tell When Something is Alive*, "report a feeling of being *watched* by it. As if it were an eye. *Watched*—not with furrowed brow or jellied stare, but with its *disregard* of us, a mighty (perhaps the mightiest) indifference."

The Curse. In 1838, the Potawatomi Indians were "forcibly removed"—even that is far too sanitized a phrase—from the areas surrounding Lake Manitou, and "marched" to what is now Kansas along a path that has come to be called *The Trail of Death*. Jack L. Santiago, a self-proclaimed descendant of Potawatomi chiefs (though his ancestry has been disputed), asserts in a spoken word piece, first performed in the Eric Dean Gallery at Wabash University, that the Square is a "sign of a curse issued by the Potawatomi nation," a curse only now coming to fruition: "If you stare into the great square for long enough, you will see inside it the slumbering monster of the lake, Meshekenabek, who lived not in the water but in the air above it. It will awaken, to the great terror of all European peoples."

The Amplifier. Some people claim to hear strange music coming from the Square, as if it functioned like a stereo speaker. Such people often are moved to dance around the lake. *Dancing in the spirit*, they call it.

The Pixel. Conspiratorial theories abound. Perhaps the most interesting come from adherents of the so-called "simulacrum theory:" "If there were any remaining doubts that we are all living in a simulation, a computer program of some unimaginably sophisticated type, the Square should dispel those doubts once and for all. For what is the Square if not a *burnt out pixel?* A fourth or fifth dimensional pixel—one that can only be seen from certain angles, from certain sections of three-dimensional space and time. For the first time ever, we have the proof we've been looking for: *a permanent glitch in the matrix!*" Jolie Clark, "Computer Screens in Five Dimensions," from the debut issue of the now widely-circulating periodical, *Simulacra*.

The Covenant. Religious discourse surpasses all other discourse about the Square, at least in terms of sheer volume. Some believers say the Square must be a doorway to Hell; others, like Rebecca Morgan in the preface to her book, *Late Apocalypse*, see something different: "The rainbow in the sky marked the Covenant between Noah and God (and we often forget to imagine just how strange that experience must have been, when humans saw rainbows appear for the very first time!). The Square is some new sign, a sign of changing times—a sign, perhaps, that the old order no longer obtains. Everyone must now put to themselves the question: *What is God asking of us?*"

The Poem. From Jalal Lage's book, *Religion, Poetry, Hell*: "Many poetic utterances deploy the *failure* of words to good effect. A word is only poetic, that is, if it is not quite right. One definition of poetry might be: *Language exploiting its own failure, seeking it.* Indeed, there might be times when a word is available to me that means exactly what I want to say, but I reject it: there's no *failure* to it, so I keep looking. As a poet I want my language to *collapse* sometimes. […] But the Square is a failure in an even more objective sense: it is a *failure in/of the sky itself.* Let us be clear: the Square is an artwork, a poem. It shows Nature, and whatever signifiers Nature has at its disposal, put to the very point of collapse. Nature itself has evolved, and is now making art."

The Mistake. This is your favorite name for the Square, your favorite interpretation of it. It came from your father, shortly after the Square first appeared in the sky over Rochester. "The square doesn't mean anything," he said to you, "it's just a hiccup. The universe is nothing but a big machine, it's bound to make mistakes every now and then. It stands to reason that one of those mistakes will blunder its way to our world and then just stay there. We should be happy it's not worse."

It may be a literary error to mix metaphors, but one can string together similes one after the other and no one makes a fuss; in fact similes may grow more robust the more diverse their company. This idea flashes upon you after you observe how easily the Lake Manitou Tour Guide—for yes, you return to that spot, you want to see the Square again, though now it's a commercial affair, men of business have descended on the lake, which has come to be clogged with boats—*perspires* while gesturing up to the Square. Evidently it excites her, and you too, in ways neither of you fully comprehend. And then, in your mind, and because you are bound to fall in love with her, you liken the sweat on her temple to the glassy plane which glows over the purest and most finished marble, and to the halos atop smooth opal. Then you decide that her lip faintly gleams like wet plum skin, like dew, like an April rose or the waxy stalk of flowering hogweed, like pearl, like a shelled oyster, like snow softly beaming in the sun, like a rosy soap bubble, like stars, like a horse's eye, like a barely-glimpsed sea from far away, so very far, and cold, cold as if the distance were what made it cold, and warm and glinting as if the world made it warm and glinting.

In that moment you hear a strange, faint music. You think it's coming from the Square.

On a later occasion, while you are making love and both of your faces are covered in sweat, you liken her face to the Square itself—the Square, so devoid of sheen it shines.

It then occurs to you that even an empty black square can be filled up with human meaning, and become a sign of love. Or maybe love, like a shape that just appears in the sky, can happen for no reason.

One day, without any ceremony or warning, without so much as a swish or even a pop, there disappeared from the sky above the small town of Rochester, Indiana, directly over Lake Manitou, a motionless black square.

The *Gehenna* of Saint Augustine

"The better a thing the worse its ruin," Augustine said, but tenderly, to Porphyro, his last pupil. "Angels and men, when they fall, become more wretched than monsters."

When Saint Augustine spoke these words he had less than an hour left to live. At the time—the year was 430, Visigoths and Burgundians hounded the empire on various fronts, and Vandals laid siege to Hippo—he was still but Aurelius Augustinus, not yet a saint; but his voice, though rattling from illness, sounded nobly in the still-proud Latin of Rome, and projected the special authority he'd gained during his life, as if his vocation (as bishop, as a statesman of Roman Africa) would not yet relinquish him, and as if he were somewhat more than a man dying.

Lifting his arms from his sides—he lay in his bed, almost still—and raising his cold fingers to lend emphasis to the words, he said to Porphyro: "Our natural goodness is a gift from God. There can be no worse evil than to squander it."

The church was quiet. Porphyro looked about Augustine's chambers and saw that psalms had been hung from the walls. Augustine, with a hand half-palsied, reached out and clutched Porphyro's wrist.

In that moment, nearly a thousand years still stood between Augustine and his sainthood. Neither he nor Porphyro, of course, could have any inkling about that. Nevertheless the student swore that he could feel his teacher's soul radiating all about him, and he knew that it had been specially touched by God, and his eyes filled up with tears.

At this, Augustine paused, suddenly aware of the shortness of his time. It may surprise you, but the man who wrote *City of God* and the *Confessions*, and who had long warned congregations in Hippo and Carthage of the corruptible body, had not given much thought to the subject of his own bodily demise. (It should be granted, at any rate, that the strictly *physical* fact of death, at least as a theological matter, could be of only minor interest to someone like Augustine.) What strange new thoughts now came to him?

One need not be a varlet to know the knight's armor clatters before a campaign; likewise, one needs no special wisdom to predict that a man of old age—even one as notable and pious as Augustine—will, when harried by death, feel consternation about it. It is one thing to talk about dying, or about long eternities; it is quite another when rot creeps upon you. When Augustine looked up at weeping Porphyro, and felt his own heart quicken, he knew, for the first time and truly, that he was going to die.

"I've written a book that I've kept secret," Augustine said abruptly. Porphyro wiped his eyes. "I'll tell you where I've hidden the manuscript. You must promise me you will find it and destroy it, and not show it to anyone."

Porphyro was taken aback, but nodded.

"You must promise me that you will not read the book, either, but will destroy it at once."

Augustine's student looked pained. Eventually he said: "My teacher, I fear my interest in your book will be too great. Perhaps if you tell me its contents, my curiosity will be diminished, and I will be able to destroy it without reading it."

Augustine lay silent with his hands clasped for a long time. At last he spoke:

"It was not long ago. I had recently finished writing Book XXI of *City of God*, where, among other things, I attempted to deduce the qualities of hell. As you well know, I wrote in that book that hell is a place of fire, and that the souls consigned to that domain have bodies which suffer burning. I wrote that these bodies do not perish in the flames, but are doomed to suffer them forever. I theorized, too, that any repentance in hell is fruitless, not only because the source of such penitence would be *pain* as opposed to *goodness*, but also because the *evangelium* proclaims it to be so: *their worm does not die and the fire is not quenched.*"

Augustine paused, coughed, and adjusted himself in his bed.

"At that time, just as I was about to begin work on Book XXII, a man came to visit me. I knew straightaway that this man was an unnatural being, for he appeared in the exact form of my old acquaintance, Faustus from Mileve, whom I knew to be long dead. The man said to me, 'I came to speak with you about hell,' and then he grinned, and I knew it was the devil."

Augustine fell silent for a moment. Porphyro raised up slowly in his chair, and barely breathed.

Augustine continued: "Very well do I know of the devil's forked tongue, and how he uses flattery, and enjoys the fruits of his manipulations; so I paid him no mind when he told me he was a great admirer of my work. I ignored him, again, when he complimented me for the good I'd done for Rome and the world. Finally, he said to me: 'When it comes to the subject of hell, however, you're simply off the mark. May I offer you a glimpse?' He then took my hand and kissed it. And then, without ceremony, he left."

Augustine adjusted himself again, and took a moment to rub his eyes.

"That night I had a dream, a dream that was more than a dream. It was a vision. A vision of hell. The hell that I saw, however—or rather that I now found myself *in*—was not a place of fire, but of *water*. 'The water of knowledge,' a voice whispered to me. 'It encompasses everything.' It was as if I'd been sent to the bottom of the sea, only, it was not dark; the water was limpid and bright, and it functioned somewhat like the sun, making all things visible. Moreover, I found that I could move through the water with ease, and I walked about on the ground normally. Nothing floated or swam. And yet I could *feel* the water at every moment. It moved over me, and its vibrations were like something alive.

"This hell that I saw, the landscape of it, was much like our own world, with creatures and plant-life and mountains and stones and plains; indeed the whole of beautiful nature was there. Nearby me stood a tree; I approached it. At that moment I understood how the 'water of knowledge' had earned its name.

For what flashed upon me, from many of the water's vibrations, was not just the sight of the tree in its current state, but in every stage of its existence. I saw it through the seasons, and as a seedling, and then as an acorn; I saw the changing life of the soil which nourished its roots, and the spread of the tree's ancestors in distant woods; I saw the flattening of mountains to make room for it, and before that the receding of ice, and fire and explosions that were terrifying to behold—all things that took place over eons, and seemingly for the sole purpose that I might now gaze at these simple branches. As if I, like some cossetted prince, were meant to be the beneficiary of all that's ever happened in the universe.

"Just then a voice spoke from behind me: 'The water shows you everything.' I spun on my heels and saw that it was Faustus of Mileve once more. Whether this was the real Faustus, or the devil again, I could not say. He continued: 'The water makes sure that we see the absurdity of God's generosity wherever we look.' And then he smiled at me, and it was just the way he would smile many years ago, when we discussed theology.

"Without ado, he cheerfully began to criticize what I'd written in *City of God*. 'Your first mistake,' he said, 'was assuming the primary substance of hell should be fire. The very lightest of elements!' Faustus laughed, and I could not help but laugh too. 'Even the simplest of principles,' he continued, 'ought to have suggested to you the opposite: that here, in this lowest place, the heavier elements, earth and water, should predominate.' Again I was moved to laugh. He went on: 'Your second error was conceiving of hell under that most human of ideas, that of *retribution*, as if hell were but a dungeon for the paying up of debts. But no, there is no paying of debts here. In truth, if there is a single axiom of this place, it is that: *No debt is ever paid.* Even to try is foolishness.'

"I then asked Faustus if hell was not a place of punishment after all. His answer astonished me. 'But it's all there in Genesis already,' he said. 'God did not punish. *Knowledge* did. And perfect knowledge is perfect punishment.' He paused to allow my confusion to settle somewhat. He continued: 'It is just the same as with riches: the more you're lavished with knowledge the more fruitless the abundance becomes.' My incomprehension must have been evident; he explained further: 'Just as there are solitudes that are accessible only in crowded cities, so does a general *blur* become possible when everything is thrown into relief equally. Where everything is luminous nothing is. It is not only in the dark of night that all cows are black, as the saying goes, but in the bright and full day, too. Or as we sometimes put it in one of our proverbs, *There is more nothingness in a clod of dirt than in the empty air, and even the buzzing richness of nature only talks over itself.* Call it the nothing of plenitude. There's just so, so much. It humiliates you. It reduces you and even itself to naught.'

"We both laughed. I don't know why we laughed so much. There was something preposterous about it all. And then, while laughing, Faustus suddenly cried out: 'Oh you charmed creatures still on the earth! If only you knew how much passes right through you! If only you knew how faintly you exist! Here in hell we are dense, we collide with everything.' Faustus's smile then faded, and he said: 'In hell it is evident that nothing we could ever do, even given infinite lifetimes, could earn the abundance bestowed on us. Even gratitude feels like foolishness. Nay, more than that. Gratitude is impossible here. We have too much.'

"We continued talking for some time. Faustus recited for me some more of hell's proverbs, and he told me what society was like there, and he showed me a dark molten sea where people sometimes boiled themselves, if they burned with too much guilt (somehow they found this soothing). We discussed more theological concerns, too, such as whether one can sin in hell, or pray, or repent, and how vast a place it is, and what manner of demon resides there, and if hell be eternal or not, and how much the damned can recall from their lives on the earth, and so forth.

"When I awoke from this vision, I immediately set about to writing it all down. This labor took three days. On the fourth day I rested, but fitfully. On the fifth day I resolved to keep what I'd written secret. I reasoned as follows: Either my vision was a lie, or, if it contained some part of the truth, it was nonetheless that part that the devil was desirous for us to know. Either way, I figured, it must be suppressed. Why I did not destroy the text myself in that very moment, I cannot say. Pride, perhaps, or doubt. Sin, in either case!"

Augustine then told trembling Porphyro how to find the manuscript, and admonished him one last time not to read it, and then waved him away.

...

Later that day Augustine lay dead, while Porphyro stole into a hidden recess underneath the baptistry. He found his way down a dark stair and through a low-arched hall, as instructed, and then moved aside the third stone to the left from a sign of the cross that had been carved on the wall. The only copy of *De Gehenna* lay revealed. He took the text into his hands. "I have a home for you," he said, "in a library in a low place;" and then he fled away through the secret door, and over the mosaics set so carefully in the floors of the basilica.

The Ambivalent Moller Gitch

Moller Gitch, the essayist, teacher, somewhat-famed art critic and literary theorist, author of *Modes of Expression* (now in its fifth printing), and my old mentor from my school days, took his own life more than a year ago, though sadly—or mercifully—I only learned of this fact yesterday.

An aphorism comes to mind (composed, I think, though I'm not sure, by Baltasar Gracián in the seventeenth century): *Every face is an enigma, and the lives of others are like rivers on the opposite end of the world.*

Leafing through my old copy of *Modes*, I find myself marveling at how the death of such a man, all at once and instantly, alters the significance of his work. *Modes of Expression* is no longer just a book about the philosophy of art; it is now (at least for me, and much more profoundly) a preserve of *traces* of a mind, a mind that, but for such faint remnants, has vanished completely and won't ever exist again, even if time goes on forever. I'd like to say that it's not even a *book* any longer; the moment Moller Gitch made away with himself (I shall not dwell on the shocking particulars of his death), the text turned into something like an *artifact*—archaeological evidence, as it were, of the fathomless adventure of a *consciousness*, but also of the terrible certainty that, whether we've written books or not, the *totality* of our thoughts, their concerted and living shape, must go with us to our graves.

The thesis of that now magical book—some said it was undaring, others insisted it went too far—can be stated simply, and is so stated in its opening paragraph:

> The fundamental mode of all art is *ambivalence.*
> Art which only loves, or only hates, or only
> celebrates or denounces, is not art but propaganda.
> And art which merely records—does not exist.

The method Gitch proposed, as every student of literature knows by now (certainly if they are of my generation), lay in searching out, in any given text, the various sites and sources of such ambivalence. The primary task of a critic or theorist, in other words (and the key to unlocking the mystery of any artwork), was to ask:

> What is the artist, or the work in question, *most conflicted* about? Where does the love/hate passion burn brightest? The essence of the work—the essence of humanity—resides there.[*]

Among the last words I ever heard Moller Gitch say (it was during my dissertation defense some twenty years ago): "No passion is pure. Even God cannot love absolutely, it would destroy Him." I remember protesting; surely this was too romantic an idea, i.e., that anyone, much less God, should die from love. At the time he only smiled. Later it dawned on me that for Gitch the principle of ambivalence was more ontological than sentimental: "A pure or simple force or object," he declared in *Modes,* in his sweeping, well-nigh Hegelian fashion, "can never sustain itself":

> Existence is already a contradiction, one that leaves nothing innocent. Add to that the dividedness of the human soul and all of *Being* may

---

[*] The comparisons with deconstruction were inevitable (I remember hearing them, like accusations, when I was in graduate school), though Gitch consistently maintained that his views were easily distinguished from those of the likes of Derrida or de Man. During his last interview (a brief and meager exchange with an editor from the journal, *Literature in History*), he said: "Deconstruction was concerned with *oppositions.* I have never held any interest in such logical structures. My work has been occupied instead with love and hate, with good and evil, and how they mix—*in the heart.*"

appear to be at its own throat. Even light is two opposite things at once, and must be.

…

About two years ago I began receiving a series of strange, typed letters. They were unsigned, and without any return address. They were postmarked from all different cities in western Europe. They consisted mainly of poems—poems about philosophers. At the time I had no idea what to make of them. When I learned yesterday of Moller Gitch's suicide, however, I understood instantly: they'd come from him.

Altogether there were about twenty letters. As a sample, I reproduce a few of them here.

Dear Joachim,

Ah the salad days of the twentieth century.

LEVINAS

I am interested only in the younger
Levinas, the precocious phenomenologist.

Something almost juvenile about his method:

Find those human experiences in which BEING
feels oppressive—

> like insomnia (involuntary
> wakefulness), or madness (an
> onslaught of consciousness, thoughts
> that don't feel like your own), or
> pain (the feeling of being riveted to
> your own body)

—and then, look for the escape hatch: the
power to sleep, the movement towards the Other
or God, breaking loose from the strictures of
subjectivity, and so forth.

Before Derrida, Levinas waged a war on PRESENCE.
(A formula comes to mind: All pain is
presence inescapable.)

It is of course only natural for those who
experienced captivity to dream this way.

I often think of Levinas's famous soft
face. That fat soft face. That limping rabbit
of a face.

I sometimes wonder if he ever found the
escape hatch he was hoping for.

Fondly,

NOBODY

```
Dear Joachim,

As life weakens we cling to it less.

EPICTETUS


One can build a quiet life,
in which DESIRE is but a small animal in the
     corner.
(One might be moved to ask: Is a pet a slave?)

Make no mistake, you know it's there;
it growls and bristles from time to time,
you have no choice but to tend to it-
but still it's only an animal after all,
lesser than you, and,
like any good dog,
it learns quickly,
if only the house is kept quiet enough,
to sleep often.
In time, it will sleep more and more.
The gist of it: an old man dozing peacefully in
     a chair
has triumphed over life.
No matter how little he did.
Whether or not he intended to.


Fondly, and perhaps victoriously,

NOT ANYONE
```

Why Gitch sent these poems to me is a mystery. I suspect he probably sent them to many people. Perhaps he mailed them out more or less indiscriminately to figures from his past; perhaps he wrote hundreds, or even thousands of them. Maybe I'll find out at some point.

More perplexing to me, however, was the final letter. Or so it seems to me now. Like the others it contained a poem; this poem, though, was not about a philosopher. Or I should say it *was*; for it was about Moller Gitch himself.

Dear Joachim,

At times one might even wish there were a
line, one soon to be crossed.

"I'll be deployed to the front next week,
probably I won't return."
"I've received my diagnosis. In all
likelihood I'll be dead in a month."
"They're bringing me to jail tomorrow, a
ten-year sentence."
"My mind's going. Soon I won't even
recognize you."

If there were a line I soon had to cross,
I'd have no choice but to tell all of you
plainly:

I love you.
I'm so sorry.
Thank you for being my friend.

As it is, life blends muddily from this
part to the next, shapeless as the blue sky.
And here I am, seventy-years-old, lickety-
split, with all the disbelief that accompanies
old age, and most of the people I've known are
dead already, and I've hardly said anything to
anyone.

Sometimes I wish there were a line, one
that I'll soon have to cross.

NO ONE

I can't decide: was this final poem an *expression* of the philosophy of ambivalence, or was it raging against it? The longing for a *line*, like some uncluttered absolute: did Gitch fantasize, in his last, miserable days, about a kind of *purity* after all? Did he dream of simplicity, a state of existence without the mischief of duality? Did Death, that monotonous ghost, appear to him in some inviting form, like the promise of such a state?

Another aphorism comes to me, I don't remember whose it is: *Death is the vengeful proof of monism; the dust to which everything returns is everlasting, and it is all the same.*

Perhaps, in spite of himself, like some loving god, and at the price of great violence, he found it—the refutation of his life's work.

When the Ghostmen Came to Mothview

1.

prologue

After President Polk's envoy was rebuked in Mexico City during the fall of 1845, a humiliation which was followed, not long after, by the inglorious Thornton Affair; after the outrage in Congress, the calls for expansion, the Whigs' half-hearted protestations; after the United States warred with Mexico and took lands; after the ink had cooled on the Treaty of Guadalupe Hidalgo—there came to the highlands in a region no longer in dispute (that part the Spaniards had called Colorado) free trappers and hunters, or so-called "mountain men" of the fur trade, who went about their gory business all on their own, separate from the brigades and *boosway* of respectable outfits—companies too regimented for wild and solitary sorts like them—but who knew the habits of beaver and deer as well as anyone, and who were well-accustomed to sleeping by themselves on the ground, and under every kind of sky, and with hands and faces thickened by the elements, and buckskins and beards begrimed; men who, having equipped themselves with rifles and traps and pack mules, went up into the foothills and mountains southwest of the Royal Gorge so that they might get hides from the wildlife there. For that rich but treacherous territory was now America (in the strange new sense of that word), and it was therefore fair game to any and all brave enough to help themselves to it. Harlon Gaddis, the serial murderer at the heart of our tale, came among those early brave.

How a monster like Gaddis, whose melancholy brow and red-lipped sneer seldom inspired confidence in strangers, managed nonetheless to convince someone to teach him the arts of trapping and skinning, and also how to shoot down a sprinting buck; how a murderous man like him, though born wealthy, came to blend so well among that modest class of hunters and foragers; how a killer like him, somewhere in the belly of the nineteenth century, and with scarcely a dollar to his name (having long since fled his family's lavish home in Massachusetts—not in order to escape his crimes, exactly, but rather in a half-conscious attempt to negate what his transgressions had revealed about him)—how such a killer, I say, though nearly penniless, found his way down the Ohio River and from there into the prairie (where, still undetected by the law, he extracted a living as a farmhand and a thief), before going further west across the lowlands and plateaus of Kansas (where wages were scarce but where a man as heavy-pawed and wide-shouldered as he was could always earn a few coins taking a fall to the local boxing hero, who sometimes was a slave), and then at length finding himself even further west, all the way past the coal fields of the Raton Basin, and with a view to the distant peaks of the San Juan range; how a man like him, seduced by those prolific mountains (and by their seeming remoteness from all the rest of the world, and by the prospect, perhaps, of soothing his conscience there), ended up climbing the lesser slopes and hillsides that lay just eight or nine leagues to the east of the mountains' outer ridge, and all around the valley known as Mothview (at the time a mere outpost, holding only some sixscore souls), and then stayed there, or in that vicinity at least, and without killing anyone, for more than twenty years—these are all details we shall leave aside. We shall leave aside, too, at least for the most part, at least on this present occasion, the morbid particulars of the crimes performed by his younger self. (There shall be murders aplenty in this story, even without them.) No, instead of recounting those bloody deeds we shall simply find him there in Colorado, among the mountains already, a grown man nicely established in his role as a getter and seller of skins, his every year segmented into the same three parts: six or seven months alone in the wilderness (to collect furs), a month to get his haul to the Denver merchants with whom he'd long had arrangements, and then four months or so in Mothview, taking a room above Jin Jin's Saloon and drinking until his money ran out.

We shall find him, in fact, in that town of Mothview, and at that very saloon, once his proper story begins.

2.

the origins of Mothview

We shall return to Mr. Gaddis—whom I've introduced prematurely, perhaps, though that is for you to judge—in due time. For now allow me to concede that I've already led you astray. For it would be too simplistic to suggest, as I did in the very first of these paragraphs, that anyone had actually waited for formal annexation of lands before moving into the disputed territories. The procession of settlers going west had long been underway by then (well before the war with Mexico), and hunting expeditions into those wilds were nothing new. The widespread slaughter of bison proceeded apace, there and elsewhere, as did the general displacement of the Indians (the bloody deed of centuries). The resolution of the Mexican-American conflict, in other words, produced hardly any change at all, at least as far as the movement of peoples upon the continent was concerned. Certainly there occurred in those years nothing like a turning of the tide. For a true shift in the current, one likely would have to look at least three-hundred years further back in time, back to when Europe first cast her gleaming eye in earnest on that newer half of the earth. But then, the text you are reading is a work of fiction, not of history: sometimes even the time and the place are lies. Or as the antique saying has it (putting it the other way around): *Historia fabulosa semper.*

History is indeed fabulous; she is also mightily jealous of her secrets. In chapter 7 of Bruel's dry and perhaps justly obscure work, *Developments in the English Corporate Form, 1717 – 1789* (New York, 1961), the evidence is laid out that, many decades before American independence was declared, certain stealthy partnerships and joint-stock companies based out of London, some of them armed even with letters patent from the British crown (but all of them prepared with terrific sums of capital), had begun funding explorations into the deep west of the North American continent (close on the heels of French fur traders), and began building up small outposts and even the rudiments of towns here and there along the rivers and the more scenic mountain ranges. This was done, of course, "in anticipation of the migration to come" (Bruel 254), which those with keen foresight had already deemed inevitable.[*]

Needless to say, the events of 1776 required the abandonment of most of those endeavors, leaving behind in remote places half-built hotels, piles of timber, escaped horses and befuddled cattle, limp tents strewn about like scales shed from serpents long since slithered away. But all they left were not ruins; some of the edifices—intended to be stores, custom

---

[*]   In that same chapter, for example, Bruel cites the following passage from a report made to the clandestine London Congress For The Development Of The Unorganized Territories In America, written by one Phineas Arbuthnot in 1742:

> Once the Colonies, being over-full, spill out their excess Populace, those adventuring west shall require posts in the wild: Lodgings, gross Supplies, Bases from which to launch further expeditions, Guides & Maps, Churches, Graveyards, Courthouses & Jails, Physicians & Apothecaries, Livery Stables, General & Dry Goods, Constables, Publick Houses. We warrant that, should our several propos'd plans be carried into execution, it will be our Doors & Rooms & Stock that greet them, with our Interests extending not only to the Storehouses & Establishments, but to the very Towns themselves. We shall build up not just stations, but Oases in the wilderness, capable of drawing Multitudes to them as well as any Boston or New York.

houses, stables—had been built to completion. Many of those finished structures stood soundly and, astonishingly, remained undiscovered for years. By the turn of the century, however, people had come upon them once more, and rightly took them over.

Of those half-flowered seeds of future towns and cities, the last to be rediscovered, and the remotest, and perhaps the most impressive, were those sown in the valley of Mothview.

What would you have seen, had you come to that place the same year Harlon Gaddis arrived? Let us imagine that you did go there, that you did see that place, and in that same year; let us imagine it, therefore, in the form of a memory. Some of the details no doubt have grown vague in your mind, considering the time that has elapsed—for example, you can no longer say just how many drab tents had been pitched alongside the main way leading into the town, or whether the first low-roofed and weather-beaten cabin you encountered on that route boasted a hand-drawn sign for dry goods or leatherworks or a barber. Somewhat less vague in your memory are the well-built but empty stockyards that lay just visible in the distance (awaiting their charges, as it were), and then, somewhat closer, the vast livery stable, with gleaming and sturdy roofs and deep-planted pillars, almost empty but with room enough for at least forty horses, and seemingly unattended but for a brave from the Ute who lay asleep in the straw (you can no longer remember just how you knew of his presence there; perhaps someone told you).

Much clearer in your mind are the three prominent peaks that rose out of the distance like sibling giants, and which everyone referred to by the single name of Martha. You recall that, when pressed, a local man divulged to you the mountains' individual names: The Lesser Martha (the shortest), Martha Proper (the most foregrounded), and Martha Greater (the tallest but also the most distant of the three). And then your own gentle epiphany: the name of the valley, "Mothview"—which, you deduced, must originally have been "Martha View," but which became condensed over time, as all things so become—the name

"Mothview," you realized, must have stuck, at least in part, because the three mountains, when looked at askew, sometimes resembled a moth, or some similar broad-winged insect, especially if you directed your gaze there about an hour before the dusk, when the lesser and greater Marthas, washed gray by the sun, and flanking Martha Proper, gave the appearance of being fine wings set upon the back of their sister peak.

Even clearer among your memories is the preacher, whom everyone called Brother Ambrose, and who, without the benefit of a church or so much as a pulpit, but with honest lofty speech, lectured to the few faithful there under the open sky. Short and square and humbly dressed, he was also known to have hard fists and had no objection to standing his ground against any man with a heresy in his mouth. "A stone-knuckled man of God" was the hero of a ballad shared by frontiersmen later that century; the song, you are quite sure, had been inspired by good Brother Ambrose. You yourself once saw him humble a drunken heckler when he drew his bible hard across the rascal's cheek, leaving him asprawl and sputtering (Ambrose resumed his sermon as calmly as if he'd shooed away a fly).

All in a haze in your recollections, though, float the images of the other few establishments in the town; all in a haze are the dugouts with hide-flaps as doors, the squalid shanties, the horses tied to posts, and the several people, mostly men, many of them trappers and hunters like Harlon, some of them explorers, others mere riotous beasts who'd fled the law or serfdom or some mischief they'd done back east, milling about and of varying degrees of filth, and some of them near-savages (or so it seemed to you).

But clear as the bright blue day in your mind is the image of the great saloon in the middle of everything, that tallest structure, that great presence, as beautiful and sturdy a drinking house as ever you'd seen, all white and wooden, and with the simply-serviceable placard above its swinging doors: GIN WHISKY ROOMS. Doubling as a hotel and four stories high, the saloon loomed over everything in the valley, like a palace or a fortress;

behind it stood the stills, whose smoke and steam only added to its holy aura. From within its depths there floated low, grumbling voices, and the clink of glass upon glass, and also laughter, and shouting sometimes.

Entering that place for the first time, or so you recall, you found yourself in a great room, with a good many tables and chairs (far more, you would quickly learn, than ever there had been people inside), and a long wood bar tended by a woman everyone called "Jinny."* A balcony overhung the great room from three of its walls, and was itself enclosed by a whited balustrade draped here and there with bison hides. Two perfumed and strong-backed women reposed there, upon pillow and cool calfskin, and waited for business.

In addition to the usual appointments of a public house, the saloon also contained a handful of oddities—objects and furnishings which felt out of place considering the circumstances. A lavish brass-framed glass mirror, for example, hung from a random part of a random wall; an old British musket and, even more oddly, a Turkish *yataghan* were displayed over the bar; a too-lovely cuspidor got passed around but had not yet ceased to gleam.

Supreme among those peculiarities, however, was an oak china cabinet, as tall as a man, full of porcelain and silver, standing somewhat-too solemnly at the rear of the great room. Long-unopened and only occasionally wondered-at, the cabinet stood as one of the few remnants of some London consortium's heady vision for the town. How it survived unpillaged for so

---

* Her real name was Elizabeth Browne. At the time the saloon was known simply as "Gin's," because of its sign, but later took on the nickname "Gin Gin's;" finally, after several years, a board was put out front that read: "JIN JIN'S SALOON AND ROOMS." Elizabeth Browne—who, for all you knew, had simply occupied the place and declared it her own (an outcome made likely, perhaps, by the fineness and fame of her whiskey, or perhaps because she'd shot dead two men already for disputing her claim)—Elizabeth Browne had been so synonymous with the establishment that people just started calling her "Jinny."

many years, in a place with no shortage of unsavory men, always remained a mystery to you. Perhaps it was the very unlikeliness of the item which, in the eyes of the townsfolk at least, made it appear somehow unbreachable; or maybe the locals only feared Jinny's quick rifle. Or perhaps this was just one of the ways the past clung to the present, that is, in the form of objects gradually receding into the décor.

Let us end this short journey into your memories of Mothview with the following catechism. Question: Who put that brilliant saloon there? And the stockyards and the stable? What missing men, I mean, with weary limb and calloused hand, actually raised them up? Were those laborers British, or colonists, or native, or enslaved, or just early wanderers migrating from the south? Answer: Only Oblivion knows their names now, and keeps them with her in her sleep. (The day will come, dear reader, when your name, too, is known only to her, just as every other name and every other flake of life will eventually settle and fall still upon her placid seabed.)

3

Harlon Gaddis and Brother Ambrose become acquainted

Harlon Gaddis, a murderer fleeing himself, and Brother Ambrose, the preacher, quickly struck up something of a friendship. It came about naturally: both had a tendency to hold forth for long intervals; both exhibited great patience while listening. Both had a penchant for the abstract and the metaphysical. Probably no one else in Mothview could stand them in private hours, or possessed the stamina for their long roosters' songs.

The two men were also bonded by something that occurred shortly after Harlon first arrived in the valley. It was during the latter part of the winter, at that far point in the season when the patience of less-civilized folk sometimes got tested. A man drew on Ambrose in the saloon after a theological dispute; Harlon leapt up and sunk his blade into the man's gut before he could get off a shot. Luckily, the man survived; and, as with most violence of that sort in those days, the whole matter was forgotten by the time the snow packs thawed. But Harlon and Ambrose could often be found together after that, at least during the winters when Harlon took up residence above the saloon.

But these were just minor events, more or less ordinary in such a town. Harlon Gaddis's real story still has not begun.

4

the obscure being of Harlon Gaddis

What more could I tell you about Harlon Gaddis, but while still remaining within the confines of this long preamble? The story I have in mind for him has not yet begun, as I've said (we are so far only dressing the stage). We've established, of course, that he was a killer; but no one is only one thing. There is more to him that I want you to see. Yes, I want you to *see* him—not just his appearance but his obscure being—before any proper action commences. But what can I say, without spoiling anything, so that you do? To begin with, I could try giving you a glimpse (though it couldn't be much more than a glimpse) of his half-wild life as a man of the mountains. I could give you a glimpse, for example, of long journeys through the foothills, the tedium and strain of the climb up to a sweet spot on one of the higher peaks, the horse's heavy load of traps and dry goods and the elements of the camp; I could give you a glimpse of the whole business of getting hides, of collecting castoreum for bait, wading into frigid streams, plunging the traps for beaver (resetting those that were false-licked or had returned only a chewed-off paw), stalking a pack of mule deer with a double-barrel smoothbore, flaying the carcasses, perhaps salting and smoking the meat, throwing camouflage onto caches gently dug so as to leave no visible trace, hunkering down beneath mountain storms or the early snows he could smell coming three days away, staying mute (or mostly so) for weeks at a time, all while keeping wary of Indians. I could give you a glimpse, too, of furtive comforts: the flavor of a pipe under the stars, reading Shakespeare or the Bible aloud in the shade of a tree, skies as perfect-blue as the idea of blue, custard-colored flowers and the pillowy green of never-trodden grass, all the comic little life underfoot, the timid hares and the marmots and pikas with their soft haunches and inquisitive noses, the smell of the campfire, indeed the whole magic company of human smells, of coffee or roasting meat, almost pungent against the softer fragrances of the wild, and even the solitude itself, unappealable on those days when there likely was no other soul for a hundred miles, or on the late-season September nights when the moonlight was so full and pale it lay like snow on the trees, and the air, still sugared by mountain pigroot and the fading summer heat, carried the soft-fussing strains of wildfowl up from the roosting grounds below (though whether to soothe him or to confirm that this was indeed no true place for a man, Harlon could not say)—it was while in the throes of pleasures like these that Harlon would swear he had no memories, this was all he ever was, there was nothing to remember but the mountain, nothing but the wood and streams and the faint paths and old Indian trails he'd sniffed his way through, no home to think of but the skin-hut he'd pitched imperfectly from an overhanging rock, no roof but the stars, no fellows but the knife and the rifle ever within his reach, no audience but the blue spruce trees nodding vigorously in the gales. And besides, all remembering was really guessing, he could never be sure he remembered his past right, no one could—and what was his boyhood or a youthful love or even his mother's face to him now, now that he'd come this far? His every memory was a speculation, especially the far-back ones, the ones that flew over distances in pursuit of him, all the way from Boston, unfathomable city of his birth, where, he could only assume, his mother and brothers still thrived in a great house on Beacon Street amid the coaches and elm trees and parasols and clinking china and, just half a league away, the maddened stir of merchants and seafarers and tradesmen, all that bustle of maritime commerce, the arriving Irish and Italians, the effluvia of the fish trade and the stink of the mill basins, the queer discipline of crowds, but also the blasphemies and rude speech from men heated by work, indeed all the different etiquettes for the different human layers, including of course his family's own preposterous code, that decorousness they practiced from pew to parlor—venison on Sundays, so much needless silver, coat and vest buttoned up to conceal the damp body beneath—and all the other physical courtesies they observed without fail as if to buttress against the abstraction of Massachusetts Bay, or as if to make of love, even familial love, something secretive and dark— and indeed had anything in his life been darker or more secretive than his early love, or rather the failure of it: him standing in front of an elm tree in the falling snow, his hands pale and soft, a just-dropped knife steaming in the cold, another young man sitting against the tree, his head pitched to the side and still, and Harlon struck, first, by how little death had changed that slumped figure (for his face was still lovely), and second, by the fact that the passion he had hoped would evaporate in that moment had not in fact gone away, but remained, and even smoldered more intensely than before (call it "jealousy" if you like, though the individual form of it, that particular mixture of love and bitterness he found in his heart at just that instant, was but one among an infinite series of such passions, each one its own creature, and it was therefore nameless, properly speaking)—but then all this was just a memory, a sequence of guesses, maybe none of it really happened that way after all. *Every memory is a speculation*—that had become for him the meaning of birdsong, and of the west, and of the rivers and the clay and the smell of pine, and of his own free stench, and of the death caked onto his hands from all the skins he'd pulled loose and treated

with ordure or animal brains and smoked over fires made from
deadwood, and of the fish he'd snatched from the waters and of
the elk and other hooved creatures whose livers he'd chewed raw
there on the spot while the blood was still warm, and of the
slow—and then quick, and then slow again—corruption of those
dead, and of the deadly bear, and even of the occasional famished
or just unscrupulous mountain cat come to menace him—there
was nothing before any of this, all these seeming ephemera of
nature were in truth spirits, eternities into which he (himself a
thing plucked loose from time) had vanished long ago. No, not
long ago. There was no long ago. But still, long ago. The so-called
mountain men of the western frontier, especially such lucid
specimens as Harlon Gaddis, were not just the uncouth, thick-
bearded recluses of lore; they were properly a separate form of
life. Or better: A separate form of life struggled to come into
existence in them. We may be assured that, in some cases, it
succeeded.

5

the Ghostmen

Some years passed—twenty or so—since your anachronistic
visit to Mothview. There was now a church there; Ambrose, ever
the tough root, was the pastor, though everyone still called him
Brother. There was a mayor and a sheriff, and two lawyers and a
fur company and a few big ranches off in the distance. There
were land speculators, and various businesses and stores, and
even a small bank. There were the common cabins and tents, the
odd roving salesman, and a regular supply of prospectors and
transients passing through on their way to Utah or California.
Some of the more bellicose Ute, who'd come from the west and
were still seething from skirmishes with Mormons, made off with
cattle from time to time, and occasionally exchanged gunfire

with settlers. Jin Jin's Saloon was still the heart of the place (with Jinny ever at the helm); hunters and trappers came and went. Colorado was a state now; President Grant had only recently signed the proclamation. The vast dead of the recent war haunted everything, even this far west, even now.

Harlon Gaddis, outlasting the ebbs and flows of the fur trade, still got skins for a living. As in all the previous twenty years, he drank during the winter months, and exchanged doctrines with Brother Ambrose. His story still has not begun.

Speaking more generally (looking beyond the valley), these were also rather good years for that fading way of life known as *brigandage* (a last good gasp, perhaps, before its death throes in the century to come). The Bulgarian *hajduci*, for example, about whom many songs have since been sung, were still plotting their bold heists from hideouts in the Balkan Mountains. Black Bart, the poet, who never once fired his rifle during a robbery (and was by all accounts a polite and affable bandit), was still very much at large in northern California. The bushranger Ned Kelly eluded capture in the south of Australia, and hounded the Victorian police. The Swampmen Seven, bushwhackers who'd come up from the wetlands of Alabama, made off with more than two-hundred horses. Sándor Rózsa, from the Great Hungarian Plain, continued wreaking havoc upon passengers in trains and coaches. What few *klepthes* remained in Crete and the Grecian highlands went on with their romantic theme of being wild and fearsome outlaws who had helped to throw off the Turkish yoke once and for all.

The well-armed band of pale and mostly-mute men that rode into Mothview at this same time was not, technically speaking, a gang of bandits, since they never pillaged; they were only guns for hire, which is to say, assassins. But a problem that commonly beset brigands also affected them: for killing, like banditry, was seasonal. What ought a band of outlaws do in the snowy winter months, when orchestrated crime became a more difficult prospect, and clients grew sparse? "Find a town," instructed the great *hajduk* chieftan, Panayot Hitov, in his invaluable memoir,[*] "some remote and provincial cluster of farms or peasant families, let them know you mean them no harm, that you stand against tyrants and not pure and honest folk; teach them your songs and join in their rituals and rites, settle in among them not as brigands but as heroes; regard them not as your prey but as your blood, and, like two families bound thereby, each will come to defend the other." Some version of this wisdom, it may be opined, brought the Ghostmen to Mothview, just as winter was about to set in.

Their infamy preceded them. Though known by several names—The Pale Men, The New Orleans Eight, The New Orleans Wraiths, The Wraiths, The Haints, The Jameses (though that name was based upon a confusion with the James-Younger gang after the Massacre at Fort Sota), The Ghostmen—their singular reputation had nonetheless been assured by the War Department, which promised a bounty of $5,000 per head for their capture. The Ghostmen, it turned out, somehow had carried off the assassination of the famous Union general, William "Bull" Nelson, at a hotel in Louisville during the war (after being contracted for the job by Robert Lee himself[**]). Even before that noteworthy murder, the Ghostmen had distinguished themselves as cold and reliable killers, and well-cheap ones, too. (According to reports they abducted Wade Hatch, mayor of Marshland, Mississippi, for a mere hundred dollars before feeding him alive to swamp alligators.)

---

[*] Hitov, Panayot. *Kak stanah haydutin: familiarni zabelezhki* [How I became a hajduk: familiar notes]. Sofia: 1959.

[**] Lee had long resented Nelson, a good Kentucky man (and to whom Lee personally had appealed), for ultimately siding with the north. The account of Nelson's murder that has been entered into the history books—that it was Jefferson C. Davis, a Union general himself, who fired the point-blank shot—is apocryphal. Note that the historical record shows Davis was never punished or tried, nor arrested or even detained for the crime.

The Ghostmen were recognizable, even as far west as Mothview (and even by the provincial folk there), in part because of the fame of their so-called "first rider," the one who always headed up the pack. He was something like the "face" of the gang, and accordingly he too went by many names: The First Rider, White John, John the Grim, Skinny Pup (the appellation generally preferred by the residents of Mothview), The Death's Head. A paper in Kentucky once referred to him as "the Paganini of the outlaws," on account of his sickly pallor and frail-looking form, his prodigious speed on the draw, and because of his sunken cheeks which looked as if they'd never once puffed out for joy or even for breath. All the men, in fact, were pale and sick-looking in this way, with dark gloves and their hats pulled low— all, that is, except for the one known only as Sam: a talkative and squat blushing beet of a man, boisterous by comparison to his fellows, and noticeably cruel to his horse. Sam's hands were always bare; instead of a hat he wrapped his bald head with rags (which he soaked in water when the temperatures rose, and which lay coiled atop his head like a crude turban). If left to himself he would mumble and laugh through clenched teeth like someone half-mad. According to rumor he was the slowest on the draw but also the best marksman of the bunch: "I heard he 'an hit a rabbit mid-jump from two-hund-fifty yards 'way," a hunter said to Harlon shortly after the Ghostmen arrived in town. Harlon scoffed, of course, but not without a certain telling twitch in his eye.

So they were killers, and everyone in town knew it. Their arrival naturally made the mayor nervous. He didn't fear the men themselves so much as the bounty on their heads. "Last thing I need is some drunk elk-hunter thinkin' he's gonna cash in, and sparkin' gunfights in the street." The mayor consulted the sheriff: "Could we make 'em constables of a sort? You know, like honorary men of the law? People might leave 'em alone if they knew a cage was waitin' for 'em if they started somethin'."

The sheriff declared he couldn't very well deputize a gang of known assassins, and would sooner throw down his badge than do so. So the mayor went to talk to one of the lawyers in town, to discuss possible legal options. For the most part he hoped only to acquit himself of whatever duty he owed to the townspeople—though he was also keen to find out if, should he simply abandon them, a jail cell might lie in his future.

Just then—by one of those coincidences that will sound extravagant should you ever have to recount it in front of an audience—four men from the Wyoming Langston Boys, on the run from the law and all of them bandits true, having abandoned their dying horses right there in the middle of Mothview, burst into Jin Jin's Saloon with weapons drawn. They let poor Jinny know in no uncertain terms that she was going to help them hide, or they'd put a bullet into her ear canal—and to drive the point home one of them took hold of her left ear and ripped it clean off.

Someone from one of the rooms upstairs managed to scramble away and informed the mayor of what was happening. And since the sheriff was nowhere to be found—he'd hid already in the stockyards—the mayor went to Skinny Pup and implored him for help. (Whether or not money changed hands is a matter of some dispute.) Shortly after their meeting, one of the Ghostmen—no one can recall just which one, only that it wasn't Sam—slowly walked over to the saloon.

According to the legend that survives in Mothview to this day, the Langston boys started laughing when a ghostly-thin, frail-looking man entered Jin Jin's great room and very casually drew his gun.

Of course, no mere band of freebooters, however riled-up and hot-faced, and whatever ballads had been sung in their honor back in Wyoming, could have matched even one of the Ghostmen in straight gunfire. At that range in the saloon, anyhow, marksmanship wouldn't have much to do with it. It would come down to who feared death the least. And on that count, the Ghostmen had few rivals.

After it was over the Ghostmen took the Langston boys' corpses and dragged them out back by the stills. Their heads were severed and nailed sideways to their saddles and then shipped back to Wyoming in a crate that read, PROPERTY OF THE LANGSTON CREW. None of the surviving Langstons was ever fool enough to seek a reprisal.

A legal instrument was drafted later that day by the mayor and his lawyer, granting the Ghostmen immunity for the murders (at least as far as any local authorities were concerned), in exchange for the Ghostmen's guarantee to leave the local folk alone, and to protect them against any future criminal invaders. The document was signed by all the relevant parties that very evening.

The mayor beamed with pride. Not only had he avoided disaster—indeed the town was probably safer now than it ever had been—it was also certain that, after the deadly display in Jin Jin's Saloon, no local man would dare try to collect a bounty on the Ghostmen, no matter how loudly the government men back east howled, or how much they offered.

The Ghostmen, like a sleuth of bears, settled in for the winter.

6

Harlon Gaddis and Brother Ambrose discuss the Ghostmen

Some more years passed. The Ghostmen never left Mothview during this time, except for a handful of weeks here and there when they ventured out to do a job. Harlon Gaddis and Brother Ambrose often discussed the topic of the wispy assassins who'd settled in among them so comfortably. They both agreed there was something strange about them, something almost inhuman: "It's like they're not full-and-true *there*," Harlon once said. Brother Ambrose explained it differently by saying that they had "none of the wealth but all the indifference of rich men;" and what he meant, Harlon eventually gathered, was that they shared with high-class folk a certain relationship to the *future*, "a mule-hard expectation of fine outcomes." Or at least they appeared to, even when there was rough going, even if they lost a man during some particularly dangerous campaign; even then they showed a nonchalance that one normally wouldn't expect from killers, the kind one might get instead from a drunk or a well-fed dog, or from the blither women in Ambrose's congregation (those ladies who, if only beneath their bonnets, rejoiced rather than winced at the prospect of a reckoning), or from those even more serene and princely types that passed through from Denver sometimes, sons and daughters of senators and cattle-men who always knew what strings to pull to get themselves out of a jam. The Ghostmen had just such a carelessness about them, a sort of disregard for the odds, almost as if they doubted the existence of the future, though in their case it was without happiness, without any hint of the ecstasy of drunks or Christian women or dogs confident of their supper, and with little more than fifty dollars between them all. Over time Harlon learned to find this quality in their faces; he could spot one of the Ghostmen from a hundred yards, and often by nothing more than the man's placid brow or his lowered chin or the passive glances he exchanged with other members. To such faces, to such unmoved men (or so Harlon thought, and not without envy), the future couldn't be more than a phantom, and a laughable one at that, every bit as sparse and light as smoke— far sparser and lighter, at any rate (or so their eyes seemed to say), than that other and realer phantom, which is any given *present* instant, than that sun or those rummaging blackbirds or this cool gulp of morning air, all the *actual* fortunes of time, ever done-up and fixed-pretty in the current of consciousness (that strictest place of the present, really the only place the present ever *is*), and all but emptied clean of guesses about the morrow or any farther-flung outcomes of days or months or years. The certitude of the simple here and now; to Harlon it seemed they bathed in it.

Then again, perhaps the Ghostmen had little choice in the matter. Theirs, after all, was the blunt empiricism of all killers from that era: in the end, who kept their gun and who bled were the only truths that held any weight.

Brother Ambrose and Jinny both would say that the Ghostmen had watchful eyes, "like the Indians." Harlon knew better. Look into the face of one of the Ute or Blackfeet or a Crow, he'd say, and humanity itself gazes back at you, eyes rich with the past. The Ghostmen, by contrast, had eyes like lonely planets, like clean stones, as if they had no history at all, as if they'd been rubbed dry of it—not lifeless, exactly, not dead eyes, but like they'd not yet seen life, like the glassy, violent eyes of hatchlings. They squinted, those eyes, even in the moonlight.

"'Ghostmen' ain't the right name for 'em," Harlon once said to Ambrose, while possessed by the fleeting genius of Jinny's spirits. "We only call 'em that on account there ain't a word for a ghost that's come before it's died."

7

in Jin Jin's Saloon, Harlon tells Ambrose the story of how he recently became lame

"I hadn't the stomach to bleed my horse the end of that winter," Harlon Gaddis said to Brother Ambrose, and not for the first time. "The cause of it goes back to that, I suppose."

Brother Ambrose, as he had the last time Harlon began in this fashion, played along: "Bleed 'im?"

"Makes 'em hardier in the springtime. All the trappers know it. 'Specially if your aim is to drag him up a mountain come April. But somehow I couldn't bring myself to do it."

Ambrose squinted and pursed his lips as if Harlon had just said something very mysterious.

"I know," Harlon continued, "ain't no real sense to it. I've skinned more things than any two men in these or any other parts. Twenty years a trapper. Done my share of huntin'. All up and down those accursed hills. Every hide you can imagine, too. Beaver, elk, even a few bears. What's a little blood to me? But goddamn if that horse didn't look at me a way." Harlon paused and gulped down half a glass of whiskey before finishing his thought. "Made me reckon, maybe he knows something I don't.

"Anyway, it was on account of that I took my time gettin' up the mountain that year. Didn't wanna tax the horse overmuch. 'Course that meant the company men, who followed me up almost every season—so they could find my places—already drove their stakes into all my usual spots. And some of those company fellas ain't quite so kind, you know. So I had no choice but go further west, find some new place to set up camp. I go all the way around Martha Proper, all the way to the north side of Martha Greater even. Had no plan, just followin' my nose really. And sure enough, after a few weeks a searchin' I come up on this part with heavy forest, and there's a wild stream there, an angry frothin' mess, and I'm thinkin' there's no way there's any beaver, but just before I despair I hear some barkin' behind me—and sure enough, just there, hidden behind a flat of alder and pines there's another stream, all calm and green and shaded, and it goes on for miles into the wood, and it's full of these big fat beavers like I never seen before, their fur all bright blue like the wings of butterflies. So I set up camp and trap a few. I smoke the hides, and some reason the fur turns this soft purple color, like a deep sunset, or like nothin' else I can think of, and it's for sure the prettiest fur I ever got, and I can barely stop lookin' at it. I spend the whole season there, fillin' my cache with purple pelts, and lucky for me that year the fellas from Denver decide to throw an actual rendezvous, like back in the old days, with lots of different buyers and sellers at once, and I got the most beautiful skins of anyone. Best catch yet. Tripled my money from the year before.

"Naturally everyone wants to know where I found them blue-bellied dogs. 'Course I'm not tellin'. But the company men…they start followin' me up the next year like always, and I know just what they want. They keep their distance, and I pretend like I can't see 'em, though they ain't so damn sly. And it occurs to me that this time they might not play nice. Once they find the stream and them blue beavers, who knows what they do to me. After all, it's wide past nowhere out there. So one morning—we're 'bout halfway there—before the sun comes up I shed most of my dry goods and my heaviest trap, and then me and the horse make a dash for it. I don't get far before I hear the yellin' and screamin' behind me, that damn-fool stir and clang of company men on my tail. I'm so eager to get away I lose my footin' by the Threddin' Gulch and sure enough me and the horse roll down into it. Break my leg bad. The men find me hollerin' and drag me out, put the horse down. Had to be done.

"And now I'll never again get up those mountains. Funny thing is, if those men hadn't hung on our heels I would've croaked in that pit for sure. All the same, only reason I ended up there in the first place was on account of them. I guess nuthin's good or bad but time says so."

"I think that's from a play," Ambrose said with a grin.

"Maybe so, I get 'em all confused in my head."

8

with little left of his life, Harlon decides to reduce the evil in the world by one cruel man

So it was that Harlon Gaddis—who, being lame, was no longer fit for the life of a mountain man, and had reached already the beginning of old age—found himself running out of just about everything: money, time, health, virility, prospects for work, novel ideas, hair on his head, the desire to stay up past eight o'clock, good erections, long and deep sleeps, any great urge to bathe, well-functioning liver cells, conversations worth having, credit at Jinny's bar, all the old anger of youth and hot manhood, friendships (though perhaps he'd never really had any), clear memories (we've touched on this already), feelings of purpose (the greater sort and the lesser too), faith (and anyway in what?), love (could he even pronounce the word?).

Harlon Gaddis's story can now begin. For it was at this same time that a well-equipped prospector, who'd been passing through Mothview on his way to Silver Reef, Utah, in order to stake a claim there, was found murdered near the stills back behind Jin Jin's. The crime was a grisly one, and had been carried out, it seemed, with both a hatchet and a flaying knife. If there were witnesses to the murder, none came forward.

The only likely suspect was Sam from the Ghostmen, who not only seemed deranged as a general matter, but also had argued with the man in the saloon earlier that night.

Neither the mayor nor the sheriff was particularly disposed to do much about it, of course. The dead man, however, was well known in Denver; a banker from there had been funding his expedition. When word of the murder reached that city, a lawyer and a couple of bailiffs were dispatched to Mothview, and began asking questions.

No one from Mothview volunteered anything. Even if one of the townspeople had seen the murder he likely wouldn't have said so. Harlon Gaddis, however, with little left to live for, suddenly decided it was his destiny to do at least one good thing before he died. He would reduce the evil in the world, if only by one cruel man. So he went to the Denver officials and claimed he had witnessed the murder from the window of his room above the saloon. He put the blame on Sam.

Sam, who happened to be passed out drunk in the saloon at the time, was taken into custody without incident. Later that month, Harlon testified in a courthouse in Denver. Sam was found guilty for murder, and was promptly hanged for it. Witnesses reported that he cursed and hissed through his teeth before the plank beneath his feet gave way.

Harlon Gaddis returned to Mothview, and to his room above the saloon, and resumed his daily routine of drinking and early retirements to his bed. He had nothing left to do now but wait for the Ghostmen to come kill him.

9

the slow reprisal of the Ghostmen

Weeks passed. Months. No one came for him. Sometimes Harlon would pass a man or two from the Ghostmen in the street, and they might gaze at him, or whisper to each other, or grin coldly, or even point a ghastly finger in his direction—but still none of those men ever called upon him.

"Reckon they're just tryin' to torture me a little before they get me," Harlon said to Brother Ambrose during a quiet winter afternoon. Ambrose could only sigh gravely.

"You could always leave," Ambrose said.

"Nah. I can barely walk with this damn leg. I accept my fate. Just wish they'd get it over with."

Some months later, on a late-spring night, under a round moon, and while Harlon Gaddis slept fitfully (for he was down to his last few dollars and didn't have an idea as to where he would go once Jinny threw him out), someone from the Ghostmen finally paid him a visit.

Harlon started awake. There in the open window was a man, in a long coat and a downturned hat, with knees bent and his hands limp and crossed beneath his chin. He was motionless, like a gargoyle or a stone golem. For what seemed like several minutes Harlon's eyes stayed fixed on that shape in the dark, perched in the window like a vulture with wings halfspread— like it might yet fly at him.

Suddenly the shape was no longer in the window; it was crouching on the bed by Harlon's feet, and with a gun drawn. Harlon's heart pounded.

Finally, in low languorous tones, the shape spoke.

"You know we're plenty solemn about our vocation. Ain't a one of us who'd ever take a life, 'less we was paid for it. And that went for crazy Sam too." The shadowy man kept the gun pointed at Harlon, clicked his tongue and swallowed audibly, and then continued: "But to do a murder in *that* way…that Denver fella all hacked to bits…well, I'm not saying we ain't done a thing or two in our time…*if* someone hired us to do it. But there's crimes so bad only someone pure of principle can be trusted to commit them. That bastard Sam had the scruples of a coyote. We wouldn't have given a job as bloody as that to a man like him."

The crouching man holstered his gun, but slowly, carefully, like he was sheathing a sword.

"But then," he added with a tilt of his head and a smile that seemed to twinkle even in the dark, "I think you knew that already."

"And how would I have known that," Harlon rasped, barely able to muster up the words.

The man sighed and moved his face half into the moonlight. Harlon could see that it was clean-shaven and punctuated by a long and bony jaw. The man's sunken cheeks puckered and sucked softly as he breathed. Harlon also caught a glimpse, or so he thought, of unnaturally long and jagged teeth, though in the half-light it may have been an illusion. The man's eyes were still covered in shadow, thanks to his hat, but the untroubled blue lips wore the same sort of fiend's grin as before. After a long pause the man said: "Needn't worry. By and by it'll get sorted. *Res nolunt diu male administrari.*"

The man reached into his coat and pulled out a stack of bank notes. He tossed the money onto the bed next to Harlon. "For your debts," he said, before vanishing out the window like steam sent up into the air.

Harlon didn't quite know what to make of it all. But the next day, after carefully grooming himself—he even shaved off his beard for the first time in twenty years—he went about and dutifully settled all his outstanding obligations, and was even able to extend his stay at Jin Jin's for another month. Every few days after that, in the middle of the night, he would start awake to find one of the Ghostmen perched in his window with gun drawn; but always, instead of firing, the man would tilt his head, as if discerning something, or rather as if looking for something, and then, not finding it, he would vanish again.

After a while, Harlon began to think the Ghostmen weren't going to kill him after all. "Perhaps they take their contract with the town all too serious," Harlon opined aloud to Jinny. Jinny just smiled and said: "You know, you been hiding that handsome face a' yours all these years. Who would have thought it." And she reached out and touched his bare cheek.

Both the remark and the gesture were fleeting and insincere—expressions of mirth, and not of anything deeper. But the sound and feel of those words passed through Harlon's body like a bolt of energy, like an invisible wave that bent every one of his cells just a little, as if leaving its tiny mark on every part of him.

Scoff though you may, dear reader, Jinny's was the first tender remark Harlon had heard about himself since he'd fled Boston, some forty years before—the first time in forty years anyone had touched him in a gentle way, the first time he'd felt soothed by another human being. And just then and there, as he sat at that dirty table in the great, half-empty saloon, and as Jinny got up to tend the bar, he felt changed—transformed from root to leaf—like something marvelous had happened to him.

And then Harlon turned his head and saw Skinny Pup sitting in the corner, staring at him and grinning.

He'd seen everything.

10

the death of Harlon Gaddis

Skinny Pup rose slowly, trudged over to Harlon's table like an old elk, and sat down. He said: "You know you're a tricky sort, you mountain men." He reached for the bottle of whiskey on the table and pulled it toward himself, though he did not drink. He continued without raising his eyes. "I sometimes see somethin' of myself in you scurryin' mountain types. Them hills do things to a man, don't they? They can make him wise…or turn him wild. But sometimes…sometimes they just empty him. Get inside him and it's like they replace all what's wet and livin' with dry earth and stones. Make it so he don't got nuthin' left of his own self, so his stories don't much feel like his own anymore." Skinny Pup then raised his head and drew it forward over the table; his face was long and pallid, and his chin hung and wagged like it had popped loose. The empty eyes gazed in Harlon's direction, but only vaguely. With a great vein-blue grin Skinny Pup then said: "Sometimes that's just what a man wants. Ain't that right?"

Harlon felt an old stifled fury inside him start to build; he gritted his teeth, barely able to contain himself. He looked around the saloon, at all the faces he didn't know, at Jinny, and then at the old china cabinet on the far wall. The previous forty years suddenly felt like a mere shadow, like they'd barely happened. He felt his face get hot and he began breathing deep through his nose; and then, with a voice he was barely able to muscle down, he managed the following words: "A man like that…nothin' but dirt and stones inside…why he's capable of just about anything, ain't he? You would better take care around a devil like that."

"At last," Skinny Pup whispered, his eyes widening. "There you are."

The two men sat for some time, their eyes locked. Finally, Skinny Pup said: "I know you care for this place, and for good ol' Jinny too. We don't have to do this here and make a whole big affair 'bout it. Why don't we go on outside? We can finish our business among the trees out back where no one'll see us."

Harlon stood up instantly and, without a word, began limping towards the door. Skinny Pup sauntered slowly behind him, and followed him out.

By the time the two men reached the tree line past the stills, Harlon was gripping tight the knife in his belt.

Whatever its truths, the illusions of sense-perception are by far the more abundant, and often they are the more terrifying as well. Harlon would have sworn that the blood which spewed from Skinny Pup's neck, after he lodged his knife there, was not warm but ice-cold, and black, with a foamy, almost granular consistency, and that as the man dropped to the ground and slumped against a tree he gurgled and squawked and hooted in ways that hardly seemed human. The sight of it felt familiar to Harlon; or rather, he saw all at once that there was significance in it, the way one might intuit, with only a glance, a simple geometrical shape. And then, for the first time since he broke his leg, Harlon found himself longing for the mountain, for that place without audience or intrigue—call it the wild, if you like, or Nature—where once again he might have no memories, no past and no future.

(Nature, you see, has no story, because it is the complete absence of evil. By the same token—and here I only follow Plato and the Hebrew bible—human sexual love, with its artifice and finery, its great jealousies, its mismatches and its cruel dispensation, is the supreme *unnatural* thing in us, and the inspiration, therefore, for every true tale. Even this one.)

Harlon Gaddis, covered in blackish blood, and moved by old instincts, began limping slowly westward.

By then the sun had declined in the sky and there were soft reds left in its wake like those found on the breast of a house finch. These reds first appeared singly in streaks and filaments, but then joined with each other and with the clouds, and in one full expanse, like a wave. For a few minutes the whole valley seemed to glow, though dully, as if the red sky had filled it, and all the colors of the earth became closely alike. The saloon, the town, even the deep green and blue firs along the upper slopes of the mountains all turned to red and rust, and a man shambling towards the foothills might have wondered, if just then and there he raised his eyes up, whether these were the colors of decay or of some new onrushing life, and whether the wave had yet to crest and consume him, or, without his knowing, had done so already, and was now bearing him away to the next place.

Harlon Gaddis died of a gunshot wound to the heart, believed to have been self-inflicted, while residing at a boarding house in San Francisco in 1903. He was eighty-nine.

Acknowledgments

I am grateful to the editors and magazines that were the first to publish my work. "A Note on a Note on the Paraclitans" was first published in *LitMag*; "The Book of Ahaziah" was originally published in *Wrongdoing Magazine*; "*Les Maux de la joie*" first appeared in *The Georgia Review*; ""That Which We Truly Don't Know, We Don't Know That We Don't Know," by Glenn Trollip (a review of *The Idea That Never Was*, by Hiram Junker)" was selected as a first-prize winner in the Lazuli Literary Group's Summer 2022 Writing Contest, and was published in the literary magazine *AZURE*; "Some Pages Concerning the Demise of Dr. Conrad Faintly" was first published in *Philosophy and Literature*; "The Devil is a Shape in the Brain" was first published in an anthology titled *Strange Religion*, issued in 2022 by Tdotspec; "The Eighteen Possible Plots" and "Being and Fiction" were both published online in issues of *The Rupture* (formerly *The Collagist*); "Missive on an Old Refutation of Time" first appeared in *Inscape*; "HAPPINESS" was first printed in *The Moth*; "Epilogue" was selected as the winner of the January 2024 short story contest at Palisatrium's Short Story Substack, and was published there; "The Black Square" first appeared in *The Vanishing Point Magazine*; "The *Gehenna* of Saint Augustine" was first published online in *Sci Phi Journal*, and then again in the print anthology, *Tales of Sley House 2023*; "The Secret of the Tulip" was first published online and in print in *Cutbow Quarterly*, and then again online and in print by *Apricity Magazine*; both "The Ambivalent Moller Gitch" and "When the Ghostmen Came to Mothview" first appeared in *Santa Monica Review*.

I am also grateful to some brilliant scholars who helped me with translations, especially Anthony Corbeill and Judy Klitsner. Any errors of Latin or Hebrew in these pages are entirely my own.

V. Joshua Adams, Scott Shibuya Brown, Brian Rivka Clifton, Brittney Corrigan, Jessica Cuello, Barbara Cully, Alison Cundiff, Neil de la Flor, Genevieve DeGuzman, Suzanne Frischkorn, Victoria Garza, Reginald Gibbons, Joachim Glage, Caroline Goodwin, Kathryn Kruse, Meagan Lehr, Brigitte Lewis, Jenny Magnus, D.K. McCutchen, Jean McGarry, Rita Mookerjee, Mamie Morgan, Alexis Orgera, Karen Rigby, Jo Salas, Maureen Seaton, Kristine Snodgrass, Cornelia Maude Spelman, Peter Stenson, Melissa Studdard, Curious Theatre, Gemini Wahhaj, Megan Weiler, Cassandra Whitaker, David Wesley Williams

jacklegpress.org